THE
CUT UP

Also by Louise Welsh

The Cutting Room
Tamburlaine Must Die
The Bullet Trick
Naming the Bones
The Girl on the Stairs
A Lovely Way to Burn
Death Is A Welcome Guest
No Dominion
The Second Cut
To the Dogs

THE CUT UP

LOUISE WELSH

CANONGATE

First published in Great Britain in 2026
by Canongate Books Ltd, 14 High Street, Edinburgh EH1 1TE

canongate.co.uk

1

Copyright © Louise Welsh, 2026

The right of Louise Welsh to be identified as the
author of this work has been asserted by her in accordance
with the Copyright, Designs and Patents Act 1988

No part of this book may be used or reproduced in any manner
for the purpose of training artificial intelligence
technologies or systems. This work is reserved from text
and data mining (Article 4(3) Directive (EU) 2019/790)

British Library Cataloguing-in-Publication Data
A catalogue record for this book is available on
request from the British Library

ISBN 978 1 83885 986 2
Export ISBN 978 1 83885 987 9

Typeset in Perpetua Std by Palimpsest Book Production Ltd,
Falkirk, Stirlingshire

Printed and bound by CPI Group (UK) Ltd, Croydon, CR0 4YY

The manufacturer's authorised representative in the EU for
product safety is Authorised Rep Compliance Ltd, 71 Lower
Baggot Street, Dublin D02 P593 Ireland (arccompliance.com)

To Willy Maley

. . . the darkness pulls in everything –
shapes and fires, animals and myself,
how easily it gathers them!

'You, Darkness', Rainer Maria Rilke

One

THE EYE SEES what the eye expects to see. What my eye saw was a pile of rags fluttering against the north wall of Bowery Auctions, in the blind spot where Rose's CCTV spy lens does not reach. It was four-thirty in the afternoon, October dark. The working day was done, and I had locked the saleroom doors. I almost walked away, but our district is on the up, and gentrified neighbours had been complaining about fly-tipping and removal vans blocking access. I cursed under my breath.

I knew before I knew. It was just fabric, mussed and damp from the intermittent showers that had punctuated the day. But there was a familiar shape to it, an ancient outline.

'Ah Christ,' I swore again.

Now was the moment to turn my back and head for the pint that had been hovering on the edge of my mind all afternoon. The bundle was motionless, the man — for some reason I knew it was a man and not a woman — sound asleep.

Glasgow has more than its share of rough sleepers. People need somewhere to kip, so why not our place? But Glasgow is not known as Tinderbox City for nothing, and old auction houses like ours are prone to burning down, even in the dank end of the year. The sleeper might wake and decide to light a fire to warm themselves.

I paused on the edge of the shadow cast by the wall. 'You okay, mate?'

The bundle shivered but did not move. I drew closer, and saw that it was his hair that trembled in response to the breeze. The man was not huddled in a sleeping bag. There was no cardboard cushioning the tarmac, no small dog to raise the alarm. He was wrapped in a raincoat that, now I looked closely, I thought I recognised. I squatted level with him and saw that one hand was outstretched, the gold signet ring set with diamonds still on its middle finger.

'Are you okay Manders?' A faint whiff of whisky scented the air between us. 'You can't sleep it off here, Mandy. Sorry, pal, time to head home.' I reached out and touched his shoulder. He did not move. The rain started, and I was tempted to retreat, but it was cold and Mandy Manderson was not a young man. 'Fuck's sake, Mandy. It's been a long, bloody week.' I gave him a gentle shake. His face turned towards me, and I saw the reason why Mandy Manderson, jewellery dealer, man-about-town and thorn in many sides was lying on the ground in the rain.

If I had been asked to take a bet on how Manderson would snuff it, I would have put a heart attack top of the list, a stumble down a pub staircase close second, followed by a hit and run, some fast and joyless ride. He was obnoxious when sober, unpleasant when drunk, but I would not have thought him important enough for murder.

Manderson's mouth was slack. The left side of his face was painted with blood, the right side pale except for a few spatters. Something was up with his left eye. It was the wrong shape, oversized and purple. He looked like a damaged cyborg from some low-budget sci-fi show. I sucked air into my lungs and let go of the body. His skull banged against the ground. I crouched there in the shadows, trying to calm my breath, and then turned his face towards me.

Someone had pierced Mandy Manderson's left eye with a Victorian hatpin. The tip was an amethyst decorated with gold oak leaves and seed pearls. It might fetch £95 to £150 in auction. The stem was 14-carat gold and long enough, I knew, to extend beyond his eye socket and into his brain. It was a classic duelling move, displayed in old sword fencing manuals as a perfect coup de grâce. I recognised this hatpin, had seen it earlier that day – nestled in my boss Rose Bowery's shiny black hair.

Two

I TOOK MY phone from my pocket and rang Rose. The call went to voicemail. I did not know if it was more incriminating to leave a message or to hang up. I settled for 'Something's happened. Call me when you get this.'

Mandy had been a slimeball, too sure of his own superiority to be popular. Rose disliked him, but not enough to play KerPlunk with his brain. He stared up at me. One eye rolled back in his head, the other purple and faceted, unnaturally round and large. I closed my own eyes. I did not doubt that Rose was capable of killing a man, but my boss was a controlled explosion. If she was to stab someone, she would clear up after herself and make sure not to leave silly evidence lying around. Yet here was silly evidence, staring me in the eye.

I thought about the way the pin had gleamed gold against Rose's hair, the scores of people who had passed through our saleroom that day, the years of beef between her and

Mandy Manderson, the way police and courts were quick to jump to conclusions that sent people like us to jail.

Somewhere a motorbike engine screamed. The dodgy arc light by the car park's entrance flickered on and off, casting flashes like TV static. The wind rose, and an aluminium can tumbled tinny across the tarmac. Then, as if a hand had stopped all motion, the breeze died, the can stilled, the arc light cut out and the motorbike throttled and faded into the distance. The night was calm, except for the jewel gleaming in Mandy's eye socket.

I took another deep breath and pulled on the cotton gloves I use for handling delicate objects. I rocked on my heels, glad I had skipped lunch, and, whispering *jesusfuckingchristalmighty*, placed my left hand over Mandy's violated eye, clasped the amethyst with my right hand and tried not to think of jelly as I eased the hatpin free.

I was fond of the air of 1930s detective on the prowl my grey gaberdine lent me, but I took it off and draped it over Mandy, covering his twisted body and ruined face. The polis would give me a hard time for corrupting evidence, but I was a stunned, sober citizen and the coat would excuse any traces of my DNA.

I did not have to make a show of looking shocked for the CCTV cameras as I crossed the car park, unlocked the auction-house doors and went inside. Luckily Rose prefers privacy to security and there were no cameras in this part of the saleroom. I went to the kitchen, washed the hatpin with warm water and squeezy liquid and dried it with a paper towel. I tried phoning Rose again and received the same message.

'Rose, you better come over to Bowery. Something's happened. Something bad.'

I dialled Rose's on-off squeeze, Inspector Jim Anderson, but his phone went to voicemail too.

'Anders, there's a murdered man in our car park by the name of Mandy Manderson. I'm about to phone your lot, but I'd consider it a favour if you could come over and hold my hand.'

I was as uncomfortable with Glasgow's finest as I was with a murdered jewellery dealer. But there was nothing for it. I phoned 999, asked for police and gave my details to a call handler who made it sound like a dead body was no big deal. I promised to stay where I was and hung up.

The hatpin weighed nothing, but it was a load in my pocket, bigger than a Brink's-Mat gold bar. I went to the tables where lots for the following day's sale were arranged in tempting display. I intended to slip it into one of the cartons of bric-a-brac piled beneath the tables but spotted half a dozen silver and gold Victorian hatpins fanned out on a black velvet cloth. Rose must have helped herself from the collection. I placed the hatpin beside the others and rearranged the display so it was hidden in plain sight.

Sirens sounded in the street beyond. Blue lights flashed against the auction-house window. I texted Rose, *You're needed here*, and went out to greet the police.

Three

'HOW DID YOU say you knew Mr Manderson?'

It was the third time I had told the police inspector that Mandy was a client, a jewellery dealer who operated mainly at antique fairs but also did a bit of business online.

'He was a regular client, buying rather than selling. We didn't socialise, but I saw him most viewing and sale days.'

'Do all right for himself, did he?'

'He kept afloat.'

We were sitting in Rose's office, two mugs of coffee between us, a uniformed officer sitting on the sidelines taking notes. A television production company, devoted to afternoon TV, had been in to do a bit of filming that morning, and I had found a selection of wrapped biscuits in the kitchen. The inspector picked up a Blue Riband, turned it absentmindedly between his fingers and returned it to the plate.

'How well did he keep afloat? Buoyant or looking for a life jacket?'

The constable grinned, as if the inspector had said something clever.

I cradled my mug. My fingertips tingled, remembering the suck of resistance Mandy's eye had given as I pulled the hatpin free. 'His expenses were low. He had good knowledge, good connections. I've no idea how much he turned over, but he was a regular buyer.'

The inspector nodded. His name was Murchison. He was in his late thirties, underweight and sallow. The kind of man whose stomach plays up.

The internal windows of Rose's office looked onto the saleroom where a couple of uniformed officers were loitering, casting suspicious glances at the neatly labelled lots laid out for tomorrow's sale. The big lights were on, the displays glimmering. It was only a matter of time before one of them spotted the hatpins and put two and two together.

I touched the tobacco tin in my pocket. 'Is there anything else?'

Murchison slid his tongue over his front teeth. 'Probably.'

Beyond the office windows, a couple of figures dressed in the white coveralls I was familiar with from news reports and cop shows approached the saleroom, lowering their hoods.

I nodded in their direction. 'Shouldn't they have taken those hazard suits off outside?'

'Why?'

'Contamination.'

'It's the other direction we have to worry about.' Murchison stretched a hand towards the constable and clicked his fingers. The man passed him the notes he had been making. Murchison read them, took a pen from his pocket, scored something out and made a correction. He glanced at the uniform. 'Learn where to put apostrophes.' He handed the paper to me. 'Your statement. Read and sign if you agree everything's in order.'

The constable had used phrases I never used and written in block capitals which gave a hard-of-hearing vibe. The statement did not sound like me, but the facts were as I had told them.

I signed and returned it to Murchison. 'When can I go?'

'We need a keyholder on site until we've finished.'

There was no point asking how long that would take. 'All right to go outside for a smoke?'

'As long as you stay away from the locus.'

The white-suited scenes of crime officers were at the window. One of them rapped against the glass. Murchison nodded and they entered. Two men, raindrops glistening against the unnatural fabric of their coveralls. The room shrank.

One of the newcomers, a pale ginger with red, slapped-looking skin, said, 'That's us done. Van's on its way.'

I had assumed that Manderson was already en route to the mortuary. 'He's still there?'

'The body will be gone soon. We've put a tent around it.'

Inspector Murchison slid his pen back into his inside pocket and gave me a weary look. 'I'm meant to ask if you'd like to be put in touch with Victim Support.'

I abandoned my last dreg of coffee and set the mug on the table. 'You're all right.'

Murchison nodded as if tea and sympathy were beyond the dignity of men like us. 'It would have been better if you hadn't put your coat over him.'

I got up from my chair and took my tobacco tin from my pocket. 'I wasn't thinking straight.'

Murchison gave a dry smile. 'It's pissing down out there. You're going to get soaked.'

I took a dustcoat from the back of the door and shrugged it on. 'There's always something lying around the place that'll do the job.'

The second scenes of crime officer, the one who had not spoken yet, met my eyes. 'Good to know.'

The air was cold and damp, and it took a moment for my cigarette to light. I stood on the fire escape beneath the overhang of Bowery's roof and looked out to where a white plastic tent shielded Mandy's body. It made me queasy to think of him lying there, ruined eye staring. A policeman in a hi-vis vest stood guard. It was after seven, over two hours since I had found Mandy, and Rose had still not appeared.

The tent and hi-vis shone fluorescent beneath the arc lights. The perimeter was strung with blue-and-white police tape. It fluttered, ragged, in the breeze. A team of officers had carried out an unsuccessful search for the murder weapon and were conducting door-to-door enquiries. Something else for our aspirant neighbours to moan about.

I had never liked Mandy Manderson, but I felt guilty about screwing up the investigation into his murder. I took out my mobile and phoned Rose and then Anderson. Neither picked up. I wondered if they were together. Anderson was still asking Rose to marry him at roughly three-monthly intervals and she was still saying no. What would Anderson do in my position? I had known the police inspector since we were boys, but he had grown harder to read as the years progressed. He might conceal the hatpin for Rose's sake or trust the system to do its job and hand her in for questioning.

I had read enough news reports and seen enough movies to know that women like Rose do not fare well where justice is concerned. The taboos that drew Anderson to her – her exotic looks, contempt for authority and quick, combative wit would not sit well with the law.

The fire escape door opened, and a man wearing a full-length waxed coat and wide-brimmed hat stepped out. It was a practical getup, but it gave him the look of a Witchfinder General. It took a moment to recognise him as one of the scenes of crime men who had been with Murchison in Rose's office.

He nodded towards the tent. 'You found the body.'

My lungs felt soggy. I pulled smoke down into them and coughed. 'I thought he was a bit of rubbish someone had fly-tipped.' I took another deep inhale of smoke. 'Sounds bad when I say it out loud.'

'Must have been a shock.'

'You could say that.'

'That why you covered him?'

I stuck to the story I had concocted. 'I'd left my mobile in the office. I had to go inside to phone your lot. It didn't seem right to leave him exposed like that, where anyone could see him.'

The man stared out across the empty car park. 'Not exactly a busy thoroughfare.'

'Like you said, it was a shock. Guess it's all in a day's work for you.'

'Most murders are old pals falling out. Nine times out of ten the perp's still hanging around greeting his eyes out when we turn up. This is a bit of a novelty, what's known in the trade as *up close and personal*.'

'Nice to know you've got a name for it.'

'We've got a name for most things.'

I asked a question that had been bothering me. 'You think he knew his killer?'

Rain slid from the brim of the man's hat. 'We have to keep an open mind, but it's a reasonable guess. Whoever did him knew your friend well enough to get within kissing distance and hated him enough to put a spike through his brain.'

'He wasn't my friend.' It sounded damning, and I backtracked. 'He was just a client.'

The officer buttoned up his coat. 'Killer was a cool customer. Had the presence of mind to take the weapon with them.'

I took another drag of my cigarette, hiding my expression in a wraith of smoke. 'Any idea what it was?'

'The weapon?' He stared at me, and I got the impression he was committing my features to memory. 'A kebab skewer maybe?'

'Easy to lose.'

'We might find it yet. The boys are out checking gutters and stanks.' He gave me another quick, appraising look. 'Don't remember me, do you?'

It was my turn to look at him: square jaw, dark hair cut short, but not unfashionable, grey-blue eyes, heights with me at six feet, but broader, more athletic. Good-looking but not advertising the fact. The kind of man who could melt into a crowd if he hunched his shoulders and kept his eyes down.

'Should I?'

He smiled, revealing a slight gap in his front teeth. 'Don't worry about it.'

A white van drove slowly into the car park and backed towards the tent, reverse-warning beeps penetrating the silence.

The fire-exit door opened, and the man's red-faced partner appeared, also in civilian clothes. 'That us?'

'Looks like it.'

The tall man turned to me. 'Keep an eye out for anything that could have done the job.'

Asking me to keep an eye out was not diplomatic, but now was not the time for banter. I nodded. 'Kebab skewer.'

'Or similar.'

The two investigators walked at a leisurely pace through the rain, towards the van. I waited until they had crossed the car park and then returned to the saleroom. I had no desire to see Mandy Manderson make his final journey.

Inspector Murchison and his troops were getting ready to leave. The hatpin was sending sonic waves in my direction. Murchison buttoned a blue, three-quarter-length coat that had the air of M&S menswear. 'Remember, we need your CCTV recordings and the names and addresses of anyone who attended today's viewing.'

He had already asked for the same information. I had told him I did not have the right computer login, that paperwork was Rose's department and had reluctantly surrendered her phone numbers and address.

I played with the tobacco tin in my pocket. 'Like I said, Ms Bowery will be in touch. We don't keep a list of everyone who enters the salerooms, but she can send you a record of anyone who registered for a paddle number or submitted a lot for tomorrow's sale.'

An officer had been sent to her flat and reported no one home. Rose's private life was her own business, but I was starting to get worried.

Murchison pulled on a pair of leather driving gloves. 'We'll be back first thing. I'll station a couple of uniforms outside the auction house overnight.'

'You think the murderer might come back?'

He gave a weary smile. 'That would be convenient, but no. Murder makes people nervous. It helps the community to see we're on the job.'

'What about tomorrow's sale?'

He looked at me as if I had lost my mind. 'Cancel it.'

Four

ROSE LIVES IN a square of Georgian townhouses arranged around a neglected pleasure garden. I took the subway and walked the rest of the way through rain that shimmered beneath the uncertain glow of streetlights.

One of the square's houses had been a gay bar in dim and not so distant days, when being gay was illegal in Scotland. The old club had a derelict air. I noticed that its front door did not sit right in its frame. It would be an easy thing to slip inside, but I was on another mission, and sometimes it is best to leave the past to the past.

The square had the haunted air of a black-and-white movie, a thriller with a score that told you something bad was on its way. I could make out the shape of the long-dead fountain in the centre of the garden which was rumoured to cap an abandoned mineshaft. A breeze shimmered the bare branches of the trees that marked the garden's perimeter, strafing shadows across the street. I caught a glimpse of a figure ghosting on the other side of the park, there for a moment, then vanished in the dark.

This was one of the earliest sections of Glasgow's West End, built on the site of old mines and quarries for city merchants who had grown rich on the products of Caribbean plantations and compensation for freeing enslaved peoples who received no reward.

Geology, like history, has a habit of reasserting itself. In the 1970s and '80s the old mines had made themselves known, sinking pavements, cracking walls and dragging the occasional building down into their depths. Banks refused to lend; the neighbourhood slipped into decay. Rogue landlords moved in, and it became a red-light district.

The square and its surrounding district were still home to recent immigrants and artists whose craft barely paid their rent, but recently the place had gone up in the world. Young professionals and students whose parents had deep pockets had started to move in. A new neighbour had complained about Rose's habit of sunbathing in her underwear in the central garden. The students downstairs had objected to loud music after midnight.

The front windows of Rose's flat were dark. I slipped down the lane at the back of the building. There was a light on in the kitchen, but that meant nothing. There was always a light on at Rose's place. I waited a while to check that no one else was surveilling the street and then pressed the entry buzzer. There was no response. I tried the students on the ground floor, who buzzed me in without asking who I was. The keys to Rose's flat were in their usual place, hidden beneath the statue of Pan on the turn of the stair. I knocked and, when there was no reply, let myself in.

*

I was asleep in the winged chair by the sitting-room window when I heard the key turn in the lock. The police had already woken me twice, banging their signature assault against the apartment door while I hunched in the dark like a fugitive.

Rose was silhouetted in the light from the entrance lobby. She reached for the light switch.

I caught her hand in mine. 'It's me. Don't get a fright.'

She shoved me away. 'Rilke, for fuck's sake.' Her breath smelt of brandy. 'You almost gave me a heart attack.'

I let go of her hand. 'Mandy Manderson is dead.'

'You broke in and waited up just to tell me that?' Rose went to her cocktail cabinet and started clinking about amongst the mishmash of glasses and bottles. Enough light shone into the room from the streetlamps outside for me to see her set two glasses and a bottle on the table. 'Still, always sad to see a big spender go, even if he was a cunt.' Rose poured us each a glass of brandy. 'Mandy had a tidy stock. We should try and find out who it'll go to and encourage them to use our services. It could make for a good specialist sale.'

'Someone murdered him.'

Rose flung her coat over the couch. Underneath she was wearing something tight and long that would look good on Morticia Addams.

'What happened? Mugging gone wrong? I always said it was a bad idea to splash the cash the way Mandy did.'

Any fears I had harboured about Rose's guilt were evaporating. I would have preferred a whisky but took a sip of brandy. 'It was more elaborate than that. He was killed in our car park. Someone pierced his brain with the hatpin you were gadding about with.'

Rose produced a box of matches and lit one of the candles

on the table. Its glow illuminated her dark eyes and red lips, the fine lines beneath her make-up. 'Ha-bloody-ha, not funny.'

'I'm serious.'

She looked up, match still burning between her fingers. '*Serious* serious?'

'Yes.'

'How?'

I pointed at my eye. 'Straight through his left eyeball.'

'Christ, that must have stung.' Rose remembered the match and waved it in the air, killing the flame before it could burn her fingertips. 'That's why we're hiding? That stupid hatpin?'

'Yes . . .'

Someone started hammering the brass door knocker. Rose blew out the candle and reached for my hand. She whispered, 'I only wore it for a few hours while we were filming. Shit . . .' The landline started to ring. Rose grabbed her mobile and turned it to silent, just as it started to buzz. She shoved it under one of the cushions on the couch and clamped her palm over her mouth. We sat silent in the dark. After what felt like a long while her phone cut out and we heard footsteps going down the stairs. The front door slammed.

I said, 'No one knows about the hatpin. I gave it a quick clean and put it back on display.'

'You did what?'

'I planked it.'

Her lips turned down in a Grimaldi grimace. 'You took it out of his eye?'

'I used gloves.'

Rose looked like she might throw up. 'I wore it on camera.'

'I know, you already said, and anyway I saw you wearing it. That's why I hid it.'

'It's worse than that, Rilke.'

A sick feeling lodged in my chest. 'You didn't do it?'

'You're not seriously asking me that, are you?'

'No.'

'I wouldn't touch a hair of his cheesy head.' Rose got to her feet and lifted her coat from the back of its couch. It was white and shaggy – the kind of garment Douglas Fairbanks might have twinned with a straw boater. She took her mobile phone from under the cushion. It was almost out of juice, and there was another delay while she hunted in the dark for a charger. Rose glanced at her messages. 'I'm popular tonight.'

I sank the last of my brandy. 'The ones that aren't from the polis are probably from me.'

Rose poured us both another drink and pecked at the buttons on her phone, still attached to the wall plug by its umbilical cord. 'You should have waited till I answered before you called the police.'

'He was dead, Rose.'

She muttered, 'One of the advantages of being dead is you're not in a hurry.'

'Murder doesn't wait. I phoned Anderson. He didn't pick up either. I thought maybe you were together.'

Rose gave me a withering look that told me she and Anderson were on one of their regular 'breaks'. 'I was out with Moira and Pimm from Penny Ante Productions. Pimm promised to send me the scenes from this morning.' She turned the screen of her phone towards me and pressed play. 'We were discussing hatpins.'

Rose is photogenic. Her black hair gleamed glossy on the phone's screen, her dark eyes smoked. She smiled at the presenter, and I caught a glimpse of amethyst and gold in her hair. The presenter lifted a hatpin from an array on the table and held it up so viewers could see its long stem.

'This is bigger than I expected, at least six inches long.'

Rose has a smutty sense of humour. I could tell by the way her lips pursed that she was trying not to laugh. 'Edwardian hats were huge. In those days ladies had a lot of hair, which they wore piled on top of their head, so these long pins were necessary to secure everything in place.'

The presenter's voice was bright, her eyes wide with enthusiasm. 'They served more than one purpose though, didn't they?'

Rose mimicked the other woman's wide-eyed expression. She looked like a maniac. 'That's right, Sue. People think #MeToo is a new phenomenon, but Edwardian ladies had similar problems to twenty-first-century women. Some of them had entered the workplace and were travelling on their own by public transport. They encountered the same kinds of creeps women and girls encounter today: men who don't know how to keep their hands to themselves. And when they did, they had a handy weapon they could rely on.' Rose pulled the amethyst hatpin from her hair and turned it around so that viewers could appreciate the jewelled ornament and then its pointed tip. 'This is a lovely example, beautiful and lethal. Sharp as a blade.'

'Were any men seriously hurt by these pins?'

Rose held the hatpin in front of the camera again. 'This is basically a form of stiletto. I'm not talking shoes; I mean a dagger with a deadly needle for a point. In medieval times knights used stilettos to finish off their opponents once they'd knocked them off their horse. They would slip the blade between their enemy's helmet and armour, then plunge it through his eye, into his brain.' Rose wiggled the blade as if she was cleaning out a winkle shell. 'Most ladies merely wanted to protect themselves and make men think twice before they harassed anyone again, but there were reports of men having their faces permanently scarred. And, of course, suffragettes armed themselves with hatpins when police tried to arrest them. I'm not sure if anyone was actually killed by one, but it would definitely be possible.' Rose clutched the hatpin like a dagger and stabbed it towards the camera, laughing. 'Don't mess with the ladies, or you'll get an eyeful!'

Rose stopped the video. 'Does that look as bad as I think it does?'

'Worse. What did you do with the pin once the filming was over?'

Rose touched her hair, as if feeling for it. 'I don't know. I think I left it lying on the desk, but I'm not sure. It was a busy afternoon. I lost track.'

I thought back to the viewing. The door to the office had been open, the saleroom crowded. Anyone could have sneaked in and helped themselves.

Rose took a deep breath. 'I told Manderson to fuck off out of my way during the viewing.'

'You did what?'

'I told him to get to fuck most viewings. I had to. It's the only language he understands.' She paused, recalling that he was dead. 'The only language he understood. He was a sleazeball. He'd wait until the place was crowded and rub up against you. I told the girls to give him a wide berth.'

'Did anyone hear you?'

'Anyone in the main saleroom at the time. He pretended it was a running joke between us, but he knew.'

'For fuck's sake, Rose.'

'Easy for you to criticise. It wasn't your bum he was squeezing.'

'It wasn't you who pulled the bloody thing from his eye. I can still hear the noise it made as it came out.'

Rose made a face. She reached out and touched my hand. 'You're a good pal, Rilke.'

I returned her squeeze. 'What do we do?'

Rose sat up straight. 'I'll phone the police like a good citizen, hand over our CCTV and client list, then we'll do what we always do. Keep schtum and hope no one finds out.'

Five

BOWERY AUCTIONS BRISTLED with knives and needles. Scissors with blades sharp enough to geld a man. Brooches braced with pins, brass-nibbed fountain pens, tacks and nails and paperclips that only needed unfolding to become sly agents of injury. Manderson was not my first dead body. He was not even my first murdered body, but I could not shake the memory of the suck and pull of jelly as I slid the hatpin free.

The phone was busy all morning. Word had got round about Manderson's murder. Punters wanted to know when their lots would be auctioned. A couple of dealers asked if we would be handling the sale of his stock, but there were no enquiries about the date of the funeral. Times were tough, and empty wallets make for short tempers. Manderson was a dead prick who was making lives harder by putting our fortnightly sale on hold.

The crew had already been questioned and sent home by the time Rose turned up. Inspector Murchison had claimed her Hans Wegner swivel chair. She sat across the desk from him on the visitors' seat, wearing a 1940s suit, provocative in its buttoned-up modesty. Rose had once told me that rows of buttons send heterosexual men's minds towards unbuttoning. The constable taking notes leaned forward in his seat as if eager for a whiff of Chanel, but perhaps Murchison preferred zips. His expression remained all police business.

I watched Rose and Murchison from the other side of the saleroom as I pretended to work my way through a selection of old auction catalogues. Even from a distance I could see that Rose's routine, a dance of sugared insults and flattering looks, was failing. Murchison was a detection machine, immune to seduction. Eventually she signed her statement and joined me at the big table where I had laid out the catalogues. I lifted a pile of papers from one of the Singer sewing stools. 'How did it go?'

Rose perched on the stool and crossed her legs, as if she was sitting at a cocktail bar. 'Who knows? He asked about Mandy. I told him I don't like to speak ill of the recently departed but he was a handsy lech and we didn't get on.'

'Bold approach.'

She tucked a stray strand of hair back into her bun. 'Anderson says it's good to come clean sometimes. Makes you appear honest.'

'You told Anderson what's going on?'

'There's enough polis around without Anders poking his truncheon in. I should have listened to my dad. He always told me to keep clear of the law.'

Rose's dad, old Jim Bowery, had not stayed as clear of the police as he liked to make out. I remembered the days when loot that should have been secured in a police evidence room occasionally wended a crooked path to Bowery, courtesy of the thin blue line. If the robbed householder had got wind of it, Jim would have blamed an anonymous punter. The villains who had lost their prize to the police weren't going to complain.

I preferred the way things were now. The route to Bowery Auctions was not a Roman road, but it was straighter than it used to be.

Rose said, 'Anderson knows me too well. He can tell when I'm lying.'

'An impressive superpower.'

'Maybe if you'd left the hatpin where it was . . .'

'You're going to be on national television this lunchtime using it to demonstrate how to kill a man.'

'It's afternoon TV. No one watches except the afflicted – students, stoners and chairbound pensioners. With any luck it'll pass the polis by.'

Rose harboured ambitions of becoming a regular on the show. She had watched every episode on catch-up and analysed the antique experts' outfits and eccentricities. Wishing the programme to obscurity was a measure of how worried she was.

I glanced at the auction-house clock, gathered the catalogues into a neat pile and got to my feet. 'Time for me to go.'

Rose looked at her watch. 'Doesn't feel like six months.'

'Maybe not to you.'

Rose fished in her handbag, found her purse and counted out ten twenty-pound notes. 'Give him that.'

I folded the notes into my wallet. 'Ta, I'm sure it'll be much appreciated.' I saw Murchison watching us from across the room and tucked my wallet swiftly into my inside pocket. 'Do you really wish I'd left the hatpin where it was?'

Rose glanced at the police inspector and then turned her gaze back to me. 'Anderson and I discussed police corruption once. He said covering something up is self-incriminating, but then so is having a hatpin I declared a weapon against lecherous men on national television shoved into a lecher-I-told-to-fuck-off's brain. You did me a favour, Rilke. I'm just hoping it's not a favour that lands us both in jail.'

Six

LES WAS WALKING along a residential street of neat ex-council houses, carrying a transparent plastic bag stuffed with clothes and books. I pulled the van into the kerb beside him and rolled down the window. 'Fancy a ride?'

Les is usually quick off the mark with a double entendre, but he gave me a look that said I was late, opened the passenger door, flung his bag into the cab and climbed into the seat. Some men come out of prison pale and doughy from too little sunshine and too many pre-processed carbohydrates. Les was the colour of bone. Six months had carved new lines into his face. He looked older, more ascetic than before, with an edge that invited no japery.

I swung the van out onto the road and drove west. 'How's things?'

'Fucking peachy. I've got forty-six quid in my wallet and an appointment with probation services. I'm out on licence, so one wee slip and I'm back inside before you can say pronto. Oh, and that sod Scanlan has it in for me.'

Thurso Scanlan was the policeman who had arrested Les. Their paths had crossed during lockdown when he had stopped and searched Les, who was masquerading as a key worker while bicycling little bags of boredom relief to socially distanced doorsteps. The judge had let Les off, but Scanlan had borne a grudge and arrested him a second and then a third time unlucky.

Traffic lights shifted from amber to red up ahead. I braked to a stop, slipped my hand into my inside pocket and pulled out a bundle of neatly folded notes – four hundred pounds.

'That's from Rose and me. It's not much, but it'll help keep you going until your benefits come through.'

'Cheers.' Les turned the van heater up. It had been summer when he was taken down, and he was wearing a sky-blue suit that was too light for the season. He stuffed the money into his pocket. 'Did you bring me a change of clothes?'

I nodded to a holdall in the back of the van. 'As requested. Where do you want to go? Home?'

'Naw, Turkish. Then a haircut.'

We selected loungers behind the glassed-off partition of the Arlington Baths' Turkish suite, where we could talk without being overheard. Les unfastened his towel and stretched out, pale and naked. The nearest Les generally gets to the sea is a day trip to Largs, but his body is decorated with tattoos that recall pre-war Hamburg sailors. Some of their detail was lost in the blue-black bruises that marked his chest, back and calves.

He saw me looking and gave a wry smile. 'It's tough inside, Rilke.'

'How did the other guy look?'

'Like a fucking nonce.'

Les has been handy with his fists since we were boys in the playground. He has a big mouth and a sense of humour that gets him into trouble, but he has survived decades as a small-time drug dealer with a penchant for female attire by being savvy about clans and alliances. His cottage industry, as he likes to call it, relies on a level of respect Les is not shy to encourage with the aid of a baseball bat.

He lay back, relaxed. 'Think Rose would give me a job?'

'I've more chance of becoming First Minister.'

Les snorted. 'You're a big bender but you're not that bent.' He ran a hand across his chest and regarded the sweat on his palm. 'Seriously, probation are going to be on my back, and I need something for spends.'

I stared up at the small red and blue stained-glass windows, dotted like stars across the ceiling. 'Sorry, Les. Rose has her own problems.'

'Spill the beans. I need something to cheer me up.'

I had intended to keep Mandy's murder to myself, but lulled by the dry heat, coloured glass and afternoon silence, I told Les about discovering the body, Mandy's wandering hands and Rose's response. I mentioned the killer had pierced him through his left eye but kept the hatpin out of the story.

'Sounds like he got what he deserved.'

'Harsh.'

'Law of the jungle, Rilke. Keep out of folk's personal space if you don't want to get bopped.'

'We're not in the jungle.'

'We're in Glasgow, same thing. I wouldn't put it past Rose. Remember when she aimed that World War One bayonet at you? Almost diced your melon.'

He was joking, but it was true. Rose could be vicious when her blood was up. I did not want Les associating her with murder, even in jest. 'That was years ago. Everyone had been drinking.'

'Aye, happy days. Think I'll give Bowery a body swerve if it's crawling with polis.'

'I'm hoping they'll sling their hook soon. We've got a sale waiting to happen.'

Bowery Auctions lurched from hurdle to hurdle, an outside chance whose odds grew longer with every year. The cost of living crisis meant no one was moving house, which meant no one was clearing out their gear or looking for new objets d'art to brighten their new abodes. There were still deaths, of course, bringing a steady stream of stock, but the quality was variable, so combined with increased energy and fuel prices we were living hand to mouth. The staff had asked for a wage rise we did not have. Rose's expensive wardrobe was regarded with disapproval by workers who were worrying whether their wages would pay the rent. There had been dark mumblings about strikes. Downed tools and a picket line could toll our death knell.

Les swung himself into a seated position. 'I wanted to talk to you about something.'

He sounded uncharacteristically serious. I sat up and wrapped my towel around my waist, ready to go to the showers. 'What?'

Les's hair had grown longer than usual during his six months inside. It hung over his face, concealing his features. 'I met someone inside.'

'I'm happy for you.'

He looked up at me. 'No, not like that. I shared a cell

with a bloke called Hari. A good lad. In for aggravated GBH.'

'Sounds like a prince.'

'Landed six years for beating up the guy who put his kid sister on the game.'

'Must have been quite a beating.'

'Near enough killed him. Thing is, now he's in there and she's out here with that fud running the show.'

'People have free will, Les. That includes the right to be a sex worker.'

'I get that, but it's murky, Rilke. I told Hari you'd be a good guy to get on the case.'

I had heard my share of sad stories. They had got me into trouble. I knotted my towel at the waist. 'Since when?'

'Since you cleared those other matters up.'

I had been snared by two mysteries that I would rather have left alone. They had cost me bruises, sleepless nights, and brought me attention from the authorities I could have done without. 'I'm concentrating on leading a quiet life.'

'She's only a kid.'

'Not like you to get emotionally involved.'

Les made a sour face, as if he had reached for white wine and picked up a water glass by mistake. 'It's been my bedtime story for the past six months. The pimp's a guy called Richard Bird, they call him Dickie.'

'And where was your pal Hari while she was being corrupted?'

'Australia.'

It was not the answer I had expected. 'Australia? What was he doing there?'

Les blinked and wiped sweat away from his eyes with the back of his hand. 'Something to do with green energy.

It's over my head. Hari's a self-improver. Went to uni, took a job in the oil industry in Aberdeen, got sick of fucking the planet, went into renewables and hooked himself a job down under. He came back to Glasgow for a visit, rolled up to the old homestead and found Lolita instead of the sweet kid he'd left behind. He did what any decent man would do. Put the corrupting fucker in hospital.'

I got to my feet. 'Sounds like a sad story, right enough. Get a journalist on the case. Someone like Lucy Paolozzi. The police will pay attention if it's all over the newspapers.'

Les puffed out his chest like a bantam cock about to take his pick of the hens. 'That's why I need you. I'm a drug-dealing ex-con, a questionable source. You're a taxpayer. Someone like her would listen to you.'

I scanned the Turkish room beyond our glass enclosure. There were a couple of middle-aged guys stretched out, sweating silently with towels over their faces. They were probably asleep, but I kept my voice down. Even with the glass wall between us I was cautious about being overheard. 'Have you forgotten how things ended last time? If it wasn't for young Abomi, I'd probably be rotting in a shallow grave in Galloway Forest. I'm still looking over my shoulder in case Razzle Dazzle Diamond decides to set his dogs on me.'

'That's what I'm saying, Rilke. You're a connected man. You sail close to the wind and come out smiling.'

I got to my feet and headed towards the showers. 'I'm a clean-living auctioneer for a well-respected firm. Sorry, Les, your pal will have to find someone else to help him out.'

*

Les emerged from the Arlington Baths wearing a black kilt, tartan Doc Martens and a T-shirt bearing the slogan *Get Your Rosaries Off My Ovaries*. I drove him towards a chrome-and-mirrors hair salon in the centre of town, radio blaring to drown out the sound of his proselytising about Hari's sister.

He brushed his hair back from his face and put one of his boots on the dashboard. 'Young lassies like her, neglected lassies, are desperate for love. They're easy pickings for the likes of Dickie Bird. This is your chance to make a difference, Rilke. Get back on your white horse and do your knight-in-shining-armour routine.'

'Did Hari try talking to her?'

'Course he did. She told him to fuck off out of her business.'

A works van tooted as it passed, and a trio of painters in white overalls made a fist-up gesture at Les who curled his tongue at them.

I smacked his foot off the dashboard. 'I packed you a pair of boxers.'

'I'm a true Scotsman, Rilke. Anyway, since when did you join the fucking Taliban?'

I parked on double yellow lines outside the hairdresser's. 'Thurso Scanlan would love it if you were nicked for flashing.'

Les drew his knees together. 'That fucker is going to suck all the joy from my life.' He brushed a fleck of dust from his kilt. 'Ever wonder why Scanlan's so keen to get his claws into small fry like me?'

'He's prejudiced against wee men in high heels?'

'Get to fuck. It keeps his arrest rates healthy while he turns a blind eye to the sharks higher up the food chain giving him bungs. The man's got a caravan at Heads of Ayr and a Subaru. He went on holiday to Puerto Pollensa last year. You don't get all that on a polisman's salary.'

'You had him under surveillance or something?'

'People talk in jail. You're tight with Anderson. Tell him to have a look at Thurso Scanlan. He's a bigger crook than me, dodgy fucker.'

'Rose is tight with Anderson, not me, and he doesn't take advice from her on police business.'

'He might. He's cuntstruck.'

'No doubt, but it's not your cunt he's struck on. If Scanlan was picking on Rose, it would be another matter, but arresting you for dealing? Anders probably thinks it's a risk of your chosen profession.'

Les snapped, 'I chose fuck all. I was one of Maggie's millions, I made the best of it.'

I did not bother to remind him that Margaret Thatcher had resigned over thirty years ago. Les would remind me that her influence still tainted our existence, and he would be right.

Les nodded towards the carrier bag stuffed with his belongings he had tossed in the back of the van. 'Be a pal and drop that off at the flat for me.'

It was on the tip of my tongue to ask what his last servant died of, but Les was already out of the cab and heading into the salon. A stylist with a tangled mane of hair met Les at the door and pulled him into an embrace. He ran a hand through Les's locks and said something that made them both laugh.

I drew the van into the afternoon traffic and drove west, in the direction of Bowery. Finding Mandy had left a bad taste in my mouth, but it was the thought of Hari's sister that was making me feel queasy. Les had not told me her name and I had not asked for it. I wondered where she was, somewhere in the city I called home. A place that boasted of its warmth and good humour but could gut you from chops to navel and tip your body onto the pavement without a second thought.

Seven

ROSE'S PHONE KEPT buzzing with notifications from friends and clients who had seen her TV appearance on the antiques show Bowery's porters had christened *Bargain Cunt*. She kept glancing at her mobile, checking WhatsApps as they pinged through, nervous that someone would put two and two together and identify the murder weapon.

Our doors were open again. Murchison had given the go-ahead for the sale and Bowery had a festive air. The consensus was that it was okay to speak ill of Mandy Manderson, who had had the bad manners to delay everyone's payday by getting himself killed on the premises and who no one had liked anyway.

Mrs Keenan, a retired private boys' school headmistress, whose good eye for porcelain boosted her retirement, grabbed my arm as I headed for the podium. Her lipstick matched her bright red coat and raspberry beret.

She grinned like an Ensor mask. 'It'll turn out to be a

Murder on the Orient Express situation.' I must have looked bewildered because she added, 'Where everyone stabbed him. He was that disliked.'

I nodded to the back of the room where Murchison and a couple of plainclothes officers loitered, fooling nobody. 'Careful what you say. Sherlock and his crew are keeping their eyes open for clues.'

She followed my gaze. 'You're not up on your Agatha Christie, Rilke. You mean Hercule Poirot. He's the one who investigates *Murder on the Orient Express*.' She gave the inspector a second look. 'That's Sandy Murchison, one of the better boys in his year. Not much imagination, but dogged. I wouldn't have pegged him for a policeman. I would've predicted the law, like his father.'

'His dad's a lawyer?'

'Top judge. Have you heard of the Murchison Anti-Corruption Report?'

I had not but said, 'It rings a faint bell.'

'Alexander's father chaired the inquiry. Fairly toothless – the usual misogyny, racism, homophobia, blah, blah, blah – no surprise to anyone and no big solutions, but of course the force didn't like it. I wonder how his son is getting on in the ranks.'

'Pretty well. He's an inspector.'

'He's got his work cut out for him this time.' Mrs Keenan gave the porcelain cup she had been examining a disparaging look and set it back on the display table. 'Not much for me in this month's sale. I'd better say hello to young Sandy before I head off.'

I watched as she crossed the room, bright as a warning light, and took the inspector by the arm. His face registered polite bewilderment followed by alarm. His colleagues looked amused.

Rose flapped a hand in my direction and pointed at her watch. I nodded and made my way to the podium. It was time to get the show on the road.

The hatpins were lot 147, towards the end of the first section of the sale. Under normal circumstances, I would have made a quip about them featuring on national television in the hope of raising their price, but Rose and I had agreed not to draw more attention to them than was necessary. The pins appeared on the big screen and simultaneously on the various screens of virtual buyers. Hannah lifted the velvet display tray and angled it towards the assembly.

I had delivered my spiel to the bathroom mirror, whispered it beneath my breath as I dressed, practised it in the car on my way to work. The trick was not to remember the way the amethyst had gleamed in Mandy's face, how fatty-white his flesh had been, the suck and give of his eyeball as I pulled the pin free.

I snatched a quick glance at the police officers stationed against the back wall: a trio of clean-shaven men, dressed for outdoors in shades of black and navy business casual. Something Zen gangster about their neutral expressions. A familiar you-make-the-first-move-and-we'll-finish-it air that explained the discreet, bad-smell space around them in the otherwise busy saleroom.

'Our next lot is one hundred and forty-seven, a fine collection of Victorian hatpins. Who will bid me three hundred? Three hundred pounds for this collection of Victorian hatpins.' The amethyst pin alone was worth a cool one-fifty, but the punters kept their hands in their pockets. I looked at Lucy to check if there was any interest online. She shook her head. 'Okay, ladies and gentlemen and ministers without portfolio, who will give me two-seventy-five? Two hundred and seventy-five for this fine collection of hatpins? A rare selection here, not often seen these days, two hundred and seventy-five . . .' I am not a suspicious man, but I come from suspicious stock, and it occurred to me that the punters might sense bad karma emanating from the amethyst pin. '. . . Two fifty, two hundred and fifty pounds . . .' A hand went up at the back of the room and we were away, the price slowly rising. 'Two-seventy-five, three hundred, three hundred and twenty-five . . .' The room was alive now. I glanced at the policemen. The sight of the pins had raised no obvious alarm; they wore the same stony faces as before.

A door opened at the back of the saleroom. A blast of fresh air swept through the fug as Les entered, his hair styled in a blond pixie crop that made him look fallen-angel devilish. He was wearing skinny black jeans and a cropped black jumper under a silver bomber jacket. His earlobes had a diamond sparkle. So much for staying under the radar.

I kept the bid going, numbers climbing. 'Three-fifty, three-seventy-five . . .' The lot was nearing its full potential. The room faltered and I dropped the increments. 'Three-eighty, three-eighty-five . . .' I glanced at Les, then at the trio of policemen, but they were on opposite sides of the room, oblivious to each other's presence. 'Three-eighty-five, three-eighty-five . . .' An online bid. I raised the gavel in my right hand. 'Am I bid any more for this fine collection of Victorian hatpins? Going, going . . .' I scanned the room, looking for a final bid, taking everyone in: the punters and the police, Les in his shiny new incarnation, Rose pale with anticipation, Lucy following the virtual punters on her computer screen. 'Going . . . going . . .' I had avoided the sight of the hatpins, but I glanced at them one last time as a I brought the hammer down.

The black velvet display tray trembled in Hannah's hands. I smashed the gavel down – 'GONE!' – and the tray flew from her grasp. The pins seemed to hang for a moment in the air, proof that time and space are not fixed, then landed in a jumble on the floor. The assembled punters broke into a round of applause. Hannah and Rose knelt on the floor by my podium rescuing the fallen items. Rose was swearing under her breath. Hannah started to cry. I held a hand in the air and made a weak joke, 'That's the problem with gravity, folks. It doesn't let up for an instant.'

There was a shimmer of silver, and suddenly Les was in my eyeline. He grinned and tapped a finger against the side of his nose. I resisted the urge to jump from the podium and strangle him. Les was too sharp for his own good. Too sharp for my good.

Rose rearranged the rescued hatpins on their velvet tray and held them out to the audience, smiling like a *Sale of the Century* model. Hannah dashed into the backroom. Our head porter Frank took her place and held the next lot up for the audience to see. I slid back into my spiel. 'Ladies and gentlemen, what will you give me for this fine pearl and rose gold ring . . .'

I was an automaton, a mechanical doll fleshed with skin and blood. One day they would replace me with an AI, but perhaps I would be in prison by then, locked up for my role in concealing who had murdered Mandy Manderson, a man no one cared enough for to mourn.

Eight

HANNAH WAS STILL crying. Her peroxide-white hair had recently been cut into an Angie Bowie mullet with hot-pink dip-dyed tips. She had a new piercing above her right eyebrow, to balance the one in her nose and the other in her bottom lip. 'I didn't mean to drop the pins. I just saw them and . . .'

The sale was over, and the three of us, Rose, Hannah and me, were squashed into the kitchen at the back of Bowery Auctions. It was a poor hiding place. Policemen are known for their liquid diets. Rose had planked the whisky. Sooner or later one of them would come in search of Tetley and a kettle.

I handed Hannah a glass of water. The surface of the water trembled as if some terrible beast was approaching. 'No harm done. It's not like you to get in a state about a wee thing like that.'

The girl sniffed and wiped away more tears with the back of her hand. I reached into my jacket pocket and pulled out a freshly laundered handkerchief. She dabbed her eyes, blew her nose and offered me the hanky back.

I shook my head. 'You keep it.' I wanted to ask if she knew something about Mandy's death but was nervous of alerting her to the role the hatpin had played. 'It's been a hard week. Are you upset about what happened to Mr Manderson?'

Hannah blew her nose again. She dabbed the cotton square gently around the silver ring speared through her septum. 'He was a pig.' She glanced at Rose. 'You told us to keep away from him, but we'd have needed eyes in the back of our heads. I'd be busy working and then suddenly there he'd be, breathing down my neck. Did you notice he always wore trainers? Men his age usually wear boots or brogues like Mr Rilke, but Mr Manderson wore trainers so he could creep up on people.'

I said, 'He was a good fifteen years older than me—'

Rose snapped, 'No one cares . . .'

Hannah's eyes met mine, brimming with tears like a Bragolin child. 'You're not old, Mr Rilke.'

I patted her hand. 'Did you tell someone else that he was bothering you? Maybe one of the porters?'

'They knew. They thought it was funny.'

I made a mental note to give our head porter Frank a stern talk about the need to drag the crew into the twenty-first century. 'Anyone else?'

Hannah was a mischievous girl, popular with customers despite or perhaps because of her impudent streak. I had threatened her with the sack more than once, but she had too much potential for me to get rid of her. She had a good eye, an appreciation of craftsmanship and a memory for provenance. It was not like her to keep quiet when asked a direct question, but she looked at the floor and said nothing.

Rose muttered, 'This is a bloody waste of time.'

I shot her a look. 'Rose, would you do me a big favour and check on Les? He sloped in at the end of the sale looking like a cat in search of a canary.'

She got to her feet. 'For fuck's sake. That's all I bloody need.'

I waited until the door swung shut behind her. 'You'll feel better if you tell me what's bothering you.'

Hannah rolled up the sleeve of her blouse. Pink peonies and blue forget-me-nots shone on her tattooed skin. 'It's nothing.'

'The police are all over this. If they find out you know something you've not told them, it could go bad for you.'

'Maybe it will go bad for me if I tell them.' She took a deep, wavering breath. 'I think maybe I was the last person to see Mr Manderson alive.'

I kept my expression sombre, careful not to reveal my sense of relief. 'That's probably something you should share with Inspector Murchison.'

Hannah cradled her water glass. Her hands were small, her nails painted with blue nail varnish, chipped at the edges, her fingers stacked with silver rings. 'I don't want anyone to know.'

'Murchison doesn't strike me as a gossip.'

'I'm ashamed.'

My relief vanished. 'Are you telling me you did it?'

Hannah had set her water glass aside and was picking the blue varnish from her nails. It was difficult to imagine her childish fingers pushing the hatpin into Manderson's brain.

'Did what?' It dawned on her. 'Killed him? Of course not.'

The swing from relief to fear and back again made me impatient. 'So what's the problem?'

'Promise not to tell?'

I zipped my fingers across my lips. 'Not unless you give me permission.'

'Especially not Lucy.'

I repeated, 'Especially not Lucy.'

'Or Rose.'

I gave the usual liar's reassurance. 'Your secret's safe with me.'

Lucy and Hannah were the only young women employed at Bowery. They had both been to art school and completed degree projects on the auction house before joining the team. They were each other's friend and ally. If Hannah's secret was too shameful to share with Lucy, I was not sure I wanted to know it.

Hannah sipped her water. She looked towards the cupboard above my head, reluctant to meet my eyes. 'Mr Manderson saw me and Lucy looking at those hatpins. They're really pretty, but we hardly make enough to eat these days . . .'

The conversation was in danger of taking a familiar turn. 'Did he say something?'

Hannah looked away. 'He was a dirty old pervert.'

'What did he say?'

She took another sip of water and set the glass down on the counter beside her. 'The usual stuff.'

'Mr Manderson's dead and gone. He won't bother you anymore.'

Hannah's eyes met mine. 'He said he'd buy us a hatpin each if we gave him a kiss.'

Mandy had been prone to licking his lips. I pictured his mouth. It had been thin and ungenerous. He was a sloppy shaver, and white bristles often edged it. It was not a mouth made for kissing, but the hatpins were tempting, the girls young and short of money.

'He shouldn't have done that.'

Hannah shook her head. 'Lucy told him to get stuffed. I did too.'

I took her hands in mine. 'I've done plenty of things I regret. Sometimes there's nothing you can do with regrets except put them in a box and fasten the lid.'

Hannah gave a little sob. 'He stank of garlic.'

It was always smell that conjured the bad memories. A particular brand of aftershave, stale sweat, burnt petrol fumes.

'What happened?'

Hannah looked at her feet. 'I went out to get filled rolls for the crew. It wasn't my turn, but whoever goes gets their roll for free, so I volunteered. I was almost at the gates when Mr Manderson called me back. I should have kept going but I stopped and asked if he wanted me to get him something.' She met my eyes. 'He held out a fifty-pound note and said he'd give it to me for a little kiss. He was old. I thought it would just be a peck on the cheek.'

Hannah had been educated at private school. Until recently she had lived with her grandmother who, she had let slip, was paying the mortgage of her new flat. Hannah was a girl who people cared for. She did not know yet that even young flesh is cheap; had miscalculated the currency of her round vowels, pretty face and firm body.

'But it wasn't just a peck?'

She started to cry again. 'I thought I was in control, but his hands were all over me. I tried to push him away, but he was stronger than he looked. He stuck his tongue in my mouth.'

I took her hand in mine again and stroked it, hoping the story ended there. 'You're right. Mandy was a dirty, old pervert. Where did this happen? Presumably not in the middle of the car park.'

'In the gap between the wall and the side entrance steps. I thought I was going to be sick, but then someone opened the main door and started to come down the steps. He was distracted, and I managed to wriggle free. I ran all the way to the roll shop.'

'Did you see who it was?'

Hannah shook her head. 'I didn't look back. I pulled my hood up and hoped they didn't recognise me.'

There was a knock on the door and Abomi stuck his head into the room. The young porter had started going to the gym. He was growing into himself and looked less gormless than when he had joined us two years ago as a sixteen-year-old apprentice.

'Sorry, Mr Rilke, Rose says she needs you in the saleroom.'

'Tell her I'll be there in a moment.'

Abomi looked worried. 'She said to bring you back with me.'

'She'll just have to wait.'

'Please, Mr Rilke, she'll have my guts if I don't bring you back.'

'So keep out of her way. Go and check there's no stray bits of police tape still hanging around the car park. It's bad for business.'

'As long as you tell her I tried.' Abomi let the door swing shut behind him.

Hannah's eyes met mine. 'Do you think it was the murderer who came down the steps?'

'I don't know. But you're going to have to tell the inspector a version of this story.' I paused, thinking it through. 'You don't have to say anything about the money or the kiss, just that you were going to the roll shop and you noticed Mandy in the car park. You think you heard someone coming down the steps, but you were in a hurry and didn't bother to check who it was. Do you think you can manage that?'

Hannah touched her lip piercing with the tip of her tongue. 'I'm not a very good liar.'

I raised my eyebrows. Hannah was creative when it came to providing excuses for why she had missed a day's work or arrived late, but lying to the police is harder than telling everyday falsehoods.

'Visualise it in your head, try and believe that it's true and keep it simple. No extra details you might forget if someone asks you to repeat the story later.'

She gave a grave nod. 'I didn't even get the fifty pounds.'

I shook my head, mock-sad. 'First rule of soliciting: get the money up front, before you deliver the goods.' I reached into my pocket and passed her a twenty-pound note. 'Next time you're desperate, come to me. I'll try and get you some overtime.'

She hesitated, then slipped the money into her pocket. 'Thanks, Mr Rilke.'

'Sorry I can't give you a hatpin.'

Hannah wiped her tears and blew her nose on my handkerchief. She took a deep breath. 'I wouldn't want one now.' Her face was suddenly serious. 'You don't think the murderer used one of them on Mr Manderson?'

I gave the assured, lightly amused smile of a seasoned liar. 'One of the hatpins? No, we'd already inventoried them. They were all present and correct.' Hannah looked like she was going to ask something else. I changed the subject before

I could slip up and implicate myself. 'Do you want me to sit in while you tell the inspector about seeing Mr Manderson in the car park?'

'Won't he want to know why I didn't tell him sooner?'

'Say you didn't think it was important. People were coming and going all day. It just occurred to you that it might be useful.'

Hannah gave me a quick, unexpected hug. Her hair smelt pinkly of bubble gum. 'Thanks, Mr Rilke. Probs best I see him on my own, so it doesn't look like a big deal.'

She left the kitchen door open. I stood there for a moment, watching the after-sale bustle in the saleroom beyond and remembering what the scenes of crime officer had said about Mandy Manderson's killer being close enough for a kiss. I wondered who had bought the hatpins and if I should check their address – in case of what, I was not sure.

Rose stuck her head round the doorway. Her hair had come loose of her bun. 'I think we have a problem.'

Nine

LES WAS GRINNING like a loon. 'Soon as I saw Fantoosh on the TV waving that hatpin in the air, going on about stilettos and suffragettes, I knew.'

We were in Rose's car, an almond-beige Rover 3500, parked in the Bowery car park. Les in the back, Rose in the driver's seat, me in the passenger seat.

I turned to look at him. 'You know fuck all because there's fuck all to know.'

Rose pulled down the driver's visor and checked her lipstick in the vanity mirror. 'I wouldn't use a stupid hatpin anyway. I'm a steak-knife-in-the-kidneys woman.'

I doubted Les really believed Rose had murdered Mandy, but he was a man who made his living by his wits, and he knew that something was up.

Les took out his own vanity mirror. His lipstick was more muted than Rose's. Cherry blossom to her scarlet. He clicked the mirror away and leaned forward into the space between Rose and me.

'I reckon this was an impulse crime. Death by accessory. This guy got in your face, and you took him out with the nearest thing to hand. You'll get off with manslaughter. Three years if you're lucky, six if you're not.'

I could see the corner where Mandy had breathed his last. The tent was gone, but a scrap of crime-scene tape flopped dismally against the wall. Abomi had missed it.

I said, 'An imagination's a great thing. You should start writing for the soaps.'

Les grinned. 'I'd be great at that, by the way.'

Rose started the engine and pulled out of the car park. 'These hatpins aren't as robust as they look. They're sharp, but the stem would bend to buggery if you stabbed someone with it.'

Her voice held all the assurance of a seasoned bullshitter, but Les was practised in the art and not ready to buy what Rose was selling. 'Through flesh maybe, but your pal took it in the eyeball. There's more give there, unless you hit bone, and from what I heard it was a clear shot. Kudos.'

I held onto the door panel, steadying myself as Rose swung the Rover too fast into the main road. 'Since when did you become CSI Glasgow?'

Rose shook her head. 'The poor man's not even in the ground. This is in bad taste, even for you.'

Les snorted. '*Poor man?* You hated his guts.'

A BMW cut in front of us. Rose tooted her horn and gave the driver the finger. Les rolled down his window and shouted, 'Wanker.'

Rose glanced at him in the rear-view mirror. 'I'm not over

fond of you but I'm not thinking of creative ways to take you out.'

Les huffed, 'Mibbe so, mibbe no. Put it this way, I wouldn't want to be on my own with you.' He looked out of the window. 'Where are we going, by the way?'

Rose gave him a sparkling smile. 'Partick Police Station. I'm sure they'll be interested if you have information that will help their inquiries.'

Les did not miss a beat. 'Bring it on.'

Roadworks and temporary traffic lights had reduced a long stretch of Dumbarton Road to one lane. We made slow, stop-start stuttering progress past pubs and beauty salons, restaurants and cafés, newsagents and charity shops. Rose parked at the bus stop opposite the police station. There was a queue of people. A bus was due.

She cut the engine. 'Off you pop.'

Les grinned. 'You calling my bluff?'

'I'm saving you a subway fare.'

'I could have walked it quicker.' He leaned back in his seat. 'Good word, manslaughter, when you think about it. Man . . . slaughter. Descriptive.'

Rose turned to look at him. 'Are you going in, or are you going to sit here playing Dictionary Challenge? I've got things to do.'

Les reached for the door handle. 'You've not asked me what I want.'

Rose shook her head. 'I can't believe I gave you a bung to ease your reintroduction into society.'

'Oh aye, thanks for that. I got my hair done.'

'I noticed.'

There was a short pause while Les waited for Rose to compliment his dye job.

I turned round and looked at Les. 'These kind of rumours are bad for business. Tell your suspicions to the police or—'

Rose interrupted. 'Nasty suspicions about people who have showered you in the milk of human kindness.'

Les wrinkled his nose. 'That sounds gross.'

I pressed on. 'Tell your suspicions to the police or shut the fuck up about Manderson. It's not funny.'

Les clasped his hands around his knees. 'I saw those hatpins and I watched your faces as you punted them. There's something going on. I'm not asking for money.' His eyes gleamed like dollar signs. 'Even though I'm skint and I bet it's worth something. I just want a bit of help for a young girl who's being exploited.'

Rose swivelled the rear-view mirror and stared at him in it. 'What are you going on about?'

Les pointed at me. 'He knows. My mate Hari's sister's being turned out by this guy. I asked Rilke to help but he told me to get to fuck.'

Rose shifted her gaze to me. Whatever she was going to say was interrupted by the sharp rap of knuckles against the car's passenger window. Chief Inspector Jim Anderson peered in at us. He made a rolling gesture with his index finger.

Rose said, 'Ignore him.'

But Anderson was not above booking his friends. I rolled my window down.

Anderson's weary eyes scanned the car interior, taking in Rose and me, Les — who was sinking into the back seat, wearing the same angels-with-dirty-faces expression he has worn in times of trouble and interrogation since we were truanting schoolboys.

I smiled. 'Hello, Jim.'

The queue in the bus shelter watched us with tired disinterest.

Anderson ignored my greeting. His eyes rested on Les. 'Didn't know you were out.'

Les nodded. 'They took the shackles off yesterday. Do us a favour and don't tell your pal Thurso.'

Anderson made a face, whether it was at Les's liberty or the idea of Thurso Scanlan being his pal was unclear. He turned his attention to Rose. 'Heard about your bit of bother.'

She kept her eyes on the road, her mouth a vermilion slash. 'No great loss, except to our bank balance.'

Anderson raised his eyebrows, but he had known Rose a long time and was beyond being shocked. 'Glad it didn't derail your TV appearance.'

Rose looked up at him. 'Did you see it?'

Anderson gave the ghost of a smile. 'I watched on catch-up. You were good.'

'Did you think so?'

'Aye, I liked that bit about the stiletto.'

Les chimed in. 'That was my favourite bit too.'

Rose shot him a look like a dagger. She put a flirt in her voice and batted her lashes at Anderson. 'You would.'

Anderson's eyes crinkled. 'Finished for the day?'

'Maybe.'

'Fancy a cocktail at the Dakota? Celebrate your imminent stardom?'

Rose stared out at Dumbarton Road. The sky had darkened. It was going to rain again soon, and the street was cast in shades of Soviet concrete. 'I've got the car.'

Les perked up, suddenly eager. 'You go and have some fun, Rose. We'll take it back for you.'

Rose said pointedly, 'I thought you had something you wanted to do.'

'Nothing that can't wait.'

Rose took the keys from the ignition and tossed them at me. 'Thanks, Rilke. I reckon you should think about helping Les out. Sounds like a worthwhile project.'

She took her handbag from the footwell and slid from her seat before I could object, almost knocking a cyclist clad in hi-vis under an approaching bus. The man shouted an expletive which hung in the air behind him.

Rose sniffed. 'Bit rude.'

The bus tooted. The waiting queue moved towards it. A line of blocked traffic began to honk their horns. I got out and strode quickly to the driver's side.

Rose clapped her hands twice, like a maître d' calling for service. 'Chop, chop, boys. You can't park here.'

Anderson grinned. 'Aye, move along or I'll book yous.'

I gave them the V-sign, got behind the wheel and drove on.

Les leaned forward and slapped the back of my seat. 'You heard the boss – you're my little bitch now.'

I elbowed him in the face. 'Buckle up. You're not in Barlinnie anymore and I'm nobody's little bitch.'

Les rubbed his forehead. 'That's debatable.' But he sank back into his seat and drew the belt across his body. 'So are you going to help me or what?'

Ten

'I TOLD YOU already, it's not my thing.'

We had parked Rose's car outside her building, tucked the key inside the rear left wheel arch and were now nursing pints in a corner seat of the Doublet. Someone had left the door open, and a shaft of dying daylight fell across the floor. A table of actors I vaguely recognised, without being able to recall their names, were engaged in lively conversation about an absent friend who always suggested his scenes would work better if he was nude. Their laughter was loud enough to cloak Les and me from curious ears, but we had been spotted. A studenty man in a We Were Promised Jetpacks T-shirt sidled up and sat down without asking permission. He leaned across the table and said in a low voice, 'I was wondering if you could sort me out.'

Les gave him a dangerous look. 'I can sort you out, if you're looking for a doing.'

I took a swallow of my pint. 'Don't get carried away, Les. Maybe he's looking for a lumber.'

'Ugly grunts is more your line than mine.'

Jetpacks stared, confused. He smiled as if smiling would make everything a joke. 'I'm just looking for a bit of blow.'

'Fuck off.'

He got to his feet. 'I was only asking.'

Les's smile was an amber warning. 'And I'm telling.'

Jetpacks muttered, 'Who rattled your cage?' and sloped off.

I saw the barman watching us and whispered, 'Keep your cool. I like this bar.'

'Twats like him get on my tits. Careless talk costs lives, Rilke. I don't want to end up inside again.'

'I get you.' I nodded at Les's silver bomber jacket and exposed midriff. 'Maybe you should keep a lower profile, stop drawing attention to yourself.'

'Oh aye, blame the victim, why don't you?'

We concentrated on our pints for a moment. I looked at the bar's mascot, a small plaster soldier balanced above the gantry, dressed in a kilt and doublet, with painted black hair and moustache. If you looked closely, you could see that his mouth was bunged with a wine cork, and if you looked closer still, you might realise that he was a chorus angel stolen from the nativity scene at George Square many decades ago, before the council started putting Mary, Jesus, Joseph and their posse behind glass to prevent abductions.

'An angelic press gang.'

'What?'

I realised I had spoken out loud. 'Nothing.'

'There's nothing angelic about it, Rilke. Hari says Dickie Bird's a creep. It's a tale as old as time. Find a vulnerable kid, make them fall in love with you and then tell them you've got a wee problem that could be easily solved with a bit of dough. And, of course, they think they're in love, so off they go. *Pretty Woman*, it's not.'

'If they think they're in love, maybe they're in love.'

Now it was my turn to be on the end of a murderous look. 'He's mesmerised her. She's too young to know any better.'

I stroked a finger up the edge of my glass, drawing a line in the cold sweat that clung to its surface. 'It's like when the weatherman tells you it's fifteen degrees outside but minus three with windchill. I've never understood the point. If it's cold, it's cold. Okay, this Bird guy's a slime, but rubbishing the girl's feelings doesn't make things better.'

'I hate it when you get philosophical.' Les counted on his fingers. 'One, you've never been in love, so you don't have a scooby what you're talking about. Two, you're talking shite. Three . . .' Les hesitated, unsure what three was. 'Three, you're talking deep shite.' His phone chimed, indicating he had received a message. Les glanced at it and typed a response, fingers nimble. His nails were painted with a silver sheen that matched his bomber jacket. They glimmered like mother-of-pearl beneath the dim lights of the pub. He shoved the phone back in his pocket. 'Okay, you've not to lose the plot.'

I felt a creeping foreboding. 'Why would I?'

He got to his feet. 'Because Hari's sister's outside. Wait here while I fetch her.'

I half rose. 'For fuck's sake, Les.' But he was already cutting across the barroom. I sank back into my seat. The Doublet has a back door. It would have been an easy thing to slip through it and take the path along the riverside up to Kelvingrove.

One of the actors, a slim man in a tartan sherpa jacket and black cap, met my eyes and smiled. I couldn't tell if it was a come-on or if he had clocked what an absurd pair Les and I made. I kept my face straight and took another inch off the level of my pint. Smiles are tricky. Easy to give, not so easy to interpret. I have learned to ration mine.

Perhaps it was Les's reference to *Pretty Woman* that had led me to expect a girl in a short skirt, thigh boots and low top, or some other clichéd woman-of-the-night costume gleaned from Hollywood. Hari's sister was petite and pretty, with olive skin and hair that fell in smooth, dark curtains around her face. She was wearing a man's suede jacket over a white vest, too light for the weather, skinny black jeans and black motorcycle boots. She glanced around the bar uncertainly as she entered. One hand cradled an overstuffed shoulder bag close to her body, as if the weight of it was too much. Les was nervous, talking ten to the dozen and grinning the sharkish grin that shows his eye teeth. The girl kept her face straight. I reckoned she had also learned to ration her smiles.

The table of actors watched them as they walked through the bar, heads turning like plants caught by the same breeze. I saw the maybe-student and his mates watching too and felt uneasy. Perhaps we had been unwise to be so lively with Jetpacks.

Les put his hand on the girl's shoulder and guided her towards our seat. 'Budge up, Rilke. Make room for Cat.'

The girl slipping into the seat beside me looked a year or two older than Abomi.

Les drained the last of his pint and asked, 'What do you want to drink?'

Cat tucked her bag by her side. 'Do they serve Monster?'

Les giggled, uncomfortable in the role of uncle and brazening it out. 'They served Rilke.'

The girl glanced at me, checking to see what variety of monster I was.

I tried to look human. 'They'll do you a Coke or an Irn-Bru.'

'Irn-Bru, please, full fat.'

Les nudged me. 'You got that twenty I lent you?'

Jetpacks collected another round of drinks from the bar. He looked less studenty than before. He stared at us as he passed, then sat down next to his two mates and said something that made them look at us. There was an edge to their stares I didn't like.

'Maybe we should head.'

Les followed my eyes. 'Ah, fuck them, wee nyaffs.'

Cat was perched on the edge of her seat, ready for flight. 'What's going on?'

'Nothing.' Les held his hand out and I gave him two tens I did not owe him. 'Thanks, pal.' He ducked up to the bar.

The pub was suddenly busy with men in lycra and women in short skirts and bathing costumes over spangled tights as a subway pub tour poured through the door. I spotted Batman, Wonder Woman and Spiderman costumes, but I did not know who the rest were meant to be. The slim actor in the sherpa jacket caught my eye and grinned.

Cat slipped off her jacket. Her arms were decorated with tattoos not yet dense enough to be considered sleeves but numerous enough to declare commitment. She saw me clocking them and gave me a want-to-make-something-of-it stare.

I wanted to tell her I was not a creep, that I worked with young women and respected them, but that kind of statement never convinces. Instead, I tried, 'Les seems to think you're in some kind of bother.'

She turned her brown eyes on me. 'I don't even know Les. Why's he telling my business to randos?'

I wondered if her brother was as good-looking as she was and if Les was telling the truth when he said there was nothing between him and Hari. Six months sharing a small cell could turn anyone's head.

'You'd have to ask Les. I think maybe your brother helped him out and he feels an obligation.'

I looked at the bar, trying to indicate to Les that his presence was required. Les had fallen into conversation with a man in a tight, fluorescent-green all-in-one decorated with black question marks. He was studiously avoiding looking at the banquette where Cat and I were squashed.

'My brother's in Barlinnie.'

'That's where Les met him.'

Cat gave a quick, plosive laugh. 'And they think I'm in bother?'

The green superhero passed Les a vodka. He tipped it back in one shot, like a Cossack due at the front. There was no sign of our round.

'I don't know why Les is trying to involve me in this. You're right: it's none of my business.'

'Do you know why my brother's inside?'

'Les said he beat up your boyfriend.'

'Hari molicated him. Caught Dickie by surprise and laid into him with a baseball bat. He was six weeks in hospital. The doctors said he was lucky not to have brain damage. Hari's meant to leave me alone, but every day I get another call from another burner. Every week a three-page letter through the post.' She lifted a cardboard beer mat from the table and bent it in half. 'He's obsessed with me, has been since we were kids. And now he's got some jailbird and his pal stalking me. I could get him another three years if I told the police what he's up to. Could get him a decade if I told them what he did to me when I was a kid. Maybe I will if he doesn't stop.' She bent the beermat in the opposite direction and then looked at me. 'I'm not scared of the polis. I'll dub you and your weirdo pal in if you don't leave me alone.'

I held my hands up in surrender. 'This was Les's first time inside. He's not looking to go back.'

'So tell him to fuck off.'

'I'll tell him.'

'Make sure you do.'

The gangster attitude should have been funny, coming from this young woman, but I felt ashamed.

'I'm nothing to do with this. I'm an auctioneer. I thought Les and me were just going for a quick pint. I didn't know you were going to show up.'

Cat gave a dry, disbelieving laugh. 'An auctioneer. I'm guessing my brother isn't the only jailbird you've met.'

'I've never met your brother.'

'So what's any of this to do with you?'

'Nothing. Les is under the illusion that I'm good in a crisis.' Les was getting served at last. I tried to catch his eye, but he looked away and handed my money to the barman. 'He's a stupid bastard, but his motives are pure.' I almost added, *for a change*. 'Your brother told Les his sister was being exploited by a creep and Les thought maybe . . . He said you were too young to know what you're doing . . .' I had run out of things to say.

Cat reached into her bag. She scrabbled around for a moment, then found her wallet, pulled a driving licence from it and held it up for me to see. Her face stared unsmiling from the small black-and-white photograph.

'Do you see the year of birth?'

'Yes.'

'How old does it make me?'

'Twenty-two.'

'Old enough to make my own decisions.'

'I told Les he shouldn't stick his nose in.'

'The only reason I'm here is to tell you and your friend to back off.'

Hannah and Lucy joked about *cringe*. I felt an urge to shrink into my suit. 'Understood.'

A fat Batman shouted for the superheroes to finish their drinks. There was a chorus of *chug it, chug it, chug it*, and they started to stagger for the door.

'Maybe you should tell the polis what your brother got up to when you were kids.'

'What bit of *fuck off out of my business* did you not understand?'

I held my hands up again. 'Okay.'

Cat's phone played a jaunty jingle. She scrabbled in her bag again, swearing under her breath, and put it to her ear. 'Sure, okay, fine. No bother. I'll be there.' She stuffed the phone away. 'Tell your friend Les to leave me alone or I'll set the cops on him, I mean it.'

I resisted an impulse to touch her hand. 'You sure you're okay?'

The girl was trying to zip her bag shut. The zipper kept snagging on something. She swore as she tugged it free. 'Take a warning. I set the police on my own brother. I'll do the same to your pal and not lose any sleep.' Cat slid out of her seat. She went up to the bar and said something that made

Les step away from her. He tried to grin, but whatever she said had killed his smile. Les touched the girl's shoulder. She grabbed his pint glass and threw its contents at his face. Jetpacks and his student mates cheered. One of the actors shouted *bravo!* and their companions broke into noisy applause. Cat did not pause to take a bow. She headed swiftly for the street, her bag bumping against her hip.

The barman was gesturing towards the door. Les had grabbed a bar towel and was attempting to soak up the beer from his fancy bomber, insisting he was not responsible for mad women and complaining he had just bought a round and was damned if he was leaving. 'She's one of your fucking customers. Behave, or I'll report you to the licensing authorities.'

I finished my pint and waited for the inevitable. I had problems of my own that did not include Les's Barlinnie buddy or his sister. But I had not liked the panic on the girl's face as she answered her phone, or her swift placatory tone as she reassured the voice on the other end of the line that she would be there immediately.

There was something else. The tattoos that decorated Cat's arms and flew across her hands were of swallows and corvids, magpies and sparrows, blue pigeons, bright peacocks and birds of other varieties I did not have names for. Perhaps she was an ornithologist, or maybe this was a loving gesture towards a man she adored who, for all I knew, had reciprocated by inking himself with images of felines. The man Hari accused of abusing his sister was named Dickie Bird. I could not help but wonder if he had drawn his name across her flesh.

Eleven

WE TOOK THE back exit, Les still complaining about his squandered pint and women's lack of appreciation.

'I tell you, Rilke, this jacket's ruined. It was a TK Maxx special. You know how long it takes to find good stuff there? Hours.'

It was dark and cold in the lane leading down to the Kelvin. A breeze blowing across the river carried the scent of diesel and kebabs from the Great Western Road.

Les muttered, 'I swear to God, this is the last time I do anyone a lemon.'

I put the collar of my suit jacket up and wished I had thought to wear a coat. 'Probably the first time too.'

'I've done you plenty of favours. Christ, I've been pulling you out of holes since we were kids. Remember when big Bobby Chang was going to batter you in primary five?'

We turned into the street that edges Kelvinbridge subway car park, built on the ghosts of tenements. Mills and cottages had stood there a hundred or so years ago, but now it was a lonely spot, dimly lit by streetlamps. I glanced up to Great Western Road above us. The top deck of a bus was fleetingly visible above the parapet of the bridge, interior bright, passengers outlined for a moment, brief journeying shadows.

'I still don't know what Bobby Chang had against me.'

'Didn't like your poofy ways. Point is, I battered him for you.'

'And got me six of the belt in the process. I could have battered him better myself.'

Concrete paving stones changed to cobbles as we approached Kelvin Bridge. The curved plastic tunnel that housed the moving staircase to and from the subway glowed on our left. The wrought-iron balustrade of the Victorian staircase on our right was cast in shadow. A giant red squirrel graffitied on the wall beneath the staircase followed us with dark, malevolent eyes. A crop of purple painted flowers busied the bricks beside it, where someone had daubed the words, THEY CAN CUT ALL THE FLOWERS BUT THEY CANNOT STOP SPRING FROM COMING.

Les zipped his silver bomber against the cold. 'Bobby Chang would have taken you apart. Did I tell you I bumped into him not long before I went inside?'

I glanced up at the city crest on the bridge above. The bird and the fish and the ring and the tree. 'Oh aye, what's he doing? WWE wrestling?

'Schoolteacher.'

'That figures.'

It was wetly dank in the tunnel beneath the bridge, as if water had seeped up from the river. Our laughter bounced off the walls.

Les said, 'What do you think?'

'It couldn't have been easy being Bobby. School was full of racists and homophobes. He was only seven. Can't blame him for punching down.'

Les gave me a shove. 'Not about Bobby. About Cat?'

I was on the verge of telling Les how Cat had panic-scrabbled for her phone and the bird tattoos migrating across her arms when there was a shout behind us. We paused and looked back in the direction we had travelled. Three silhouettes stood in the mouth of the tunnel like baddies in a manga comic. I could not make out their features, but I recognised their shapes. Young and broad-shouldered, in jeans and puffa jackets. Jetpacks and his two mates had followed us from the Doublet.

Les is wiry and not quite five eight, but you don't dress like he does for over twenty years in Glasgow without knowing how to handle yourself. He widened his stance and straightened his shoulders, like a man about to encounter a grizzly.

'Hello, fuckers.'

I muttered, 'Remember you're on licence.'

'Ah, fuck off, Rilke.'

They were three to our two, athletic and fired up with beer and insults. Their shadows rose large against the tunnel walls. More gorilla than bear.

Les pumped his hips, made a give-it-to-me gesture with his hands and shouted, 'Come on, boys, bring it on. I'll send yous to the Death Star.'

He meant the Queen Elizabeth Hospital, whose nickname refers to the radiating wings of its main building and its high patient death rate.

'For fuck's sake, I'm in my good suit.'

Les glanced at me. 'That what you call it?'

If I had been on my own, I would have run for it, sped out of the tunnel, vaulted one of the fences that hem the riverbank and down into the undergrowth, but backing down is not in Les's repertoire.

The younger men were fanning out, ready to rush us like rugby players on an open field. One of them shouted, 'Look, it's Jimmy Savile and Jeffrey Epstein, dirty fuckers.'

I said, 'Told you that jacket was a bad idea.'

The other boys thought their pal was funny. They hooted into the echoes, rousing a couple of pigeons who bustled in the rafters above.

Les muttered, 'I'm going to Bobby Chang them. You take the cunt on the left. I'll get the boy on the right.'

'What about the fucker in the middle?'

'He looks like he already wants his mammy. He'll leg it soon as he sees his pals getting gubbed.'

The guy in the middle looked like a tasty fighter to me. I have never developed Les's glee for battle, but I have been in enough fights to know the best tactic is to get in first and hit hard until one of you cannot hit any more. When Les said, 'Now!' and ran towards the men, I ran with him, letting out a warrior yell. The trio let out their own battle cries and rushed towards us. The men in the middle and on the right both made for me. I stepped sideways, using their speed and weight against them.

There was another shout, and a figure came bolting from the mouth of the tunnel wielding a stick. They whirled the weapon over their head like a helicopter blade and dashed towards us. I thought it was another student and that Les and I were in for a beating, but they slammed the full weight of the stick into my nearest opponent's kidneys. Pain and surprise made him totter and almost fall.

Les was already laying into Jetpacks. The student was bigger, but he did not have Les's fearless capacity for pain and was already flagging. My boy tried to kick the feet from under me. I grabbed his ankle and jerked his leg upwards. Our eyes locked for a satisfying, fleeting second, and then he was down on the cobbles.

I recognised the newcomer with the stick: the thin man in the sherpa jacket who had caught my eye in the Doublet. He had lost his cap and his hair flopped across his eyes. He pushed it away and swung his weapon in a broad arc. His opponent had regained his balance. He feinted to the right and then lunged to the left, but Sherpa was ready for the move and hit the student a sound crack. The blow felled him.

Les shouted, 'Put the boot in, Rilke.' He was applying the full weight of his own boot to Jetpacks' ribs.

The student Sherpa had toppled was already limping away, one arm cradling the other.

I gave my boy a half-hearted shove on the shoulder with the heel of my brogues. 'You had enough?' The boy cringed, and I said, 'Take a good look at this face. You see it again, you walk the other way. Understand?' The boy nodded, and I added, 'Homophobia is a hate crime. You deserve all you got. Now leg it.'

I kept my fists tight, ready for him to try a revenge punch, but the boy edged free of my shoe's range and got to his feet. 'We were just having a laugh.'

I grinned at him. 'I don't have a sense of humour.'

The boy looked to where Les was still laying into Jetpacks. 'Tell him to stop before he kills Jamie.'

I saw the rightness of what he was saying and snapped, 'Fuck off. I'll send your pal after you.'

Sherpa moved at the same time as me. He grabbed Les by one shoulder. I took him by the other. 'All right, Leslie, you've taught the cunt a lesson. Now leave him alone before you end up back where you don't want to be.'

Les kicked Jetpacks in the ribs one last time and stepped away, panting. 'Told you I'd Chang him.'

Sherpa went to the mouth of the tunnel and picked up the hat he had lost in the tussle.

I ran my hand through my hair, smoothing it back into place and followed him. 'Thanks. Those guys were mental.'

I was breathing heavily but the other man had barely broken sweat.

'No problem. I heard them saying they'd give you a kicking and thought I'd see if you needed a hand. Three against one didn't seem fair.'

He was still holding the stick, which I realised was a broom. I nodded at it. 'Better watch you don't get barred from the Doublet for pinching the fixtures and fittings.'

He smiled. 'It was by the back door. I thought it might come in handy.'

'I appreciate it. You saved my suit.'

The stranger eyed me up and down. 'I noticed it in the pub. Nice cut. Vintage?'

I had lifted it from a house clearance the week before, along with a selection of linen shirts monogrammed with initials that were not mine.

'Nineteen forties demob.'

The stranger nodded. 'They don't make them like that anymore. My name's Ali, by the way.'

'Rilke.'

I held out a hand and we shook.

Les was squatting next to Jetpacks, who was still lying on

his side on the cobbles. He looked up at me, his face a white scrap of misery in the tunnel's gloom. 'Fuck off with the Anna Wintour chat. This guy's not breathing. I think maybe I killed him.'

Twelve

ALI HAD HIS hand pressed against Jetpacks' neck. 'He's got a strong pulse, but you gave him quite a doing. Maybe we should get him to a hospital.'

Les shook his head. 'No chance. He knows who I am.'

Ali took a bottle of water from his backpack. He poured it over Jetpacks' face. Jetpacks groaned and spluttered. His eyes blinked open. Ali said, 'Don't worry. It's over. No one's going to hurt you.'

The student recoiled. 'Keep that animal away from me.'

Les snapped, 'Watch who you're calling an animal,' but he had got a fright, and his heart wasn't in it.

Ali asked. 'What's your name?'

The student looked around the tunnel, as if he was wondering how he had got there. 'Jamie.'

Ali held four fingers in front of the boy's face. 'How many fingers am I holding up?'

The boy got the number right, but there was a pause

between the question and the answer. Ali asked him the name of the prime minister, the US president and what year it was. There was the same pause each time.

Ali looked up at us. 'He's concussed.'

Les wrapped his arms around his body, hugging himself. 'Good.'

'Not good. He needs someone keeping an eye on him overnight.'

Jamie Jetpacks tried to get up, but gravity had turned leaden, and he sank to the cobbles. 'I'm going to be sick.'

Ali rocked back on his haunches. 'He's not going to make it home by himself in this state. Right now, you gave the guy a beating in self-defence. Leave him here? By tomorrow you could be up for murder.'

Jamie muttered, 'All I wanted was a bit of blow.'

Ali patted his shoulder. 'That's the last thing you need right now.'

Les was hugging himself again. His hair was tousled, his fancy jacket beer-stained, its lining poked through a rip in the elbow. 'Fuck's sake. I'm trying to keep out of trouble.'

I said, 'Les's flat is round the corner.'

Les held up his hands. 'Away to fuck. He's not coming back to mine's.'

Jamie emptied the contents of his stomach onto the cobbles. Ali patted his shoulder again. 'It's that or the hospital. I'm not leaving him here.'

Once he was on his feet Jamie looked like any other Glasgow drunk. We took turns hooking the boy under the oxters and helping him up the cobbled incline away from the river and through a series of backstreets. Les moaned all the way about *guys that can't hold their drink* and *guys that don't know how to fight* and *fucking homophobic bastards that deserve all they get.* We eventually manhandled him up the stairs of Les's close and into his flat. Ali steered the boy onto the couch. I grabbed the washing-up basin from the kitchen and set it on the coffee table in case he was sick again.

Ali squatted beside Jetpacks. 'Who were the pals you were out with?'

The boy's forehead wrinkled. He waited his trademark pause. 'Séamie and Gordo.'

'Give me your phone. I'll text and let them know you're okay.'

I expected the boy to object, but Ali's quiet authority seemed to soothe him. He typed in his password and passed it over. Ali tapped quickly at the buttons and then set the phone on the coffee table.

Les drew the curtains and switched on the main light. He had become a follower of Marie Kondo a while ago, but his flat was more austere than usual. I spotted absences in the room. His bookshelves and racks of vinyl were sparser. The marquetry cigarette box made by his granddad from wood pockled from the *Queen Mary* was gone.

'Been having a clear-out?'

'I'm broke. I've been realising my assets.'

Ali was scribbling something on a notebook he had taken from his jacket pocket. He tore the page out and passed it to Les. 'This is a list of symptoms to look out for. Any doubt, call an ambulance.'

Les jerked his head towards me. 'I'm not nursing the wee bastard. Give it to him.'

I took a woollen throw from the back of a chair and draped it over Jamie. 'Sorry, Les, I'm out of here.'

'Seriously?'

'Early start.'

He looked at Ali, who shook his head. 'Me too.'

Les looked from me to Ali and back again. He shook his head. 'They boys were right, Rilke – you're a dirty, fucking fucker.'

I gave his cheek a gentle pat. 'I don't know what you're talking about, Leslie.'

Les's mouth curled into its devil-in-disguise grin. 'Aye, you're the Midnight Cowboy, right enough. Better watch out though, son, you might get more than you bargained for.'

Thirteen

ALI'S HOUSE WAS a red-brick new-build just off Maryhill Road, with a neat postage-stamp front garden. A fold-up bike was tucked in the hallway beneath a portrait of a ginger cat. The same cat appeared at the top of the stairs and peered down at me.

Ali hung his cap on a hook next to the picture. 'Hello, Milo.' The cat scooted past us and out through a cat flap in the front door. Ali smoothed his hair and grinned. 'Don't take it personally. Milo's a rescue. We live separate lives, as they used to say in the divorce courts.'

He led the way into a small living room, drew the curtains and turned on a standard lamp, revealing an interior styled for Instagram: leafy plants, blond IKEA furniture, stripped floorboards, bright rug and a compact, modular couch. I wanted a cigarette, but there were no ashtrays or plug-in air fresheners; a no-smoking house.

Ali had been relaxed in the cab, telling me about his acting ambitions. He was into am-dram, nursed hopes of turning professional and had been taking private lessons from one of the actors he had been drinking with. In the meantime, he was a lawyer, a member of a Glasgow practice specialising in human rights cases. 'High satisfaction rate, shitty pay. Police don't tend to pick on people with deep pockets.'

I sensed a nervous edge to him now that we were indoors and hoped he wasn't going to turn. People's kinks can surprise you, and ever since Burke and Hare discovered a neat way of smothering their victims in return for a quick buck from Dr Knox, Scotland has punched above its weight in serial killers. Most of the victims are women and young girls, but Dennis Nilsen and William Beggs both preyed on gay men. They each had a stomach-churning fascination for dismemberment and cannibalism. I tried to remember if either of them had been a lawyer or amateur actor, but all I came up with was blocked drains, fridges turned bloody by their contents and unfortunate dog walkers stumbling on beached body parts.

Ali shrugged off his jacket. He was wearing a slate-grey work shirt, untucked over black jeans, and Timberland boots. He was still smiling, but his eyes no longer met mine. The sixth sense I have honed over the years told me something was off-kilter.

He unfastened his top button. 'What would you like to drink?'

He was shorter than me, around five six with slim shoulders and good muscle definition that showed beneath the tight cut of his shirt. I had seen the way he felled the student and knew he would be a credible threat if things went the wrong way.

'What do you have?'

'I've got some decent tequila.' Ali reached into a repro twentieth-century modern cabinet and pulled out a bottle of Patrón Silver. The hand that held the bottle trembled.

This was how serial killers did it. Rendered their victims helpless through drink or drugs, a poisoned draught, then the swift plunge of a needle into the neck.

I scanned the room, looking for something I could compliment, but it was the kind of bland that is killing the auction trade, and my smooth chat deserted me. Ali took out two shot glasses and filled them to the rim with tequila. I watched as he poured, for any sleight of hand.

His face looked softer, more boyish, in the low light. 'We deserve it after tonight.'

I waited for him to drink before I raised my glass to my lips, knowing I was being foolish. 'Cheers. Nice place.'

We were still standing, awkward in the middle of the room. I wondered if he was too young for me and if straight couples indulged in this are-they-aren't-they, will-we-won't-we, is-he-going-to-kill-flay-and-eat-me? dance. But something in me responds to danger and uncertainty. Instead of wishing him goodnight and heading for the door, I took off my jacket and draped it over the arm of the couch.

Ali downed his drink in one quick gulp. 'You said you had an early start tomorrow.'

I sank my drink, feeling the burn at the back of my throat, uncertain if he was asking me to leave or about to announce it was time for bed. I glanced at my watch. 'Five hours.'

Ali dipped his eyes and gave a coy smile, classic Princess Diana. 'No point in hanging around.'

He started to unbutton his shirt. My hands moved to my own shirt buttons. I stepped towards him, but he held up a hand. 'Me first.' He pulled open his shirt, giving me a view of his chest, naked except for a sparse mustering of hair. I saw a phoenix tattoo circling scarring beneath his nipples and wondered. He pulled his shirt off to reveal hard, gym-sprung muscles. Then he kicked off his boots and socks, unzipped, slid free of his trousers and stood in the centre of the room, naked except for his boxers. He grinned, raised his arms in a strong-man pose and popped his guns. It was a classic gym-bunny move, an invitation to admire his hard-won physique.

I am more turned on by muscles acquired through toil, the lack of symmetry which writes a story of strength and vulnerability on men's bodies, but politeness costs nothing, and there was something retro-porno about the brazen pose in the dull domestic setting that was a turn-on.

I started to unfasten my belt. 'Nice.'

Ali raised his hand again. 'Wait.' His eyes held mine, and then he stepped free of his underwear.

There was an absence, or perhaps a presence. The fear that had been with me since we entered the house spiked and receded. I understood Ali's nervousness and wondered about his willingness to be so vulnerable with a stranger. My eyes met his. I hesitated, unsure.

Outside, a late-night bus rumbled and faded. The phoenix on Ali's chest trembled with the rise and fall of his lungs. My heart was strong in my chest, pumping the blood that kept me alive. I met his eyes.

Ali stepped closer and gave the smile he gave too easily. 'No need to be nervous.'

I felt the heat radiating from his body, smelt sweat clinging sour to his skin. 'I'm not nervous.' I pulled my shirt free of my trousers and unbuttoned it.

Ali reached for my belt.

Fourteen

ROSE UNWRAPPED THE kitchen roll cushioning two boiled eggs and started to peel them. The air in Bowery's kitchen turned sulphurous. I took my bacon roll from its paper bag and poured a coffee from the cafetière on the counter. Soon the place would be bustling with carriers, porters and punters delivering fresh stock that would need valued, logged and catalogued, but it was still early. None of the crew had arrived yet and for now we were the only ones in the building.

I pulled out a seat and sat opposite her at the blue Formica table that has graced Bowery's kitchen for at least thirty years. Rose gave me the same appraising stare she gives auction lots of dubious provenance. 'You're looking sheepish. What did you and Les get up to after we left?'

I added a splat of brown sauce to my bacon roll and bit into it. 'Nothing. A pint in the Doublet.'

One of Rose's eggs lay bald and naked on the counter. She looked at it with distaste. 'Did you sort Les out?'

'You know Les.'

She started to strip the shell from her second egg. 'What does that mean?'

'He's not easy to sort out.'

'That's an understatement.' Rose's fingers paused their work. Her nails were painted cobalt-blue; the colour reflected in the white of the egg. 'You're wearing the same clothes as yesterday.'

I took a sip of coffee. 'Same suit, different shirt. I got five identical, remember?'

'I don't know where you get the stamina.'

'For a drink in the Doublet?'

'For the rest of it.' Rose looked at her shelled eggs with distaste and bit the top off one. 'So are you going to help Les in whatever sordid mission he's on?'

I had phoned Les first thing to check the situation with Jamie Jetpacks, but he had not picked up. I was unsure whether to worry or not. 'It's a lost cause . . .'

'No doubt, but we can't have him going around shooting his mouth off about you-know-what.'

'He won't shoot his mouth off.'

'Of course he will. Some folk have trigger fingers, Les has a trigger mouth. He can't help himself.'

I took a bite of my bacon roll. 'What do you want me to do? Off him?'

The kitchen door opened. Inspector Anderson stepped into the room looking like he had just nicked Lord Lucan. 'Who are you planning to off? On second thoughts, don't answer that. I don't want to know.'

Rose made an effortless switch from Ma Baker to Lillie Langtry. She gave the police inspector a demure smile. 'Don't worry, Jim, it's just auction stuff.'

Anderson unfastened his coat. 'That's no reassurance. This place gets more like *The Sopranos* by the day.'

I laid down my roll and glanced from him to Rose and back. 'Here's a man who's definitely wearing the same clothes as yesterday.'

It was a tease. Anderson's coat had been buttoned up to his tartan scarf when I had seen him the day before, but he blushed, and I knew that he and Rose were back on.

Rose ignored me. She was holding her boiled egg between her fingertips with a delicacy that suggested Gabrielle d'Estrées' nipple-plucking sister. She beamed at Anderson. 'Time for a quick coffee?'

Anderson fired me a dirty look, but he was excited about something and his smile re-emerged. 'We've got him.'

'Who?'

'The guy who murdered your mate.'

'Manderson?'

'If that was his name. A patrol car picked him up in the city centre yesterday evening, for acting suspiciously. Murchison questioned him and he confessed.'

Rose dropped her egg. It rolled across the table and fell with a plop onto the floor. Neither of us moved to pick it up.

I resisted an urge to look at Rose. 'Anyone we know?'

Anderson leaned against the kitchen counter. 'Doubt it. According to Murchison, the guy's an illegal migrant from Afghanistan or somewhere. Mental health issues, blah de blah.' He looked at Rose. 'I thought you'd be pleased.'

'I am . . .'

'But?'

'It feels a bit random. How can you be sure you've got the right person?'

'He confessed, Rose. And before you say anything, no one beat it out of him. Those days are long gone.'

The sight of my half-eaten bacon roll was making me feel queasy. I pushed it aside. 'How did he get close enough to Mandy to stab him in the eye?'

Anderson looked at me. 'What?'

'Your crime scene guy said whoever did the deed had to be in kissing distance of Manderson. Mandy was an old bigot. I can't imagine him letting some down-on-their-luck asylum seeker with mental health problems get anywhere near him.'

Anderson took a mug from the draining rack and examined its interior, checking its cleanliness. He ran it under the tap and dried it with a paper towel. 'You of all people should know things aren't always as they seem.'

'What do you mean, *me of all people?*'

Anderson poured himself a coffee, took a sip and made a face. 'You know what I mean.'

Rose said, 'Sex crime gone wrong? You're barking up the wrong tree there. Mandy was as heterosexual as you. More heterosexual, if anything. I doubt he had a bent bone in his body.'

Anderson looked put out. 'I'm not sure what you're implying.'

'Nothing. It's good news. I guess neither of us expected you to get a result so soon.'

Anderson took another sip of his coffee. 'Christ, I thought the station coffee was bad.' He set his mug aside. 'We don't sit on our hands at Police Scotland, not when it comes to murder.'

Rose handed Anderson her second boiled egg. 'I suppose we should celebrate.'

'There'll be a fuller investigation and a trial to get through, but, aye, a wee glass of something is definitely in order. I'll text you when I know how the day's going.' He looked at me. 'And, Rilke, no offing anyone. I don't want to have to send you to Barlinnie as well.'

I gave a weak smile. 'Les didn't rate it high on Tripadvisor.'

'I doubt your guy will either.' Anderson placed the boiled egg, whole, in his mouth. He looked like a toad. He waved Rose goodbye and backed out of the door, widening his eyes.

Rose laughed and returned his wave. The door swung shut and her smile vanished. We sat in silence, more sombre than we had been since the murder.

I got up and went to the window. A couple of vans were parked in the car park, waiting for Bowery's doors to open. Abomi walked through the gates. It was grey outside with a damp wind that promised rain, but the boy's step was jaunty, eager for the working day to start. He looked up, saw me watching him and waved. I raised my hand in reply.

I did not like the way Anderson had described the asylum seeker as 'our guy', but he was right. Rose and I had concealed key evidence. The asylum seeker was in custody because of us. I remembered Les's bruises. The prison was less than five miles, and a world, away from us. I turned from the window and leaned against the radiator.

'What are we going to do?'

Rose looked the way she looks when Bowery's tax return is due. She took a bite of my abandoned bacon roll. 'They might have got it right.'

'The police?'

'They do occasionally get the right man. It has been known.'

I could hear the rest of the crew arriving, the building

filling up. Soon they would be jostling into the kitchen, brewing fresh coffees, wisecracking their way into the day.

I lowered my voice. 'You can't possibly think this asylum seeker guy actually killed Mandy? How did he get his hands on the hatpin for a start?'

Rose took another bite of my bacon roll. She looked miserable. 'He confessed.'

'Have you any idea how many people confess to things they didn't do?'

'How many?'

'I don't know. A lot.'

Rose crumpled the paper around the remnant of uneaten roll and tossed it in the bin. 'Anderson said it wasn't a done deal. There'll be an investigation, a trial.'

I sat down at the table. 'He's going to Barlinnie, Rose. He might be there right now. The police think the poor bugger stabbed Mandy. He's got mental health problems, maybe he even believes he did it. We're the only two people who know Mandy was killed with your stupid hatpin. We know for sure this man didn't do it.'

Rose took my hand in hers. 'If you tell the police what you did, they'll arrest you too, without letting the other guy go.'

'They might let him out.'

'You think so? I doubt it. Remember, the hatpin puts me in the frame too. I'm not sure I'd survive Cornton Vale.'

'You didn't do it, did you, Rose?'

'I can't believe you asked me that.' She looked me in the eye and said, 'I swear on my father's life, I didn't do it.'

'Joe died ten years ago.'

'Yes, but I loved him. His life was dear to me.'

I tried to think of someone with the power to pin Rose to the truth. 'Swear on Bowery Auctions.'

She laid her hands on the table where I could see them and took a deep breath. 'I swear on Bowery Auctions I did not kill Mandy Manderson.'

The door opened and our head porter Frank entered the kitchen. 'Fuck me, it's cold out there.' He looked at us and paused. 'Bad moment?'

Rose let go of my hand and smiled. 'Rilke and I were just discussing cash flow. He was telling me I spend too much on advertising.' She stared me in the eye. 'I swear on the auction house that I did not.'

Frank looked bewildered. 'You cut those underground adverts last month. I don't think they made any difference to turnover.'

I nodded. 'I believe you.'

But Rose had a temper. Her reassurances sounded too sincere for comfort, and I was unsure that I did.

Fifteen

I LOGGED INTO the computer in Rose's office and brought up the previous day's sales records. The hatpin had been bought by a J. Kopalski. Not a name I recognised. I went through to the cash office. Old Jim Bowery had employed Ina as Bowery's bookkeeper after her release from a prison stint thirty-plus years ago. She had murk in her past that would make me hesitate to join any ménage she managed, but Jim had had a soft spot for her. He used to serenade her with a nonsense song:

> Ina, Ina, nothing finer
> than to eat ham and eggs
> in Carolina

They may have had something going on, or perhaps they were bonded by tricks of the trade, profit and loss. Ina's fun side – always a dubious concept – had died with Jim. These days porters and punters called her the Rottweiler behind her back, but she kept our books in order and guarded Rose's interests above her own.

The cash office smelt faintly of curry. A plastic carton sat on the edge of Ina's desk, remnants of the previous night's takeaway microwaved for lunch. Ina was deep in her computer. She glanced at the fisheye mirror above her desk. 'What do you want, Rilke? I'm in the middle of payroll.'

The catalogue number of the hatpins was imprinted on my memory. 'Has lot 147 been picked up?'

Ina continued typing for a while then turned to look at me, her eyes swivelling in time to the creak of her swivel chair. 'How would I know?'

I nodded in the direction of her screen. 'The power of modern technology.'

Ina sighed, opened a new spreadsheet and scrolled down the entries. 'They paid for it in cash yesterday.'

'What were they like?'

'No idea. I wasn't here.'

'Bit unusual? An internet bid and a cash payment?'

'Not unheard-of. Some people want to inspect the goods before they pass over cash. Can't blame them.'

I ignored the gibe. 'Did they sign for it?'

Ina took a folder from the shelf above her desk. 'What is it? Dodgy goods?'

'I'm hoping not.'

She leafed through the filed receipts. 'Ronnie Kerrie collected it.'

'Ronnie? I wouldn't have thought he'd have that kind of money.'

Ina held out the receipt for me to inspect. 'He did yesterday.'

Ronnie Kerrie had signed his name in block capitals.

'Who was on the desk when he came in?'

'I don't know. I was off with women's troubles.'

I knew better than to ask more. Bowery's crew were so familiar with tales of Ina's womb Rose had once suggested it get its own Facebook page.

'Will you check something else for me, please?'

Ina's sigh seemed to roll from the very depths of her guts, bringing forth the scent of fried onions and cumin. 'What?'

'I need Mandy Manderson's address.'

'Why?'

Why was none of her business, but Ina can be persistent when her curiosity is piqued, and I did not want her dwelling on the reasons I might be interested in Mandy's abode.

'Rose wants me to drop off a letter for the executors offering to buy whatever stock he has left.'

Ina printed out an address in the East End and handed it to me. 'Still coffin chasing – it's a wonder you don't carry a scythe.'

When I was a lad, old Joe Bowery used to scour local papers' death columns for notices from prosperous areas then send me to post leaflets about Bowery's house clearance service through their doors. Several times whey-faced relatives, angry with grief, had accused me of coffin chasing. The memory stung.

'If I had a scythe, I might just cut you down.'

Ina smiled, pleased to have needled me. 'You'd be sorry after. I'm one of the few left who knew you when you were a laddie.'

I remembered that Ina used to be good-looking and that she had sometimes stood up for me when Joe Bowery was on the rampage. 'I'm all grown-up now.'

'The clothes are better, and you've got the height, but when I look at you, I still see a wee snotnose.'

'That's because you live in the past. I'm a man who lives in the present.'

She snorted. 'A man. You say that like it's an achievement. Don't forget where you came from, Rilke.'

'How could I do that when you're here to remind me?'

She smiled again. 'Told you, you need me.'

'Like I need a kick in the hole.'

But I returned her smile as I closed the cash-office door.

Frank was helping Abomi shift a Victorian armoire into the saleroom. I waited until they had slotted it into place and asked him, 'Did you see Ronnie Kerrie yesterday?'

Frank took a handkerchief from his pocket and dabbed the sweat from his forehead. 'Yep, he was in to collect.'

'How many lots?'

'Just the one, as far as I remember. Three hundred quid-plus.'

'Big spends for Ronnie.'

'I thought maybe he'd got lucky on the horses. Paid with fresh notes, a big smile on his face like his ship had just come in.'

Abomi put up his hand. I had tried to cure him of the schoolboy habit, but it persisted when he was excited. 'He was collecting for his friend.'

Frank perched on the arm of a cherry-red chesterfield. 'Makes sense now. I guess they gave him a bung on top for doing them a favour.'

'Brave man, whoever they were, trusting Ronnie.'

Frank grinned. 'Wouldn't be my first choice, right enough.'

Abomi was polishing the armoire's mirror with the

scrunched-up sports page of the *Daily Record*. 'Mr Kerrie's okay.'

'A nice enough man, but not someone you want to lend money to. Did he say who he was collecting them for?'

Abomi stepped back to admire his handywork. He detected a smudge and applied himself to it. 'No, but I saw them.'

'Did you recognise them?'

He paused and turned to look at me. 'I mean, I didn't really see them, but I saw their car. It was quality. A sport MG, red.'

'Fancy.' Abomi can be what we used to call touched by God, but he can also surprise with his attention to detail. 'Don't suppose you remember the number plate?'

He narrowed his eyes, thinking. 'It was something funny. It spelt a name.'

Frank looked at me curiously. 'Something up?'

Abomi was wearing a worried expression.

I put a hand on his shoulder. 'Don't worry if you can't remember. It was a long shot.'

The tension in his shoulders relaxed. 'H.E.L.3.N. I don't remember the other numbers.'

'That's brilliant, son. I don't know how you do it.'

Abomi beamed. 'I remembered because there was a girl in my class at school called Helen.'

We might have teased another boy and asked if he fancied her, but Abomi is sensitive and prone to brooding. Plus his uncle Ray Diamond is a pawnbroker who puts a lot of work our way. Razzle Dazzle Diamond is also one of Glasgow's biggest gangsters.

Frank was still looking at me. 'What's the story?'

Our head porter had seen me turn detective once before. I did not want him scenting Mandy's murder on me. 'We've got a similar lot I thought might interest the buyer. I guess I'll have to ask Ronnie if he can put us in touch.'

Frank glanced at his watch. 'Aye, well, you know where to find him.'

Ronnie Kerrie was at a corner table in the Grove, popularly known as the Grave, one of the few Finnieston pubs to have escaped gentrification. His attention was trained on the horse race playing out on the flatscreen above the bar. I bought him a half and a half and sat down on the bench beside him. Ronnie gave me an anxious nod. I knew better than to talk until the race had been run, horses over the winning line and trotting towards the paddock.

Ronnie adjusted the flat cap I had never seen him without and nodded his thanks. He lifted the whisky to his lips and chased it with a swallow of beer.

I took a sip of my pint. 'How did you do?'

Ronnie's smile was cautious. He is a wee skelf of a man, with a creased face, a beery version of the jockeys onscreen. 'I'm on a six-race accumulator. So far so good.'

'Stressful.'

'You've no idea.' His eyes were still trained on the television. 'Not your usual watering hole.'

'I dropped by because I thought you might be here.'

Ronnie gave me a suspicious glance. 'What's up?'

'You collected a lot from Bowery yesterday.'

A group of builders leaned against the bar in dusty work clothes, discussing odds, glancing at their phones, ready to place real money on virtual bets. The next race was due to begin, horses and riders positioning in the starting gate, but Ronnie turned to look at me. 'What about it?'

'You collected it for someone. I wondered who it was.'

'Something not kosher?'

I had considered my excuse in advance. 'The lot wasn't complete.'

Ronnie turned his attention back to the screen, where a skittish horse pranced, refusing to get into the gate. Its jockey dismounted, race attendants hooked a sling around the horse's rear and pulled, forcing it into the tight space. The jockey climbed over the partition and sprang, nimble, onto its back.

Ronnie said, 'The buyer will get in touch with you.'

'If they notice.'

Ronnie adjusted his cap again. 'Can't miss what they never had, and you've still got the goods. Problem solved. Everyone's a winner.'

'That's not how things work at Bowery. We have a reputation for integrity. We want to keep it that way.'

Ronnie snorted. He saw that I was serious and apologised. 'Sorry, Rilke, I thought you were pulling my leg.'

The horses were lined up. Someone gave the signal, the barriers flew open and they leapt into the race. Ronnie's attention was once more captured by the screen.

I said, 'There's twenty quid in it for you if you tell me who it was.'

Ronnie's mouth turned down like an off-duty clown. 'No can do.'

'Not like you to say no to hard cash.'

'Can't tell you cause I don't know.'

'A stranger?'

'Never seen them before in my puff.'

'What did they look like?'

Ronnie glanced at me. He held out a hand. 'Twenty quid?'

'Ten – a description's not a name.'

Ronnie curled his fingers around his pint. His nails were

yellow with tobacco. 'They had an interesting motor. You'll mibbe find them through them through that.'

'I already know about the motor. A red MG. Licence plate H.E.L.3.N.'

'Forgot you were a bit of a Columbo. Fifteen and another round.'

Fifteen and another round would come to more than twenty quid, but the horses were at full pelt. A grey beast led the chase, carrying a jockey dressed in yellow and pink silks, like a Mr Kipling's Battenberg. He swatted at the creature's flank with his whip. A sleek chestnut pulled out a final blast of energy as the riders approached the finish line. Ronnie started to mutter, 'Go on, go on, go on, go on . . .' His intensity was close to sexual. I went to the bar. Ronnie shouted, 'Go on, ya dancer,' and banged the table. The workmen at the bar cheered.

The barman poured our drinks. 'Thank Christ for that. I don't know why Ronnie does this to himself. I'm not sure I can take the strain of him losing another accumulator.'

'Bad?'

'You'd think his mammy had died. Ronnie doesn't have the temperament for gambling. He gets emotionally involved.'

We agreed the best gamblers were stone cold, though I have never met a man who did not get emotional about losing money. I ferried the drinks to the table where Ronnie was beaming like a lighthouse in a storm.

'Congratulations.'

He shoved his hat backwards on his head, Norman Wisdom-style. 'I'm riding high, Rilke. If I win the last race, I'll be back where I should be.'

I nodded, unsure if he was referring to his bank balance or some place poverty had exiled him from. I took fifteen pounds from my wallet, set it on the table and placed my beer glass on top.

'Tell me about your new friend.'

Ronnie was pumped high with winner's adrenaline. He gave a leery grin. 'I wish she was my friend. A friend like that I could do with.'

'Good-looking?'

'If you like them mature, which I happen to. Strange how that happens. I didn't fancy older women when I was young. I liked them firm and fresh then. Is it the same for poofs? I mean, gays?'

I was tempted to say that I had no idea, attraction was a strange thing and there was no accounting for it, but Ronnie Kerrie was low on the non-existent list of people I wanted to talk sex with. 'Kind of.'

'I'm always telling folk you're not all paedos.'

'Very liberal of you, Ronnie.' Attractive stable girls in jodhpurs and tight tops were leading horses round the paddock. Tiny wizened jockeys in bright silks mingled with the trainers and owners. The workies had their phones out again, placing fresh bets. 'What was this woman like?'

'Nice. She had a lovely voice.'

I wondered if Anderson had similar trouble interrogating witnesses. It was not as easy as TV cop shows made out.

'How old?'

'You never ask a lady her age, especially not one you just met. A good-looking fifty, I'd say, but who knows? She might have been older. Well-preserved. Posh. Nice hair.' Ronnie touched his cap. 'Kind of yellow colour but deeper. You could tell it was dyed, but it was subtle, like. Expensive.' He smiled, pleased with the image he was conjuring. 'Smelt lovely too.'

'What of?'

'Perfume.'

'Did you recognise it?'

'How would I recognise a women's perfume? It smelt pricey. Chanel Number Five, mibbe.'

Glasgow is fond of the bleach bottle. There were countless expensive blondes in their fifties, and I was willing to bet that every one of them smelt nice. 'What was she wearing?'

Ronnie screwed up his face, making a show of trying to remember. 'A coat.'

'What kind of coat?'

'A women's coat.'

'Was it dark? Pale? Bright?'

'What do you mean, bright?'

'A flashy colour – red or yellow or something.'

'No, I would have remembered that. She was dressed classy, like a woman from a film.'

'What film?'

'Just a film, maybe a spy movie. An old black-and-white one, like they play on the TCM channel. That's what she reminded me of – a sexy spy.' Ronnie put on a French accent. 'Leesten very carefully, I will say this only once.'

I wondered how much he had had to drink before I got there. 'So this posh French lady–'

'She wasn't French. The accent was me being a sexy spy.'

'Very Danny La Rue.'

'Piss off, Rilke. She was English, or posh Scottish. You know the type. Joanna Lumley but with more meat on her.'

'Joanna Lumley was forged in the Raj.'

'She may be radge, but she's a posh radge, Rilke. Doesn't matter how mental you are when you've got money.'

'You've got a point there, Ronnie.' We sat in silence, contemplating the unfairness of life. I took another sip of my pint. 'So this sexy spy lady was loitering next to her fancy MG in our car park. What did she say to you?'

'She didn't get out of the car. Just rolled down her window and asked if I'd be interested in doing her a favour. I thought maybe all my dreams had come true. Like one of those true-life stories you read in men's mags.' He dug me in the ribs. 'Sorry, Rilke, I keep forgetting, not your cup of tea.'

'There are more types of tea then there used to be, Ronnie. Peppermint, camomile, all your fruits. I'm partial to a nice, strong rooibos.'

He gave me a quizzical look. 'Is that right? Aye, well, each to their own. I'm more of a Tetley man myself. Four sugars, leave the bag in, can't go wrong. One thing I do remember. She was wearing glasses. But now that I think on it, they looked pretend, like they had no glass in them.'

'No glass?'

He grinned. 'Maybe that's a clue, eh? Non-prescription glasses. She was mibbe in disguise, Rilke.'

'Maybe she was a plain Jane dressed as a sexy spy.'

'Ah no, she was a looker, same grade as Rose Bowery, if you don't mind me saying so. Genuine sex appeal. You can't fake that.'

It was not worth the money, but I slid the fifteen pounds from beneath the glass and handed it to Ronnie. He glanced at the clock above the bar. 'Thanks, son.' He lifted his smartphone and brought up his gambling app. 'The last horse in the chain's an outsider, good odds but risky. I'll put this on the favourite. Means I'll win whatever happens.'

It sounded to me like he was betting against himself, but I gave him an encouraging smile. 'Who knows, eh? Maybe if you win big, the women will come flocking.'

He grinned. 'Aye, wouldn't that be nice.'

We both knew that whatever Ronnie won would find its way back to the bookies. There was nothing he wanted to do more with his money than put it on a horse.

I wondered what my fatal weakness was. A reluctance to commit had been forged in me from boyhood. But I had been loyal to Bowery Auctions for almost thirty years, been friends with Rose for almost as long. Les and I had been sparring buddies since we were boys, and Anderson had saved my bacon more than once.

It was romance I could not deal with. Or, rather, what followed romance. The constancy of day-to-day and night-to-night, time slipping away. The new friends and relatives who made your life no longer your own. Long-term lovers came with a price.

The news came on the television, footage of a fragile-looking dinghy overstuffed with petrified people, the boat barely breasting giant waves. Had the asylum seeker Murchison lifted arrived in a small boat? I wondered if he was locked up and if anyone was giving him a hard time. The clock was ticking. Sooner or later, I would have to step forward and tell what I knew.

Ronnie said, 'You should get in on the act, Rilke. Put a bet on. You could win big too.'

I got to my feet. 'Aye, I could do with a lucrative hobby.'

But life is a gamble, auctions a turn of the wheel. Shame and bad decisions can drown a man. I had no urge to add to the precarity of my existence.

Sixteen

JAMIE JETPACKS WAS the last person I expected to see sitting on Les's couch cradling a can of Tennent's. I gave him a cautious nod. 'How's the head?'

Les cackled, 'No complaints.'

Jamie looked at the floor. 'Better. The double vision's gone.'

I noticed that the boy's feet were bare and his jeans had a rumpled, three-day-wear look. I met Les's eye and nodded at the kitchen. 'Got a moment?'

Les lifted his beer can from its coaster on the coffee table. His granddad's inlaid box was back in its usual place. 'Excuse us, Jamie. Rilke's a man of many secrets, most of them sordid.'

Les's small galley kitchen smelt fragrant. A chopping board and Japanese blade were laid on the counter. A couple of shallots, Scotch bonnet chillies, garlic cloves, root ginger and a bunch of spices and lemongrass were neatly laid out, waiting to be dealt with. I glanced out at the view of the backcourts.

Windows were lit in the tenements. A man carried a black bin bag to the midden. An old white dog wandered from the building behind him and squatted on the grass. It was raining. No one else about.

I leaned against the kitchen counter. 'What's up?'

Les tapped his phone and propped it against the toaster. 'Nigel Slater. Thai green curry. I'd invite you, but there's only enough for two.'

'I'm not interested in your dinner. Why's he still here?'

Les widened his eyes, mugging surprise. 'Last time I looked, this was my flat.'

'Is he here of his own free will?'

Les shouted through to the sitting room, 'Jamie, fuckwit here wants to know if I'm keeping you hostage.'

Jamie called back, 'I'm fine, ta.'

Les lowered his voice. 'Turns out Jamie and me have a lot in common.'

'He's a druggie waster too?'

Les picked up his Japanese knife and started to chop the shallots. 'Not sure you should be so bold when I've got a cutting blade in my hand.'

It had been a long day in a long week in a year that felt like it should be over. I filled the kettle, switched it on and opened the cupboard where Les keeps his coffee. 'Have you got him dealing for you?' I spooned coffee into a cafetiere and opened the fridge, looking for milk.

Les stripped the garlic cloves and moved on to the root ginger. He ignored my question. 'Aye, help yourself, why don't you?'

The fridge was fully stocked, two chicken breasts wrapped in greaseproof paper. I grabbed a carton of milk and noticed a tartan biscuit tin, sitting incongruous next to a jar of white miso paste. I put the milk back, plucked the tin from its corner and opened its lid. It was stuffed with banknotes. A pink fifty Jack-in-the-boxed free and fluttered onto the vinyl floor.

The quick chop of blade against wood halted. Les dived for the note and grabbed the tin from me. 'I'm not kidding, Rilke. You better watch your nose before someone cuts it off.'

Jamie Jetpacks appeared in the kitchen doorway, looking third from the end in the Ascent of Man chart. He glanced at Les, who had the knife in one hand and the money tin in the other. The scowl he had worn in the Doublet returned. 'Problem?'

Les laid his knife on the chopping board and closed the lid of the tin. 'Just Heid the Baw sticking his neb in where it isn't wanted.'

Jamie put a hand up his T-shirt and scratched his chest. He might have been trying to imitate a young Marlon Brando, but he was the wrong type of sullen: belligerent instead of wounded. 'Want me to show him the door?'

'He knows where it is.' Les reached into the fridge and passed Jamie a can of lager. 'Take that through the room. Me and him have a wee bit of reckoning to do.'

Jamie looked uncertain, but he did as he was told. Les waited until he was out of earshot and shot me a gleeful grin. 'What did I tell you? I've got him trained already.'

'He's a half-baked arsehole you brain-damaged the other night.'

Les returned the tartan tin to the back of the fridge. 'Not everyone keeps their brains in their arse, Rilke.'

'You saw how he was in the pub. Playing the big man. He's a gay-basher and he'll land you inside again. Remember how much you liked it there?'

Les secured a Scotch bonnet chilli with the prongs of a fork and started to top, tail and deseed it. He gave me a patronising smile. 'That's where you're wrong. Jamie was confused about his sexuality. They call it internalised homophobia.'

'I know what they call it.' The fancy curry for two suddenly made sense. 'And you've been helping him with that, have you?'

'We all have to do our bit for the LGBTQ+ community.'

'There's more than one way to get screwed.'

Les started on the lemongrass. 'You don't need to tell me. Anyway, look who's talking. How did you get on the other night? Bet that came as a surprise.' Les adopted a drag brunch falsetto and sang, '*I know all there is to know about the crying game . . .*'

I did not feel like a coffee anymore. I took a can of lager from the fridge and popped the ring pull, more to annoy Les than because I wanted it. 'You didn't answer my question. Have you got him dealing for you?'

'Apprenticeships are back in fashion and Jamie's a popular lad. He's got a lot of mates at the uni.'

'You're off your head. Thurso Scanlan's not going to let up. He'll have you.'

Les opened a wall cupboard and took out his spice tin. 'Keep your wig on. We're being careful.'

'Scanlan will boot you back to Barlinnie before you can say sorry for being a stupid cunt.'

Les selected a couple of spices. 'As if you stick to the straight and narrow.' I waited for him to mention the hatpin, but I had rattled him. He continued, 'Scanlan's never seen Jamie. He's got zero convictions. We met by chance. There's nothing to connect us.'

'Except that he's sitting on your couch sucking a can of Tennent's. It took me two seconds to work out what's going on. Scanlan could be watching the flat right now. Or maybe your new pal's undercover polis. You don't know him from Adam.'

Les leered at me. 'He's not polis. I checked him thoroughly for hidden wires.'

'Plenty of women have been screwed by undercover polis shagging activists for Queen and Country.'

Les leaned against the kitchen counter. 'You don't need to tell me polis are dirty, two-faced fuckers, but, as you may have noticed, I'm not a woman.' He slapped the palm of his hand to his forehead, as if he had just realised something. 'Oh, I forgot, you're not great at telling the difference these days.'

'I can tell the difference.'

Les made a dive for my crotch. 'Did you go for it?'

I shoved him away, raised my can to my lips and said nothing.

Les crowed, 'You did, didn't you? Filthy bugger. What hole did you go for?'

'Piss off.'

Les slapped me on the back. 'You're still a big poofter, if that's what's bothering you. It'll take more than a bit of fanny to chase the gay out of you.' He put his spice tin away and reached for his food processor. 'There's probably enough for three if you fancy some.'

I shook my head. 'I've got to get moving.'

'Suit yourself. Why are you here, anyway?'

'You weren't answering your phone. I wanted to check your new mate was still in the land of the living.'

'What would you have done if he wasn't?'

'I don't know. Help you dispose of the body, I suppose.'
Les put an arm around my shoulders and squeezed. 'You're a good pal, Rilke.'

Rose had said the same thing only a few hours before.

Les lifted the chopping board and scraped shallots, garlic, ginger, lemongrass and chillies into his food processor. 'But to be honest, you wouldn't be top of the list if I needed help burying a corpse.'

I tried not to sound offended. 'Why not?'

'You're not really a skulk-about-deserted-woods-with-a-shovel type of guy.'

'And you are?'

'I could do it if I needed to. I could probably dismember someone if my life depended on it.'

I made a face. 'You crapped out of dissecting a frog in biology.'

'That was a long time ago.'

'And you skived off the day we were meant to dissect a bull's eye.'

Les's features hardened into his tough guy face. 'I don't like cruelty against animals. People are a different matter. Some of them deserve what's coming.' He clicked the lid onto his food processor and blasted its contents. 'Shouldn't you be off somewhere, persuading little old ladies to part with their treasures?'

I glanced at my watch. 'I've clocked off.'

'No hatpins to hide?'

It was my turn to be needled. 'I don't know why you keep going on about the hatpins. They were a legitimate item of sale.'

Les shrugged. 'I've got my own thing going on. I can't be bothered untangling whatever weird deal you and Rose are up to.'

'We're pure as sunlight soap, washed in the blood of the lamb. There was another reason I wanted to see you. I think there might be something in what you said about Hari's sister. You could be right about someone pushing her around.'

Les took his knife to a green pepper. 'Who cares? That mad bitch tipped a pint of beer over me. Bloody ruined my jacket.'

'Did you see her tattoos?'

Les put a wok on the gas burner, waited a moment for it to heat, poured in a generous glug of oil and then added the contents of the food processor. 'Aye, you said the other night. So what?' He pulled the neck of his shirt wider, showing me the two swallows that swooped towards his nipples. 'Birds are popular.'

'But her tattoos are entirely birds. The guy Hari beat up is called Dickie Bird – doesn't that seem significant to you?'

The curry paste sizzled and the room filled with the aroma of ginger, garlic and chillies. Les added the slices of green pepper to the sputtering wok and bothered them with his wooden spoon. 'You should start doing the cryptic crossword.'

The chillies were making my eyes smart. I blinked and dabbed at them with my hanky. 'It's a connection though, right?'

'Maybe so, maybe no. Point is, it's none of your business. I got pulled in by a sob story. Sorry for involving you. I should have known better. Let it drop.'

Les reached into the fridge, brought out the chicken breasts and laid them on a fresh chopping board ready to be diced. His expression shut and I knew I would not get anything more out of him.

I took my beer through to the sitting room. Jamie Jetpacks was watching a Scotland–Brazil match that had played the day before. It was early into the first half and Scotland were one down.

Jamie had just rolled a joint. He passed it to me and shifted along the couch, making space for me. 'Don't tell me the score.'

I lit up, perched on Les's vacated chair and inhaled. 'Score is you and Les are going to get caught.'

He glanced at me. 'It's only a bit of blow. Les asked me to take other stuff, but I said no.'

I wondered if the boy was naïve enough to think Scotland might gub Brazil and that he and Les would conduct a nice bit of business that would finance his studies, but I had warned him. There was no point in banging on about slippery slopes and police arrest quotas.

I took another drag at the joint. 'Do you know the girl we were with the other night?'

Jamie's eyes were back on the screen. 'Maybe I've seen her around.'

'Where?'

He shrugged. 'Library, maybe. Student union. I don't know. There's always lots of girls like her. It's hard to tell them apart.'

He kept his eyes trained on the screen and took a pull from his lager, dismissing Cat the way he might toss away an empty beer can. I set my half-finished tin of Tennent's on the coffee table, deposited the half-smoked spliff in the ashtray and got to my feet. I put my mouth close to his ear, whispered, 'Four nil to Brazil,' and let myself out.

Seventeen

MANDY MANDERSON'S HOUSE was one of a row that had once sheltered ministers of the Church of Scotland. The small garden was paved, the front door painted black, the curtains drawn. There was nothing to mark it out from the other houses in the street. It was a blank face, anonymous in the winter-dark, lamplit suburban street.

The jewellery dealer had dealt in quality goods and always paid hard cash, the currency of the crooked and the poor. I had pictured Manderson living somewhere modest, a one-bed housing association flat or not-so-new build with a view of a nearby supermarket. I checked the address in my notebook. It tallied.

Mandy had never mentioned a wife. He possessed the hungry edge common to lonely men and I had assumed he lived alone. But as I braced myself to leave the van, a downstairs light came on and a slim silhouette crossed the front room. Someone was home.

Murder has a way of drawing back the veil. I had dealt with Mandy Manderson for over a decade, but looking at the neat Victorian villa I realised that I knew nothing about him.

I took a leaflet advertising Bowery's services from the glove compartment and shoved it in my jacket pocket. It started to spit with rain. I smoothed my hair, pulled on my black Crombie and grabbed an umbrella from the back seat. A telltale scrap of blue-and-white police tape drooped from the garden gate. I wondered if police deliberately left these fragments behind to mark their territory.

Close to, the house's exterior was shabby, its stonework in need of repointing, its windowsills peeling. The door was answered by a gaunt woman who looked surprised to see me. 'I didn't think you were coming until tomorrow.' She glanced up the garden path to the empty street beyond. 'Are you on your own? Surely you can't manage all by yourself?'

I had not told anyone where I was going, but perhaps Rose had called ahead and arranged a viewing. I dredged up a sober smile. 'This is just a preliminary call—'

'Aye, well, this is as final as it gets.' The woman turned away, leaving the door open, before I could introduce myself or ask what she meant. I folded my umbrella, propped it by the door and followed her inside.

The hallway was dark and musty. The linoleum floor decorated with a 1930s brown and moss-green art deco pattern, the wallpaper heavy and embossed. The woman was wearing a neat black dress with a white Peter Pan collar. Her grey hair was pulled back in a smooth chignon. She was too old and too grey to be the sexy spy lady who had commissioned Ronnie Kerrie to collect the hatpins.

She looked at me. 'I'm glad to see you, to be honest. This place gives me the creeps. I've not visited for over thirty years, but nothing's changed.' A mound of coats was lumped on a Victorian hallstand. A puffa jacket I recalled Manderson wearing mushroomed on top of the pile. A watercolour of the exterior of the house hung nearby. The painter had got the proportions wrong, and the building had a lopsided lurch which made it look as if it was dangling in the landscape. 'You better hang your coat there.'

I draped my damp Crombie on the overloaded hallstand, where it hugged Manderson's puffa, then turned to the woman. 'We'll be glad to assist you with anything you wish to dispose of.'

She gave me a quizzical stare and turned away before I could hand a leaflet to her. 'I'm sick of euphemisms. People are too scared of offending each other. No one calls a spade a bloody shovel anymore.'

I was not sure what to say and resorted to, 'I'm sorry for your loss.'

'My brother and I hadn't been in touch since I left home at sixteen. I'm not sure how the police found me. They have better detection skills than they get credit for.' She opened the door to the front room and led me inside. 'No chance you could take him tonight?'

The lounge was lit by a central pendant light, the curtains drawn to keep out peering eyes. A three-piece suite had been pushed to one side to make space for the coffin resting on two trestles in the middle of the room. The coffin lid was propped against a dining table.

Manderson's sister stared down at the coffin's contents. 'They've arrested someone for his murder already. Apparently it was random. Frightening, when you think about it.'

I followed her stare, unable to resist the pull of the open casket. 'Yes, very.'

Mandy lay at rest on dove-grey silk, dressed in a white shirt and black suit. He had been shaved, his hair combed and gelled in place. His popped eye socket was concealed beneath a black velvet patch. He looked better than he had in years.

The woman sighed. 'I don't know what I was thinking. Not much point in a wake when there's no mourners. My mother and father insisted on open coffins. He's going in the family plot with them. He didn't leave any instructions, so I decided to stick to family tradition. I should have gone for a biodegradable cardboard box and cremated him in a cotton shroud. Your colleague at the Co-op hinted as much.'

It was not the first time I had been told I looked like an undertaker, but it was the first time I had been presented with a loaded coffin.

I took the leaflet from my pocket and handed it to her. 'I'm not a funeral director. I'm an auctioneer. We used to do a lot of work with Mr Manderson. I came here to offer our services.'

The woman's expression faltered and then she burst into sudden laughter. Her face softened and the vague resemblance to Mandy around her eyes receded. She gestured at my white shirt and dark suit. 'You must admit, it's an easy mistake to make.'

Mandy's sister was called Stephanie, Steph for short. She made tea in the kitchen while I fetched the cordless drill from the van. I resolved to tell Rose that when my time came, I wanted to be reduced to ash and scattered on the winds.

The coffin was made of oak heartwood, the densest part of the tree, resilient and resistant to decay. I did not know if it would delay Manderson's decomposition. It was strange to think of him tucked beneath the earth with his mother and father, this man who I could not imagine ever having been a child. I did not want to look at his face, but I would be the last one to see it and so I stared. Pale, clean-shaven skin, grey hair, bushy eyebrows, thin nose. Manderson had been an ill-tempered git, but despite Rose and Hannah's revelations about his wandering hands and creeping tongue, I felt sorry for him. No one, not even his sister, seemed inclined to shed a tear for the murdered jewellery dealer and now, thanks to me, an innocent man was in the frame for his death.

I whispered, 'I'll do my best to find out what happened.' It was not a prayer or a vow to deliver justice, just a feeble promise.

It was a two-man job, but I managed to set the lid on the coffin without tumbling Manderson onto the carpet. One by one I screwed the brass screws home into the heartwood, locking the murdered man in the dark.

Eighteen

A SELECTION OF sandwiches and shop-bought cakes were sweating beneath clingfilm on the kitchen table. A bottle of orange squash, jug of water and selection of mismatched glasses sat on the countertop, but there was no sign of the whisky that usually accompanies a wake. Steph set two mugs of instant coffee beside the sandwiches and peeled back the plastic. The black dress with its neat white collar gave her the look of a maid who had adopted the role of hostess after disposing of her mistress's body.

'We may as well help ourselves. I thought maybe some neighbours would come by to pay their respects, but I guess my brother didn't inspire much, even in people who didn't know him.' She waved a hand, taking in the kitchen with its old-fashioned units and magnolia walls. 'You're welcome to have a look around. There's seventy-odd years of junk to be disposed of.'

I took a ham sandwich from the plate and bit into it. The

slickness of the cold meat made me think of Manderson's snaking tongue. I forced it down.

Steph took a pink fondant fancy from the plate and examined it. 'Were you the person who found my brother's body?'

I did not want to talk about finding Manderson. 'How did you know?'

She decided against the cake and replaced it next to the others. 'The police said it was someone at the auction house. Can't have been pleasant.'

I sensed a hunger for details and pushed the sandwich to one side. 'His expression was peaceful. I don't think he suffered.'

Steph's mouth pursed. 'I'm a trained nurse. I know about death. You don't have to save my feelings.'

I set the remains of my sandwich on my plate. 'The killer pierced Mr Manderson's eye with something sharp. The coroner thought it might have been a kebab skewer.'

Her pupils were bright with lack of sleep. 'Did it go deep?'

'Didn't the police discuss this with you?'

'Yes, but you were there.'

I clasped my hands and looked down at my fingers. I had scraped one of my knuckles securing the coffin lid. 'It entered his brain.'

Steph sighed. 'No matter how fast it was, he would have seen it approaching and just for an instant known he was going to die.'

I repeated what the scenes of crime officer had told me. 'The killer came close enough for a kiss.'

'Close enough for a kiss.' Steph's breath sounded in her chest. A faint, asthmatic wheeze. 'Good of you to call the police. Someone else might have been worried they'd be accused.'

My wrists pulsed. 'It didn't occur to me.'

'Means, motive and opportunity. That's what they look for in detective novels.'

'I don't read detective novels. I have no interest in crime.'

Steph turned her full face on me: symmetrical features, high cheekbones, well-shaped mouth drawn tight by tension and tiredness. 'You know they found the person who killed him?'

Her old-fashioned dress and grey hair had led me to assume Steph was in her late sixties, but I realised that she could be younger, mid-fifties or thereabouts. She was a good-looking woman, if you ignored her resemblance to Manderson.

'You mentioned it. Did the police say anything about the killer?'

She wrapped her fingers around her coffee mug, warming them. 'Just that he was a foreigner. There doesn't seem to have been a motive. I suppose that's something.'

'What do you mean?'

'If you knew my brother, you would know he wasn't the nicest of people.'

'Mr Manderson kept himself to himself.'

'Diplomatically put. When I heard he had been murdered my first reaction was to wonder what he had done. I don't think that's a normal response, but Rodney wasn't a normal man.'

'The antiques trade allows for eccentricities. It's part of the attraction.'

Her voice sharpened. 'My father was a jewellery dealer.

He wasn't like Rodney. My father was gentle. Rodney had a cruel streak.'

The house was silent. No clock ticked, no floorboard creaked and settled in the damp air. Death lay in the next room.

'Some of our female staff complained he could be handsy.'

Steph's eyes met mine. 'A rather tasteful way to describe it.'

'No point speaking ill of the dead. He's gone.'

'He's lying next door.'

It was not the moment for discussing the possibility of a soul and, if such a thing existed, how long it might hang around for.

'The funeral is tomorrow morning.' Steph's tone became businesslike. 'I want to see him in the ground and fly back to Brittany immediately afterwards. Are you willing to look at his stuff tonight?'

'I can look, but you won't be able to sell it until probate goes through.'

She raised an eyebrow. 'Very proper of you.'

To be human is to be able to say one thing while suggesting another. I looked her in the eyes. 'We're an upstanding firm.' I smiled, remembering how Ronnie Kerrie had laughed when I told him the same thing.

Steph returned my smile. 'I've a whole night to survive. Let me show you the stock. That way you'll know if it's worth your time.'

I got to my feet. 'No harm in looking.'

Mandy had kept his jewellery in an old safe concealed behind a drab wall of grey and black suits, in a walk-in wardrobe. Judging by their cut, some of them were old enough to have belonged to his father. I have a weakness for men's vintage tailoring, but I was not tempted by the Manderson family cast-offs.

Steph pushed the suits to one side and took a scrap of paper from the pocket of her dress. The safe was a lead box on feet with an old-fashioned dial and click lock. Steph glanced at what was written on her scrap of paper, crouched and carefully rotated the dial. It struck me that she was too trusting, opening her door to a stranger on a dark night and inviting him inside to review her dead brother's treasures.

'Are you sure you wouldn't like to call someone to join us while we do this?'

'Who would I call? There's nobody.'

I wondered if she had family waiting for her in France and, if so, why no one was helping her.

'I can come back when your lawyer's present.'

'Lawyers are an expensive waste of time.' Steph tinkered with the dial. 'This was my father's safe, his father's before him. It weighs a ton. I've no idea how they got it up the stairs and into the bedroom, but I know my granddad built this wardrobe around it.

'My brother changed the combination. I tried family birthdays, historical battles, football matches, tennis tournaments – not that he was interested in tennis. I suddenly remembered he had a thing for Brigitte Bardot when he was a boy and googled when she was born.' She glanced up at me, her pupils large in the gloom of the cupboard. 'Everyone said I looked like her when I was a girl.'

Someone walked over my grave. I was glad I had screwed Manderson's coffin lid on tight.

The safe door swung open. 'The moment of truth,' Steph said.

'You didn't look before?'

'I couldn't bring myself to, not with Rodney laid out in the sitting room. I never liked to turn my back on him.'

'You don't have to worry about that anymore. He's dead.' A car drove along the street outside, its engine loud. We both started at the noise.

Steph glanced at her watch. 'It's getting late. They're collecting his body at eight in the morning. Does that give you enough time?'

'Plenty.'

I helped Steph to empty the safe and lay its contents on the pink candlewick bedspread. Trays of gold and silver rings, chains and necklaces, a series of velvet boards pinned with brooches and pairs of earrings set with pearls and gems. Yellow and rose gold, solid and gold-plated. There were strings of pearls too, and silver photo frames, velvet lining exposed where the photographs should be. A few christening mugs and chased silver boxes lay at the very back next to South African Krugerrands and some tiny gold ingots so shiny they looked like plastic but were worth real money. I resisted the urge to whistle for fear of waking Mandy.

I wondered why the jewellery dealer had lived his hand-to-mouth, cheese-paring existence. He could have sold the lot and lived large. But it was hard to imagine Manderson spending liquid cash on anything except more stock. He was like Ronnie Kerrie: addicted to the rise and fall of the chase.

Steph frowned. 'I want you to take it all away. Probate's not an issue. I'm the only heir. If you won't act for me, I'll find someone who will.'

Manderson's stock lay shining on the bedspread.

I dulled the pound signs in my eyes. 'You hadn't heard of me an hour ago. I'm just a random guy you mistook for an undertaker.'

She touched my wrist. 'You'd be doing me a favour, and there's a whole funeral buffet going to waste. You won't go hungry.'

I slipped free of her grip. 'Any whisky in the house?'

Steph made an apologetic face. 'I picked up a bottle of Cointreau in duty-free. I'll get it.'

She stepped quickly from the room and returned with a bottle and two small glasses in her hand. 'Of course, you don't need to give me a receipt for every item.'

I knew enough about seduction to put up a show of resistance. 'That would be against the law.'

'And you're an upstanding firm.'

I returned her smile. 'Very, we're well known for it.'

I texted Rose that I would be in later than usual the following day and then sat in the quiet of the bedroom cataloguing, labelling and packing the contents of the safe. The Cointreau was sweet and sticky, and after a few sips I abandoned it on a bedside table. I could hear Steph moving around, but noise travelled strangely in the house, and I could not tell if she was in the next room or somewhere beyond.

Sometime around 4 a.m. I opened a slim box and, instead of the bracelet I expected, found a piece of paper rolled into a thin cigar shape. I unfolded it. The handwriting was poor and the creases in the paper distorted the words, making some illegible, but I could make out enough to see that it was a handwritten list of names.

The ones I could make out were male and Scottish: James Campbell, Stuart Jamieson, Robert McRobert, Kenneth Mackenzie, Urquhart Murchison and Andrew Cronin. I rolled the paper neatly back into its cigar shape and slipped it into my wallet. It looked like a piece of trash, but Mandy had considered it valuable enough to keep in his safe. I would hold on to it for now, even though there was something about the texture of the much-handled paper that made me queasy.

I fell into a dwam as time passed. It was still dark outside, but I could hear the rumble of distant traffic, the sound of people taking their children to school and nurseries, the slam-slam of car doors, the waking day beginning. Soon the real undertaker would come to ferry Manderson away. I finished my final cataloguing and bagging, lifted the pile of receipts and went to find Steph. I wanted to be gone before the men in black arrived.

She was sitting at the kitchen table. I sensed that her eyes had been closed, but when she looked up her voice was strong. 'They'll be here soon.'

I had the jewellery stash neatly bagged in two Lidl carrier bags I had found beneath the kitchen sink. 'Time for me to get out of your hair.'

'Thanks for keeping vigil with me.'

I nodded, though I had lit no candle and sent no prayer up to the heavens for her brother. I laid the receipts and a form confirming her rightful ownership of the contents of Manderson's safe on the table. 'This is a legally binding document. By signing it you give us the right to sell the goods listed there.'

She nodded and signed her full name: *Stephanie Manderson*. She had kept her birth name. It had a musical sound.

I thought we would hear the hearse arrive, had not anticipated it might be electric. The quiet was riven by three strikes of brass on brass, loud enough to be heard in the back of the house, not loud enough to suggest a dawn raid.

Steph got to her feet. I hesitated and then followed her to the front door.

The undertaker was short and rotund, with a drinker's nose and a jester's mouth. The sombre expression looked odd on his face-made-for-fun. He was followed by a black-suited crew. They did not give any sign of being surprised to see the coffin lid screwed on tight. It struck me that it would be easy to bury the wrong man. The black suits surrounded the coffin and lifted it in one smooth, choreographed movement. They manoeuvred it into the hallway and negotiated the tight bend by the banister with ease.

Steph let out a sigh of relief. 'No need to come to the graveside.'

I knew that she wanted me to accompany her in the car that would follow Manderson to whichever cemetery he was bound for. A detective might have accepted the invitation and hung around to see if the real murderer showed up. But I was not a detective.

I nodded at the plastic bags in my hands. 'Best I make sure this is safely delivered. I'll email you about arrangements for the sale.'

Steph gave a curt nod. We pulled on our coats and processed together out into the deserted street behind Manderson's coffin.

She shook my hand before she got into the car. 'I don't suppose we'll meet again.'

It was cold outside, the promise of rain carried on a snell breeze that shook the scruffy privet hedge.

'You came all the way from France. You've done your bit.'

Her eyes brimmed with tears. 'Rodney was an unhappy boy who took his unhappiness out on the world. We were never close. I was glad when he went away to school.'

The funeral director opened the passenger door of the black car idling behind the hearse and she slid inside. There were no other mourners, no neighbours lining the pavement to pay their last respects, but the simple funeral was costing a lot of money. She was determined to put her brother beneath ground.

Nineteen

I WAITED UNTIL the cortège had left the street and then closed the garden gate and latched it behind me.

'Hold on a moment, son.' An elderly man dressed in a smart raincoat and herringbone cap emerged from the front door of the neighbouring house. He turned his key in the lock and tottered down the garden path, frail yet nimble, pulling a bright-red shopping trolley. 'That him away then?'

'Mr Manderson?'

'No, Pope John Paul the Second.'

'Yes, that's Mr Manderson gone.'

The old man eyed me up and down. 'What happened? You miss the cortège?'

It took me a second to grasp what he meant. 'I'm not a funeral director.'

He cast his eyes over me again. 'You certain of that?'

'I'm an auctioneer.'

He gave a sage nod. 'Ah, I get it, carrion crow.'

I resented being called a coffin chaser for the second time in as many days. I gave him a curt 'Have a nice day' and walked away.

'Hang on a wee minute, son.' He pointed at my car. 'That your motor?'

'Maybe.'

'It either is or it isn't.'

'It's mine.'

He gave a cheeky grin that made him look younger, approximately twelve years old. 'You couldn't give us a lift to the Co-op, could you? It's a bloody miserable day.'

I raised my eyebrows. 'Didn't your mother ever tell you not to get into cars with strange men?'

'My mother told me lots of things, God rest her poor soul. Much good it did either of us.'

He was right: it was a miserable day, too miserable for flirting with OAPs. I took the red trolley from him. 'Come on then.' And we crossed the road together.

His name was Jack, and he had been employed by the Post Office for most of his life, working his way up from messenger boy to depot manager. He had had a good retirement, but his wife had died three years ago, and although his two sons visited regularly, the zest had gone out of life. He told me all this on the ten-minute drive to the Co-op. 'I'll be happy to go when my time comes. I'd have hurried things along if it wasn't for my boys.' He gave me a sly glance. 'Maybe that's why I hitched a lift from you.'

'Because I look like an undertaker?'

'You look like Death himself, son. No offence.'

'None taken.' Lack of sleep, Mandy's stuff in the boot of my car and escaping his funeral had put me in a careless state of mind. 'Death is the meaning of life.'

He snorted. 'When you get to my age you realise the whole thing is meaningless.'

'Not sure you have to get to pensionable age to work that one out, but it doesn't mean we can't enjoy ourselves.'

'Now you're talking. I might be reckless and blow my pension on a pack of Party Rings.' He laid his hand on my left knee. I gently removed it. We drove on in silence for a bit. He said, 'I heard him next door got murdered.'

'You heard right.'

'Couldn't have happened to a nicer man.'

'They should put that on his tombstone.'

Jack laughed. 'Aye, right enough. He was a creep when he was a kid. He was away at that school they sent him to most of the time, but when he was here I wouldn't let my laddies play with him. And he didn't improve with age.'

'How come?'

'How come what?'

'How come he was a creep?'

'Who knows? His mother and father were decent enough folk. Some people are just wired the wrong way. I always said Rodney Manderson would come to a bad end – and he did.'

There was a small car park around the side of the shops. There were no spaces and so I parked behind a delivery lorry.

'I thought folk mellowed as they got older.'

The delivery driver rolled up the back doors, ferried himself up into the van and started to lower a trolley of toilet rolls.

Jack made no move to get out of the car. 'Who do you mean *mellowed*? Him or me?'

'You. Manderson's not going to get any older.'

Jack laughed. 'This is me mellow. You should have seen

me when I was younger. Wound tighter than a gnat's quim. I read they caught the guy who did it. One of those asylum seekers.'

News got around. 'So I heard.'

The lorry driver was pushing the trolley of toilet rolls towards the back door of the Co-op. It didn't seem much of an improvement on the days of horses and carts.

Jack gave me a wry look. 'You don't think he did it?'

'What made you say that?'

Jack grinned like Mr Mischief. 'You've got an expressive face – for a cadaver.'

I ignored the insult. 'It just seems a bit convenient finding a mad guy with no one to stick up for him so soon after the murder.'

'Aye, I get your drift. A big boy did it and ran away. But that's how it goes sometimes. The polis seemed serious about finding their man. They questioned everyone in the street. Had we seen the wee prick lately? Did we know anything about his movements? I told them I lived next door to the cunt for forty years but never had much to do with him.'

I turned off the engine. 'If you didn't have anything to do with Manderson, what makes you so convinced he was a bad sort?'

'Leopards don't change their spots. He was a sleekit wee liar as a laddie.'

'All kids lie.'

'Sure they do, but he was a cruel boy. The kind that tortures cats.'

The delivery driver returned from the shop and continued his unloading. This time the trolley ferried Tetra packs of fruit juice.

I turned to look at Jack. 'Is that a random example?'

'Wish it was. We had a beautiful cat when the boys were young. A big ginger tom. The boys named him Grigore McGregor. Don't ask me why. Thought it was funny, I suppose. Rodney poisoned it.'

I remembered what Les had said about some people deserving what they got. 'Did he admit to it?'

'Course he didn't, but the way he looked at me when I accused him told me all I needed to know. It was him. Any of your crowd going to his funeral?'

'My crowd?'

'The antique mob, jewellery dealers and the like?'

'I doubt it.'

'There'll be no one there except poor Steph and that pal of his.'

'I didn't know he had any friends.'

'Oh aye, he had a friend.'

'What did he look like?'

Jack gave me a gimlet stare. 'Why are you so interested?'

I shrugged. 'It's not often you know someone who gets murdered.'

It was a poor excuse, but the old man was lonely and enjoying our chat. 'A big bloke with white hair. Looks like the Reverend Ian Paisley Senior, right down to the suit and tie. Glasgow accent, but the look of an Ulsterman.'

'What's the look of an Ulsterman?'

Jack laughed. 'Same as the look of an Ayrshire man. A potato with arms and legs. This bloke visited him regular as clockwork, every Wednesday night. He missed the news about Rodney's murder. Turned up this Wednesday, six o'clock as per usual. I'd kept one eye open for him, had the TV turned down low, just in case. I heard the gate creak and went outside. I was gentle, like. I didn't kick off with *your pal's deid, son.* Just told him I had bad news and asked if he wanted to come into the house for a cup of tea.'

'Trusting of you.'

'Why would I not be trusting?' Jack's hand found my knee again. 'You're an awfy suspicious man.'

'And you told me you were happily married for thirty years.'

The Co-op driver stowed his trolley in the back of his lorry, slammed the door, slid home its bolts and returned to his cab.

Jack said, 'A man can have a wife and a hobby. Don't tell me you've never been with a married man?'

He was right: many a heterosexual husband browses Grindr, but I had already done my bit for Help the Aged by driving the old man to the shop.

I removed his hand and turned on the engine, ready to take the lorry's parking space. 'The guy next door got murdered. I would have thought it would make you wary.'

'I'm a good judge of character. You're not the kind to beat up a pensioner.'

'What about Manderson's friend? Does he look the kind?'

'Maybe – if he was cornered. Struck me as one of those religious types who'd be happy to see you choke on the host.'

I ignored the suggestive note of old-fashioned camp in his tone. 'Did he look upset about Manderson?'

'He was surprised, that's for sure. I don't think he believed me at first. I had to go indoors and get a copy of the local *Advertiser.* The murder was big news around here, made the front page. He took the paper out my hand and read it in front of me. I thought he might be shaken up, but I'd say he was angry. Grief hits people differently. I was angry for a long time after my wife died. Still am. If it wasn't for my boys, I'd put an end to it.'

The lorry reversed out. I swung my car into the vacant space, cut the engine and turned to look at Jack. 'I'm a great believer in procrastination. You can kill yourself any time. It doesn't have to be today.'

'That's one way of looking at it, but believe me, son, the days stretch on when you're alone.'

'What happened with your Ian Paisley lookalike? Did he come in for a consoling cup of tea?'

'No. I was pleased, truth be told. Never liked the look of him. He walked off without a word. Took my paper with him. Not that it's worth reading, but I wanted to show the front page to my sons.'

'Tell them that Grigore McGregor had been avenged?'

'They never knew what happened to him. I told them Big Ginger died suddenly from natural causes. I didn't want hate to enter their hearts too young.'

'Sounds like you were a good dad.'

He looked away. 'I don't know about that, but one thing I am sure of: there's always plenty of hate in the world. No need to add to its total.'

I waited by the shops while Jack fetched his shopping, stowed his trolley in the back seat and then drove him back. Winter had turned the gardens bleak, but Jack's lawn was mown, his hedge trim. If he decided not to kill himself, I would lay odds on his borders being bright with begonias come the spring.

Jack's face took on its boyish look. 'Fancy a cup of tea? I've got biscuits. My eldest lad's popping round after work, but he won't be here before six.'

I gave his leg a reciprocal squeeze. Kindness costs nothing. 'Duty calls.'

He winked. 'I thought auctioneers liked ancient articles.'

'Only ones I can turn a profit on.' I got out of the car and lifted his loaded trolley from the back. 'Don't go topping yourself any time soon.'

'Ach, nature will take its course soon enough.' He plucked a pack of Pepto-Bismol-pink sausages from the top of his bag and held it up for my inspection. 'Enough of these and I won't have long to wait.' He shoved the packet back into his bag. 'Why are you so interested in Rodney, anyway?'

'I found his body.'

'Ah, I can see why that would make you curious.' Jack leaned his weight against his shopping trolley. 'There's a saying that when you save a man's life, you're responsible for it forever. I don't think the same thing applies when you find a man's dead body. Rodney was a nasty piece of work. The world's a better place for his going. Let him drop.'

'Maybe you've got a point.'

'You know I do. Thanks for the lift.'

I watched him wobbling up his path, the way black cab drivers watch late-night fares who have taken the precaution of tipping. He turned at his front door and waved goodbye before he went inside.

The wisdom of the old is overrated, but he had given me a piece of good advice. It was a shame I could not take it.

Twenty

AFTER THE POLICE car tailed me the length of two streets and around three corners, I knew for sure that it was following me. I drew into the curb, and it flashed its blue lights, making a point about who was in charge. In the movies people roll down their car window and ask what the problem is, but if I am forced to meet the boys in blue, I prefer to do it eye to eye.

I got out of the car, slamming the door behind me. 'Is there a problem?' It came out more aggressively than intended. I tried for a consolatory smile. There was no point. One way or another I was probably fucked.

Inspector Thurso Scanlan was wearing a navy suit that appeared to have shrunk in the rain. It made him look like a cross between a seedy Conservative and an extra on *The Bill*. The kind of guy you might see falling out of All Bar One on a Friday night or giving a press briefing at Downing Street. He was shadowed by a slack-jawed uniform who had left Tulliallan before he had had time to be fully baked.

Thurso Scanlan straightened his jacket. 'We have reason to think you are driving under the influence of drugs.'

Cannabis lurks in the system for around twelve hours. I had smoked half of Jamie Jetpacks' joint before I left Les's place. I could be on the cusp. I cursed Les under my breath. It was his fault I was here. Thurso Scanlan was on Les's back, and now, because I was a known associate, he was on mine.

I gave the policeman a lawyerly stare. 'What reason is that?'

A young woman pushing a pram crossed the road to avoid us. Thurso followed her with hungry eyes. 'We're not obliged to list our reasons, sir.'

The 'sir' sounded like an insult. He nodded to the uniform who reached into the squad car and took out a drug-testing kit.

An involuntary curse escaped me. 'For fuck's sake.'

Thurso turned his eyes on me, still hungry. 'What did you say?'

I forced a smile. 'Nothing, officer. I'm just frustrated at being stopped. I took an elderly friend for some groceries. I'm afraid it's going to make me late for a catch-up with an old school friend. One of your colleagues actually, Chief Inspector Jim Anderson.'

Thurso Scanlan's voice was smooth and bitter, like cheap cough syrup. 'Don't worry about that, *sir*. Chief Inspector Anderson's up in Aberdeen for a conference. Your class reunion must have slipped his mind.'

My smile was an ache in my face. 'There's none of us getting any younger.'

The uniform had not quite grasped the sarcastic nuances of our conversation. He gave Thurso Scanlan an anxious look.

The inspector twitched his head in my direction. 'Test the

gentleman.' 'Gentleman' had a mocking lilt. The man was a lexicon of subtle insults.

I scraped the test against the inside of both of my cheeks and licked the blue strip on the reverse, as directed, then we waited. Eventually the uniform winced. 'It's negative, sir.'

I raised a hand in farewell and started towards my car, deliberately slow, like an untroubled man, a cowboy in a white hat moseying out of town. 'No hard feelings. Thanks for keeping the streets safe, officers.'

Thurso Scanlan said, 'Just a moment, please, *sir*.'

I took one more step and halted. I pulled on the smile I save for difficult customers and turned to face him. 'What?'

If the inspector had had a moustache, he would have twirled it. 'Your manner is giving us cause for concern.'

'Exactly what aspect of my manner concerns you?'

'You look demented.' He waved the constable forward. 'Roadside impairment test.'

Somewhere nearby a school bell rang. I glanced at my watch. It was midday. I should have been at Bowery hours ago.

'You just tested me.'

'We can do this at the station if you prefer?'

Scanlan was a nyaff, but he was a nyaff with the power to make my life difficult. I retraced my steps. A group of schoolboys with an air of future Jamie Jetpacks were dawdling down the pavement towards us, uniforms scruffy, ties askew, backpacks dangling, eyes on mobile phones.

The constable instructed me to 'stand with your feet together, tilt your head back and close your eyes'. I closed my eyes. The wind touched my face, and I shuddered. He continued, 'Tell me when thirty seconds have passed.'

I counted elephants, making an effort not to move my lips. When I got to thirty, I opened my eyes. 'How did I do?'

The gang of schoolboys I had seen approaching had surrounded us. One of them said, 'You did crap,' and the others laughed.

A short boy with red apple cheeks made for slapping put his hands in his pockets, like a miniature country squire. 'What you do, mister? Kill someone?'

A lanky boy sporting a bum-fluff moustache crowed, 'Naw, bet he's a paedo.' He pointed his phone at me. 'Show us your cock, mister.'

The other boys were hooting now.

I looked at Scanlan. 'Are you going to let them go on like this?'

He shrugged. 'What do you want me to do?'

The moustached youth echoed, 'What do you want him to do, paedo?'

A car slowed down to take in the scene, and I caught a quick impression of how I must look: a tall, thin, tired-looking man dressed like a scruffy undertaker surrounded by schoolboys and flanked by two policemen.

I raised my voice. 'Put them on a warning.'

Thurso Scanlan smirked. 'They're minors. Not much we can do, under the circumstances.'

I looked at the kid who had called me a paedo. 'I'm not a paedo, but if I was, I wouldn't let you anywhere near my cock.'

The kids hooted and the boy's face flushed. He turned to the uniformed officer. 'You hear that? He was coming on to me, fucking paedo. Said he wanted me to suck his cock.'

I pointed at the boy. 'I'd rather fuck Inspector Scanlan here than fuck you, and we'd have to be well into Armageddon before I touched him.'

The boys went *ooooooh*, and I knew I should have kept my

mouth shut. One of the smartarses shouted, 'He wants to fuck you,' and then they started to chant *copfucker, copfucker, copfucker* . . .

Thurso Scanlan barked, 'Right, that's enough.'

I took out my phone and snapped a photo of the children. 'Soon as I've finished with these officers, I'm taking this photo to your headmaster. He'll be straight in touch with your parents.'

The slappable boy with red cheeks appealed to Scanlan. 'Sir, you going to let this fucking paedo get away with taking a photo of us? We're underage, sir.'

Scanlan barked, 'Delete it.'

I held the screen up and pressed delete. The photo vanished.

Scanlan turned to the schoolboys. 'Beat it or I'll visit your school myself.'

A couple of the kids looked like they might argue, but it was starting to spit with rain, their lunch hour was vanishing, and they had had their fun. They limited themselves to a few shouts of *fucking paedo copfucker* and sloped off towards the shopping parade in search of chips and kebabs. One of the departing boys shouted, 'Hope they lock you up and throw away the key, fucking sex pest.'

An elderly woman in a blue raincoat looked at the boy and then at me, trying to decide who she was more appalled by.

Scanlan turned his wolf stare on me. 'Any reason these children would be convinced you're a paedophile?'

'Same reason they'd call me a copfucker. They're bored, homophobic wee bams.'

Scanlan grimaced at the word 'homophobic'. He pointed at my car. 'Unlock your vehicle, *sir*.'

I took one of my business cards from my wallet. 'My car isn't locked, but before we go any further it's important you know I am the head auctioneer for an upstanding, long-established auction house . . .'

Thurso Scanlan's smirk was back. He ignored the card in my hand. 'I know who you are, *sir*.'

The uniform opened my car boot and started to root around inside.

I returned my wallet to my jacket pocket. 'I have valuable stock and the receipts to show that I acquired it legitimately in there.'

The uniform was already walking towards us, looking delighted with himself, a Lidl carrier bag in each hand. He spoke for the first time. 'You won't credit what he's got in here, sir. Fucking crown jewels.'

The interview room was cold. It smelled of sick and disinfectant. The worried uniformed officer had been replaced by an athletic woman dressed in the office greys and navy favoured by plain-clothes women on TV cop shows. She sat next to Thurso Scanlan, looking like she was counting to ten in her head.

A red light flashed on a wall-mounted camera. I guessed I was being recorded and that they should probably have informed me of the fact.

Thurso Scanlan smoothed his hair with the palm of his hand and looked at his notebook. 'Let me get this straight. You, who found Mr Manderson's body and called it in, now have the contents of his safe in the boot of your car?'

I took a sip from the plastic cup of water in front of me. 'Mr Manderson was a regular client of Bowery Auctions. It's not surprising his sister turned to us to help with his estate. She signed receipts for the goods you took from my car.'

The female officer scribbled something on the notepad in front of her. 'A bit quick. The man's not in the ground yet.'

I glanced at my watch. 'He will be by now. His funeral was this morning. His sister lives in France, and she's keen to get home. I got the feeling they weren't particularly close.'

She looked up from her notes. 'Did you know Mr Manderson's sister prior to his death?'

'I didn't conspire with her in murder, if that's what you're asking.'

Thurso Scanlan said, 'No one mentioned murder.'

'You mentioned that I found Mr Manderson's body, which I did. Bad luck for me.'

'Worse luck for Mr Manderson.'

'That goes without saying. I reported it immediately, and your colleagues got on the case. I understand you already have someone in custody.' I hoped the quick pulse of guilt I felt at the thought of the arrested asylum seeker had not shown on my face.

The woman said, 'You didn't answer my question. Had you met Mr Manderson's sister prior to his death?'

'I met her for the first time yesterday, when I was invited to value some of Mr Manderson's effects.'

'And you're convinced that she's entitled to these goods?'

She was right: I had moved too quickly to be a hundred per cent sure.

'Why wouldn't I be? She assured me she was. Mr Manderson was a childless bachelor and she's his only sibling. There's no complexity regarding ownership.'

'None that you're aware of. For all you know he left everything to Cardonald Cat and Dog Home.'

I recalled what his next-door neighbour had told me about Manderson's cat-killing past. 'I doubt it. Mr Manderson wasn't an animal lover.'

Thurso Scanlan's eyebrows went up and I cursed myself for opening my mouth.

'What makes you say that?'

'He was a long-term client. You gain impressions of people over the years. Mr Manderson was focused on profit. Benevolence wasn't his style.'

Thurso wrote something down. He whispered 'benevolence' as if it was a new word in his vocabulary, one he wanted to commit to memory and reuse.

I was not yet under arrest. They had driven me uncuffed in the back of the cop car and left my own motor sitting by the side of the road. I was tired, hungry and in need of a shower.

'I'm not sure what I'm doing here.' I stretched my legs beneath the table, careful not to nudge either of the police officers' toes with mine. I had already been accused of being a sex pest that morning. 'This is beginning to feel like harassment.'

The woman glanced at Thurso Scanlan, who gave a small shake of his head. He asked her, 'Who's in charge of the Manderson case?'

She said, 'I think it's Murchison.'

Thurso Scanlan nodded. 'We should probably give him a shout.'

I pressed my palms on the table, as if I was about to rise to my feet. 'I've already been interviewed by Inspector Murchison. If you're planning on keeping me here any longer, I'm going to call a lawyer.'

The woman returned her gaze to me. 'That might not be a bad idea.'

Thurso Scanlan leaned forward. He tried and failed to smother a grin, then did the whole, 'I am arresting you on suspicion of handling stolen goods. You do not have to say anything, but anything you do say will be regarded as evidence and may be produced in court . . .' thing.

A wealth of lawyers have squandered their fees at Bowery Auctions, but I did not want to test their loyalty by asking one to defend me on a charge of stealing from the dead. I requested a duty solicitor.

My previous visits to a police cell had been brief, the results of youthful misdemeanours and retaliations to homophobes that descended into fist fights. I had learned to use my wits since then and it had been a while since I had heard the clang of a cell door. Nothing had improved. It was the same five-by-six high-ceilinged room. The same piss-yellow walls and stainless-steel lav. The same stench of previous customers.

I took my suit jacket off and lay down on the hard bench that doubled as a bed. The duty sergeant had issued me with a blanket in exchange for my bootlaces, belt and the contents of my pockets. I kicked off my shoes, shoved the blanket beneath the bunk and draped my jacket over my body for warmth. A spider was stationed on the ceiling immediately above, too high for me to shift it. I closed my eyes.

The arrested have no automatic right to a phone call in Scotland. I had not wanted to gift Thurso Scanlan the satisfaction of turning me down, so I had not asked for one. Rose and the rest of Bowery's crew would assume I had gone AWOL. Les was on his own adventure, one that might lead him to a room of the same dimensions as the one I currently occupied. No one would be looking for me any time soon, but Stephanie Manderson could confirm I had taken her brother's stock with her permission. I had filled in the right forms, completed the right receipts.

I opened my eyes. The spider had vanished from the ceiling. I stood up, shook my jacket and brushed the front of my shirt with the backs of my hands, but there was no sign of it. I lay back down again and tried to banish the crawling suspicion that it had scrambled inside my shirt.

Doubt crept into my mind, as doubt is prone to do in police cells. I wondered if Les and Jamie Jetpacks were already in custody on drugs charges. There would be little I could do about it if Thurso Scanlan was planning to add me to his vendetta.

Corruption in Police Scotland goes all the way back to the start of the century with Glasgow's own Serpico, Detective Lieutenant John Thomson Trench. Trench was dishonourably discharged for stating what the dogs in the street knew, that Oscar Slater, a German-Jewish man, had not battered Miss Marion Gilchrist to death. Glasgow police had declared Trench a traitor and fitted him up for a jewellery theft he had not committed. He died a broken man.

Whatever my old school friend Inspector Jim Anderson claimed about changed days, corruption still seamed through the force like fat through bacon. I was male and pale, but a man like me, a queer dealer in second-hand goods whose influence was confined to the lower depths, would be easy prey if Scanlan decided I was worth pursuing. And, of course, there was the fact that I was a man with something to hide: guilty of taking, and losing, a murder weapon, screwing the investigation, and propelling an innocent refugee into jail.

I closed my eyes and tried to soothe myself by recalling, one by one, the items I had logged and bagged in Manderson's house, but the image of him lying in his coffin intruded. The cell I was in was a coffin of a kind.

I thought again of the asylum seeker caught in his own coffin cell. Murchison's old neighbour Jim had reassured me that finding a body did not make you responsible for the victim. But landing a man in prison surely made you responsible for regaining his liberty. If the real killer was not found, sooner or later I would have to confess.

I was woken by the click of locks turning, the groan of the cell door being opened. The sour air of the corridor met the sour air of my cell. I sat up, rubbing my face, suit jacket rumpled on my lap. A policeman I had not seen before stuck his head into the cell. 'Duty solicitor's here. Are you willing to see them?'

I felt the bristles on my chin. It was more than thirty-six hours since I had last shaved and showered. 'Yes.'

The policeman nodded to someone in the corridor behind him. 'On you go.'

The door opened wider, and Ali stepped into the cell. The tartan sherpa jacket and black cap he had worn to the Doublet were gone. He was dressed in a trim blue suit, white shirt and blue tie. His hair was neatly gelled in a side parting. Ali nodded to the policeman, who closed the door behind him.

There was an awkward pause.

I pulled on my shoes and got to my feet, attempting to shake the creases from my jacket. 'I don't normally do second dates.'

Ali glanced at the piece of paper in his hand. 'Good, because I don't date clients.'

My jacket remained crumpled. I shrugged it on, sat down

on the bench and reached for a smile. 'I feel at a bit of a disadvantage.'

Ali's mouth kept its stern set. 'You've been arrested on a charge of reset, that is taking goods that don't belong to you with the intention of reselling them for your own profit. I understand the police would also like to question you about a recent murder connected with these goods.'

'It's a misunderstanding.' The words sounded weak, the kind of thing a thieving murderer might say. 'I've got receipts for the jewellery and a declaration of ownership which will check out. I had nothing to do with Mr Manderson's murder beyond finding his body.'

Ali glanced at his notes again. 'The police aren't convinced by your paperwork.'

'It's not the paperwork that's the problem. Inspector Scanlan has it in for a friend of mine who recently got out of jail. He's extended his vendetta to me.'

Ali leaned against the wall of the cell. His neatly pressed suit and snowy shirt emphasised my dishevelment. 'By *vendetta* you mean . . .?'

'He wants to put my friend back behind bars.'

'What was your friend in for?'

'Is that relevant?'

'If you believe it's causing you to be harassed by the police, it could be.'

I was the idiot friend of an idiot. Jailbird friend of a jailbird.

I took another shallow breath of tainted air. 'Intent to supply, impersonating a key worker and breaking lockdown.'

Ali nodded as if I had confirmed something he had suspected all along. 'Are they still dealing drugs?'

I glanced away. 'I couldn't say.'

A drunk shouted something incoherent in the corridor beyond and someone told him to *shutthefuckup*. A door slammed, and there was silence.

Ali made a face that lumped drunks, thieving auctioneers and lockdown-breaking drug dealers together. 'Inspector Scanlan's job is to arrest people who are breaking the law. That includes those engaged in buying and selling illegal drugs and jewellery they have no right to.'

I reached for my tobacco tin, but it had been confiscated along with my wallet and mobile phone. 'I liked you better when you weren't on duty.'

Ali did not smile. He sat down on the bench beside me. 'This has the potential to go beyond reset. They want to question you about your friend's murder.'

For a confused second, I thought he meant Les. Ali must have seen the panic in my eyes because he added, 'About Mr Manderson's murder.'

I had said it before, but it bore repeating: 'Mr Manderson was not my friend.'

Ali grimaced. 'I recommend you don't state that fact quite so emphatically to Inspector Murchison.'

The cell door opened, and the turnkey said, 'They're ready for you in the interview room.'

Twenty-One

THREE HOURS LATER, after a grilling by Inspector Murchison that had plucked my nerves onto the outside of my flesh, hungry, unwashed and unshaven, I stepped from Partick Police Station into the chill and petrol fumes of Dumbarton Road. Ali was by my side, a receipt for Mandy Manderson's confiscated stock in my recently returned wallet.

I texted Frank and Abomi and asked them to use the spare key tucked in Rose's desk to collect my car from the roadside where I had abandoned it hours before.

'They don't actually believe I murdered him, do they?'

Ali was wearing a navy pea coat over his still pristine blue suit. There was no hint of the broom-wielding adventurer who had evened the odds in a street fight.

'The police have to consider all angles.'

I remembered what Steph said detectives in novels looked for: 'Means, motive and opportunity.'

'You have all three.'

I took my tobacco and papers from my pocket and started to build a roll-up. 'He was killed with something long and sharp. Anyone had the means. A million people could make the opportunity. As for motive . . .' I repeated the line I had stuck to throughout the police interview '. . . I'm not a murderer, but if I was, I'd need a better reason to bump somebody off than two carrier bags of jewellery. I get a wage. I don't rely on commission.'

'No one thinks this is about diddling your commission.'

I found my lighter, lit my roll-up and took a deep drag. We walked away from the police station towards the West End, side by side, though neither of us had mentioned a destination.

'Murchison's met my boss, Rose. She'd cut me a Glasgow smile if she thought I was flying solo.'

Ali stepped neatly out of the path of a Deliveroo cyclist careering along the pavement. 'She could be in on it.'

It was too close to the truth for comfort.

'Rose has a weak stomach for blood. Can't even go to a horror movie, closes her eyes at the previews.' It was a lie. Rose was a fan of Hammer horror, vampire films and '70s schlock. We had laughed our way through many a video nasty together. 'No way could she stab Manderson, but even if she could, why would she? His stuff isn't worth risking a life sentence for. Business is good.'

I hoped no one would demand to see the auction-house books and spot the business's precarious week-to-week lurching finances that occasionally left me waiting for my pay cheque. It was part of the reason Rose had been so keen to become a regular on afternoon TV.

Ali met my eyes for the first time since we had left the station. 'The friend you mentioned, the one who recently got out of prison, is it the guy I met you with the other night? Whatshisname? Les?'

'Maybe.'

'I don't normally give free advice, but I'd cut him loose if I were you. He's a liability.'

'I'll think about it.'

People had been telling me to keep away from Les since we were kids. It was too sentimental to describe him as family, but it was hard to think of another word. We were the repository of each other's memories. Les would take my side against an outsider, even when he thought I was wrong. I would not describe him as my best friend; it went deeper than that. We judged each other, carped and fell out. When we were younger, we had occasionally come to blows. But there was unconditional loyalty between us. There were jokes only Les would understand. I would not kill for two bags of silver, but perhaps I would kill for him, the same way I might kill for Rose.

I took my watch from the pocket of my jacket where I had stuffed it when the desk sergeant returned my belongings, and fastened it around my wrist. It was after five. We were almost at the junction between Byres Road and Dumbarton Road. The Lismore was on our left.

I glanced at Ali. 'I owe you a pint.'

'Legal aid will settle my fee. You don't owe me anything.'

'Fair enough.' I stopped before we came in earshot of the smokers standing outside the pub. 'What happens next?'

'Depends on what the police turn up. Maybe nothing, maybe they'll invite you in for questioning again.'

'Invite?'

'Insist.' He took a business card from his wallet and passed it to me. 'If they do, get in touch.'

I slid the card into my wallet beside the list I had taken from Manderson's safe. 'All I'm guilty of is reporting Manderson's murder to the police and accepting his sister's invitation to value his stock.'

'You would have been wiser to decline the invitation.'

'Mandy Manderson was a client. I might not have liked him, but I owe him a duty of care.'

'Him or his effects?'

'It amounts to the same thing in my business.'

'Convenient.'

'It feels bloody inconvenient.' Ali made a face at the edge in my tone. I forced my voice reasonable. 'Sometimes you defend people you don't like. I sell people's effects, as long as they're kosher, whether I want to or not. We're professionals. We do our jobs even when we'd rather walk away . . .' I sensed a wavering in him.

'Trouble is, you keep bad company, Rilke. People are inclined to judge you by your friends.'

'Maybe they should judge me by my loyalty.'

'Blind loyalty can get a man into trouble.'

'I'm not blind.'

It came out flirtier than I intended, and I laughed. The tension between us broke and Ali laughed with me. He glanced at his watch. 'I guess one pint wouldn't hurt.'

'Folk might think you're keeping bad company.'

'I'm a criminal brief. I'll tell them it goes with the job.'

The pub was busy. I stepped up to the bar, and after a while a broad-shouldered, bearded barman, tinselled in chains like a Hell's Angel, took my order.

Ali found a small table in the corner, and I ferried our pints to it. We had nothing to talk about except my misdemeanours and bad taste in friends, and so we sat in silence for a while. I had bought two packets of crisps. I burst one open. 'Will the asylum seeker who was arrested for Manderson's murder get a lawyer?'

'Of course. If he can't afford to hire one, and I'm guessing he can't, the court will appoint one on his behalf.'

The crisps tasted stale and greasy. 'Will they be any good?'

'They won't be Atticus Finch, but most lawyers do their best.'

'So if this guy didn't kill Mandy, the chances of him being convicted are slim?'

Ali took a sip of his pint and made a face. 'It's not like TV. Most murderers are opportunists. They're careless. You do know the man had your friend's bank card on him?'

I paused, halfway to shovelling the last of the crisps into my mouth. 'What?'

Ali nodded. 'Yep, the police didn't do a random pounce. He used the card in a supermarket, and it set off an alert.'

I felt a sliver of hope and a corresponding quiver of disgust at my eagerness to damn another man. 'Mandy was an old racist. I can't imagine him letting an Afghani get close enough to murder him. Maybe if it was a mugging gone wrong . . . but this was something else . . . something more intimate.'

'Murder's as intimate as you can get.'

A barmaid paused at the next table and started stacking empty pint glasses. I glanced towards her and recognised Cat. She was wearing a black sleeveless tunic over black pleather trousers, her tattooed bird sleeves on display. I slumped in my chair, hoping she would not spot me.

Ali was still talking. 'If the poor guy has a mental illness, who knows what he thought he was doing?'

Cat was back behind the bar. The tattooed barman said something to her, and she laughed.

Ali followed my gaze. 'Is that . . .?'

I nodded. 'Yep, the girl who threw a pint over Les the other night.'

'Is that why we're here?'

'I didn't know she worked here.'

'You're an odd guy, Rilke.'

'Maybe, but I'm not a stalker.'

'What would she say if I asked her?'

'I've no idea. First time we met was the same night I met you. I haven't seen her since. Glasgow's a small town. People are always tripping over each other.'

The news was playing on the television above the bar. A politician with coiffed hair and a pained expression, floodwater sending parked cars askew in a historic town centre. The scrolling tickertape beneath the images announced unacceptably high levels of infant deaths in a Midlands hospital. Two students hospitalised by drug overdoses shortly after leaving a Glasgow nightclub. An MP had mistakenly thought their mic was off and inadvertently broadcast a foul-mouthed rant to the nation.

The tattooed barman was at my shoulder. His expression could be classified under the general heading of unhappy. His voice was low, the bar noisy, but I heard him clearly. 'A word, please.' He jerked his head towards the door.

'What about?'

'I'll tell you outside.'

Ali said, 'Want me to come with you?'

I did, but I shook my head. 'Keep an eye on my pint.' It was my way of asking him to stick around.

I was aware of the barman's bulk behind me as I walked through the bar, the eyes of other drinkers following us. It was cold outside, and the crisps I had wolfed sat oily and uneasy with the beer in my stomach. I asked again, 'What's this about?'

The barman's tattoos roamed beyond his leather jacket sleeves and shirt collar. They crept across his arms, up his neck and circled the dome of his bald head. He pointed towards Mansfield Park, a concrete square punctuated with concrete benches. Once a month it was brightened by a farmer's market, but it was empty except for a couple of smokers and a man watching his greyhound sniff and scent.

Once upon a time, tattoos were the preserve of sailors, circus freaks and prostitutes. They marked people out, dedicated them to the edge and denied them straight employment. These days inked bodies are no big deal. Barbed-wire bands and tribal markings have given way to retro pin-ups, blackout drenches and botanical drawings that Audubon might have been proud of. The barman's tattoos were dense enough for me to be unsure what they were of. I glanced sideways at him. A rose, a dice, a twist of ivy, a crow, a leaping panther.

We reached a bench, and he sat down. I perched next to him, ready to spring away if he lunged at me. We were in sight of a main road and a hundred or so apartment windows, but street fights have kicked off in busier spots.

The barman covered his shaved head with a knitted cap. An abstract whorl of colour above his left eyebrow gave him a quizzical look. His voice was quietly reasonable. 'Cat thinks you're following her.'

I kept my feet flat against the concrete. There was tension in my calves, anticipation of flight. 'I'm not following her, but I can see why she might think I am. I met her the other night with a friend who knows her brother. She took objection to him and threw a pint of lager in his face. It's just a coincidence that I'm here today.'

He nodded his head, zen. 'Stay away from her.'
'Am I allowed to finish my pint?'
'Best not.'
'Are you Dickie Bird?'

The barman met my eyes for the first time. His irises were brown and gentle. 'What's it to you?'

'I heard you got beaten up. You're a big guy. I'm wondering what size her brother Hari is.'

Dickie Bird adjusted his hat, pulling it low so it almost covered his eyebrows. 'He's not big, but he's mean. Moves fast, fights dirty. Hit me with a metal bar. Put me in the hospital and him in jail.'

There was something soft and lazy about his speech that made me wonder if he had sustained a brain injury in the fight.

'He must have been angry.'

Dickie met my gaze. 'Just stay away from Cat.'

I nodded, but I remembered the way Cat had rushed for her bag and fled the Doublet immediately after she had received a phone call. I could move fast and fight dirty too.

'You know Hari's telling everyone you pimp his sister out.'

Dickie Bird's eyes narrowed. The purple whorl of colour above his eyelid creased. 'Why are you still sitting here when I told you to go away?'

'Maybe I've got a soft spot for damsels in distress.'

'She's already got someone.'

'You?'

'Doesn't matter who. She's not interested in you.'

'I'm not interested in women that way.'

He gave me an interested stare. 'Really?'

'Really.'

The news that I was gay seemed to relax him. 'My motto's live and let live.'

'Good for you. I don't have a motto, but if I did, it might be, don't put your girlfriend on the game.'

Dickie Bird's laugh was low-pitched, like a bass beat. 'I guess it got around that skinny guys can beat my arse. Maybe I should give you a battering and get word out that I've still got two good fists.'

It was time to leave. I got to my feet. 'You could pulp me no problem, but no one likes a pimp. The news is out. I'd keep looking over my shoulder if I were you.'

Dickie Bird stood up. I braced myself, but he put an arm around me and pulled me into a hug. 'What's your name?'

'Rilke.'

He let go of me and repeated my name out loud, 'Rilke. Unusual.'

'Like the German poet.'

He made a face. 'You've got the wrong end of the stick, but you're brave. You stuck up for Cat even though you knew I could molicate you. No one tells Cat what to do: not me, not her brother.'

'Did Hari get the wrong end of the stick?'

'Hari's a dirtbag. The kind of guy who needs someone to blame, so he blamed me. If he paid attention, he'd know that Cat is doing her own thing. He doesn't like it. Maybe I don't like it. Maybe I don't mind. Live and let live. Let people make their own mistakes, if they are mistakes.'

'So Cat isn't . . . what about the bird tattoos?'

'What about them?'

'I thought maybe she got them because your name is Bird.'

Dickie Bird laughed. 'That's funny. She got them because

she wants to be free, like a bird.' He clapped me on the back. 'Finish your pint. You look like you need it.'

Cat sent me a look from behind the bar that said she was not pleased by my return. I half-hoped Dickie would pour me a fresh pint, but he gave me a final friendly clap on the shoulder, returned to his post and left me to the flat remnants.

Ali's glass was empty. I slid into the seat opposite and tipped the dregs of my beer to my lips. 'Thanks for waiting.'

He pulled his coat on. 'I was about to hit the road.'

'I guess that looked dodgy.'

'None of my business unless it lands you back in custody, and even then . . .'

He let his words tail off, letting me know he was rethinking his offer to represent me.

'He thought I was after Cat. I convinced him otherwise.'

Ali got to his feet. 'Good for you.'

My phone was ringing in my pocket. Rose's voice was bright with panic. 'I need you here, right now.'

I kept my eyes on Ali. 'I told you I was going to be late—'

She cut me off. 'Les is here. He's in a bloody state. He says some guy you know, Jamie something? Les says . . .' She took a deep breath. 'This is fucking unbelievable. Les says this guy just put a couple of students in hospital. There's a chance they might die.'

'Is Jamie there?'

'No, thank Christ, but Les is. And he needs to get gone before he pulls us all into the shit with him.'

Ali slung his rucksack over his shoulder and headed for the exit. I barged after him. The barroom was crowded. Cat grabbed my arm and hissed, 'That's right, off you trot. Don't let the door hit you on the way out.' Dickie Bird raised a hand in farewell. The TV above the bar showed a deflated rubber dinghy crumpled on a sandy shore. The camera homed in on cruel tears where someone had slashed it with a knife. The ticker tape below said, *Glasgow Students Collapsed Outside Nightclub*. Outside, a siren sounded. I stepped into the street and saw a blue flashing light racing towards somebody else's disaster. I stuck out my arm and hailed a passing cab.

The driver gave me a dubious look. 'You okay, pal?'

'Aye, I'm just running late.'

'What for? Your ain funeral?' He laughed at his joke and lurched the cab into the afternoon traffic, repeating, 'Late for your ain funeral.'

Twenty-Two

MY CAR WAS neatly parked in its usual spot by the exit gate. I hunkered down and took the keys from the rear left wheel arch where I knew Abomi had stashed them. No lights blinked on Bowery's outside security cameras. Rose had turned them off. I crossed the car park in darkness. The back of my neck tingled as I passed the spot where Mandy was murdered. The wind caught a scrap of discarded plastic sheeting, sending it cartwheeling, ghostly tumbleweed.

The heels of my boots sounded hollow against the wooden steps where Manderson and Hannah had sheltered when she sold him the kiss that had gone too far. The back door was locked. I fished out my keys and turned them in various keyholes, but it was bolted from the inside. I knocked, and when no one answered texted Rose: *outside b door*.

A helicopter buzzed above. A casualty being ferried to hospital from one of the islands, or a police search. I glanced up at it. Helicopters were prone to falling from the sky. The bolts on the other side rattled. The door opened a crack, and Rose's face peered out, a blur of white in the darkness. I slid inside, and she locked and bolted it behind us. 'Where the fuck have you been?'

I hit the light switch by the door. Rose was wearing a blood-red dress that made me think of Mary, Queen of Scots' final walk to the scaffold.

'I got caught up in something.'

'You're always getting caught up. Your life's one big spider's web.' Rose wrinkled her nose. 'Are you growing a beard?'

I touched my face. 'I didn't have time to shave.'

'You look like an old man.' A bulb in one of the overhead lamps flickered, strobing the saleroom in light and dark like a poltergeist warning. Rose hit the switch and plunged the saleroom back into darkness. 'You have to get Les gone before Anderson gets here.'

'When's he due?'

She turned away from me and walked in the direction of the kitchen. 'Soon.'

'How soon?'

'I don't know. You know Anderson. He has a habit of appearing. That's why I bolted the door. I didn't want him slinking up on us.'

Slink was not a word I would use for Anderson. His investigations might be sleekit, but he was a solid man with a tendency to barge through doors, locked or not.

'How's Les?'

'In a panic. Googling countries that don't have an extradition treaty with the UK. Cursing Glasgow Airport's limited offerings.' Rose paused outside the kitchen. 'He's seriously screwed up this time. I don't care where you take him, as long as it's far away from Bowery.'

'I'll do my best.'

'Do better than your best. If he's not gone in the next thirty minutes, I'll call the cops myself. Those kids are in the hospital, Rilke. What if they die? We could be accessories to perverting the course of justice.'

There was no point in reminding her we had become accessories to perverting the course of justice when I removed the murder weapon from Mandy's eye.

Rose opened the kitchen door and ushered me inside. 'I've had enough of him. I'll wait out here and head Anderson off.'

The bright fluorescent light stung my eyes after the darkness of the saleroom. Les was wearing a black suit and dark wine-coloured shirt, as if he was already dressed for court. His white-blond hair had been dyed black with a faint tinge of blue-green iridescence, like a bluebottle's wing. A half-bottle of Smirnoff sat empty on the table in front of him. He had the wide-awake stare of a frightened drunk.

I took a seat. 'What happened?'

Les pressed a hand to his forehead as if trying to drag the answer from his brain. 'That fud Jamie went freelance, helped himself to some stuff he shouldn't have and sold it on.' He leaned back in his chair and looked up at the ceiling. 'I know what I'm doing, Rilke. I'm practically a qualified chemist. I know the right proportions, but the little prick cut it himself.'

Les had never sat a chemistry exam in his life, but I let it pass.

'You can't stay here, pal.'

Les's phone was lying face down on the table next to the vodka bottle. He nodded at it. 'I'm scared to look. Are they dead?'

'Still in hospital. They're young. With any luck they'll make it.' It was all flimflam. I had no idea if the students would survive or not. 'Where's Jamie?'

Les reached for the vodka bottle, remembered it was empty and gave it a half-hearted spin. 'Wee cunt's fucked off. They'll get him though. Nightclubs are hoaching with CCTV. They'll bury him six feet under, and me with him.'

He gave the empty bottle another nudge.

I took it from him and set it in the sink. 'The police might not catch him. Best you can do is lie low and hope it passes.'

Les gave me an incredulous look. 'I'm not talking about the polis. I'm talking about Ray Diamond.'

I realised why Les looked like he wanted to kill himself. Ray Diamond had supplied the drugs that Jamie had sold on to the students. 'Fuck.'

Les's eyes were red-rimmed, as if he had been rubbing them with his knuckles. 'Yes, *fuck*. I seriously thought about turning myself in to Thurso Scanlan, but Scanlan's bent and, anyway, Ray's got guys on the inside that'll do me as easy in there as out here. Easier.'

I'd done Ray a few favours in my time, including employing his nephew Abomi as a junior porter, but nothing that would save Les's bacon if he took against him.

I got to my feet. 'I promised Rose we'd get out of here.'

Les nodded. 'I need you to drive me to London.'

'Jesus, Les. Did you never consider taking driving lessons?'

His voice rose a notch. 'Why would I? Driving lessons cost a bomb and I live near the subway. Just get me to Heathrow and I'll catch a flight.'

'Where to?'

'Anywhere. Ukraine, Iraq, Palestine, North fucking Korea. Somewhere safer than Glasgow.'

Rose was talking with someone in the saleroom beyond. I leapt to the door and turned the lights off, as if darkness could shelter us from what was to come.

Les muttered, 'Fuck, fuck, fuck, fuck, fuck.' His voice soft, like a prayer.

We sat in silence, and then the door to the kitchen gently opened. I resisted an urge to reach for Les's hand. The light went on, and Razzle Dazzle Diamond stood in the doorway dressed in one of his anonymous beige outfits, the camouflage that helps him live in plain sight. Rose hovered in scarlet behind him.

No one spoke for a moment, then Razzle said, 'You boys having a séance? Trying to raise the dead?'

Les shook his head. 'No one's dead.'

Ray Diamond was not a big man, but he seemed to fill the doorway. 'Not yet. Might be soon, though.'

Ray Diamond never travelled alone. I wondered who else was waiting outside in the darkness. It was not my fight, but I said, 'This isn't Les's fault.'

Ray turned the cold tunnel of his stare on me. 'Ask yourself how loyal you want to be.'

Les glanced at me. 'It's nothing to do with you, Rilke.'

Ray nodded. 'Good advice. Where's your wee pal?'

Les said, 'What wee pal?'

'Let's not waste time.'

'Legged it.'

'That's where you're wrong. Trick question. We picked up the sorcerer's apprentice three hours ago. He told us the whole story.'

Les stared at the table for a moment and then stood up. His face was slack with drink, but his jaw was set. He slid his phone into his pocket. 'Let's get going.'

I put a hand on his shoulder and pushed him down into his chair. 'No one's going anywhere.'

Rose was still hovering in the half-light behind Ray. She said my name, a warning in her voice.

Ray turned to look at her. 'Nothing's going to happen. Not here anyway. Why don't you go home to that handsome policeman of yours?'

Rose said something about Anderson being due any moment and Ray smiled. 'Best head him off at the pass then. Better for everyone – him included.'

'I'm staying here.' Rose's mobile phone glowed in the dark of the saleroom beyond as she stabbed at its keys. 'I've texted Anderson that we're working late and I'll see him at his place.'

Ray's eyes were steady behind the lenses of his varifocals. 'Fair enough. This is your establishment. I respect that. But you of all people know business is important, Rose. My business has suffered an upset. Leslie is going to help me rectify it.'

There was a studied politeness to Ray's speech. The tense, circling calm that precedes a feeding frenzy.

Rose's voice was equally calm: glassy waters with only a telltale ripple to hint at what lurked beneath. 'You have thirty minutes, then I want you gone.'

'Or else?'

'It's not a threat.'

Ray nodded. 'I always said your dad brought you up well. Thirty minutes should do it.' Rose receded into the saleroom. Ray said softly to someone in the darkness beyond, 'Keep an eye on her. If it looks like she's using her phone, take it off her. Gently, mind.' He shut the door and took a seat at the table. 'You should know better, Leslie.'

Les was staring at the table's surface again, his head hung forward like a penitent. 'I thought the little twat had more sense.'

'Your bad judgement's turned you into a liability.'

I got up and poured myself a glass of water from the tap, more to give myself something to do than because I was thirsty, but when I took a sip I realised I was parched.

'Les spent six months in Barlinnie. He never mentioned your name once.'

Ray laughed softly. 'Am I meant to be grateful or something?'

I poured two more glasses of water and set them on the table. 'He's been a loyal foot soldier for years.'

Ray took his glasses off and looked at me. 'I like you, Rilke. I don't like many poofs, but I do like you. Do you know what happens to loyal foot soldiers?'

'I have a feeling you're going to tell me.'

He nodded. 'They get shot in the first frame of the movie.'

Les got to his feet again. 'Let's just get this over with.'

I pressed my hand down on his shoulder again and forced him into his seat, keeping my eyes on Ray's. 'This is real life, not a movie. What happened isn't Les's fault. Jamie Jetpacks stole from him. That means he stole from you. If anyone needs taught a lesson, it's him, not Les.'

Les and Ray were both staring at me. Les said, 'Jamie what?'

'Jamie Jetpacks. Remember his T-shirt?'

Les gave a small grunt that might have been meant to be a laugh. 'Oh aye. We Were Promised Jetpacks. I'd forgotten that.'

Ray decided he was not interested in the source of the student's nickname. He slid his glasses back onto his nose.

'Turns out young Jamie has potential. He's studying law at the uni. His mum's a judge. Father's an MSP. Friends in high places, if you know what I mean. Not a young man who can take a beating without someone objecting. On the other hand, with a bit of training and cultivation he's the kind who might eventually make himself useful.'

I took another sip of water. 'Les has been useful to you for nigh on fifteen years.'

Ray glanced at his watch and sighed. 'Two civilians are in hospital. They might not make it. The polis are going to need a warm body and Scanlan's already got a hard-on for Les. He can take one for the team and I'll make sure he lives to fight another day.'

'What if he doesn't want to?'

Les said, 'He's not giving me any choice.'

Ray smiled. 'He gets it.'

Les raised the glass of water I had set in front of him to his lips and took a sip. His hand was steady. 'What next?'

'One of the boys will give you a lift home. You'll wait there. Let things take their course.'

I said, 'I'll take him.'

'Nice try, but I don't think so.' Ray looked at his watch again. 'Ten minutes before Ms Bowery kicks us out on our arses. May as well get moving.' He nodded at me. 'You too, Rilke.'

Les snapped, 'It's got fuck all to do with him.'

Ray raised an eyebrow as if he was not used to people swearing at him and had no desire to get used to it. 'Looks to me like he made it his business.'

Les was on his feet now. 'No, he fucking didn't.'

I touched his arm. 'Don't worry, I'm practically a friend of the family.'

'You think employing his numpty nephew Abomi makes you immune? Christ, Ray's probably got the wee gobshite lined up to take your place.'

There was a Stanley knife sitting amongst a jumble of crockery on the kitchen draining board. Ray reached for it and in one easy movement sliced the blade down Les's cheek. A jagged arc of blood splattered across the wall and dripped scarlet on the floor.

'What the fuck?' I grabbed a dishtowel, ran it under cold water and applied it to Les's face.

Les put his hand on the wet cloth and held it in place. I could smell his sweat, sudden and nasty. His face was grey, except for where blood dripped from it. He drove his boot into the kitchen cupboard, forcing the pain into the wall.

The door opened, and a large man stuck his head into the room. 'Everything all right?'

Ray nodded. 'Tell Ryan to bring the van round. We'll be out in a moment.'

Les stopped battering the furniture. His voice was tight, grit and spume. 'I shouldn't have said that. Abomi's a good lad.'

Ray gave a small, almost imperceptible nod. 'Phones on the table. SIMs out.'

Les took two phones from his pockets. He tried to prise the phone's casing apart with one hand while holding the bloody dishtowel to his cheek with the other. 'Rilke's sound. You don't need him.'

'Telling me my business, Leslie?'

'I wouldn't do that, Ray. It's just . . .'

I took my own phone from my jacket pocket. My hand was trembling. 'Leave it, Les.'

Les was still struggling to get the back off his phone. He started to slam it against the table. 'Jesus fuck.'

Ray shook his head. 'David Attenborough would have a field day with you two. Never understood why he went all the way to Africa to study monkeys when Glasgow's a quick EasyJet from London. Give it here.'

He took the Stanley knife from the counter and deftly split the casing of Les's phones. He did the same for mine and put the SIMs in his pocket.

The kitchen door opened again, and the big man leaned into the room. 'All set.'

Ray nodded. 'Come on, boys. Time to get out of Rose Bowery's hair.'

He led the way across the darkened saleroom and out into the car park, where an unmarked white van was waiting. Les and I followed like lambs. I glanced at the security cameras as we passed. They were as dead as Mandy Manderson, our exit unrecorded.

Twenty-Three

THE BIG MAN stepped from the passenger seat and slid open the side door of the van. Les climbed inside and I started to follow him.

Ray Diamond put a hand on my shoulder. 'Not you, Rilke. You're coming with me.'

'I'd rather stick with Les, if you don't mind.'

'I do mind.'

The driver asked, 'You okay, boss?'

Ray slapped the side of the vehicle. 'Yep, I'll drive myself back.'

The door slid shut on Les hunched forward in his seat, the bloody dishtowel still held to his cheek. The van sped out of the car park, leaving us behind.

Ray walked in the direction of the exit gate, and I fell in beside him. The wind picked up, sending needles of rain into our faces.

Ray took a tweed cap from the pocket of his coat and put it on his head. 'Bloody weather.'

'Never fancy retiring somewhere warm?'

He glanced at me. 'You don't give up, do you? Who do you think holds this city in place? The police? The CEOs and boards of trade? The bloody city council? They can't even empty the bins. When I *retire* there'll be a war.'

We left Bowery Auctions behind and walked through a canyon of tenements. Ray was two decades older than me, but he walked at a fair clip. I did not ask where we were going. Up ahead a black Mercedes, parked beneath a dead streetlamp, flashed its headlights.

Ray muttered, 'Stupid arsehole.' He opened the driver's door and leaned in. 'Okay, I'll take it from here.'

A nasal voice whispered, 'Nae bother, boss.'

Ray straightened up. A thin man slid reluctantly from the warm leather of the Merc into the evening rain. He hunched his shoulders and headed into the dark.

Ray nodded in the direction of the passenger seat. 'Get in.'

It was cosy inside the car. The engine started without a cough. We drove in silence through the tenement-lined streets, keeping to a steady twenty. Neither of us spoke until we reached the bright lights of the expressway. Ray said, 'Never understood why you hung around with that fuckwit.'

'We go back a long way.'

'So does sewage. You should do yourself a favour and marry Rose Bowery. Take her away from that gammon and get yourself a slice of the auction business. You're not getting any younger. Time to think about feathering your own nest.'

It was a relief to know there was a future in which I might survive to feather a nest. 'I'm not the marrying kind.'

'Ach, plenty of poofs marry women. Always have done, always will. From what I heard you're not so fussy anyway.'

'What have you heard?'

Ray kept his eyes fixed on the road. 'I hear a lot of things. I heard you've been asking questions about Mandy Manderson, may he rest in eternal hellfire.'

'Not a fan?'

'Not a fan.' Ray kept his eyes on the road and the speedometer at sixty. 'Heard you got his stock and lost it again.'

Only the police and Ali the lawyer knew what had happened to the contents of Mandy Manderson's safe. I wondered which of them had passed the information to Ray and why.

'A misunderstanding on Thurso Scanlan's part. It'll be ironed out.'

I watched his face as I mentioned the policeman's name, but Ray would make a good poker player. His expression gave nothing away. I was familiar with the route Ray was taking and knew where we were going now. To the housing estate on the east of the city where Ray lived. I had dropped Abomi there many times before the boy had passed his driver's test and been gifted a customised Mini Cooper by his uncle Ray.

We slid off the motorway, onto a long road edged by new-builds and gap sites that had been empty since I was a boy, past the occasional petrol garage shining like the American dream, fast-food shop windows a steamy glow and parades of corner shops, shuttered and dead.

Ray said, 'You're interested in more than Mandy's silver.'

It was a statement, not a question, but I answered it anyway. 'I found his body.'

'Not the first dead man you've seen.'

It was my turn to be enigmatic. 'True.'

'Why so curious?'

'You'd be curious if someone was killed on your doorstep.'

'If someone was killed on my doorstep, it would mean something. Bowery's a public building. Could be bad luck someone snuffed it there.'

'Could be.'

'But you know otherwise?'

Ray had spies everywhere. I wondered if someone had seen me pull the hatpin from Mandy's eye. 'Not for sure . . .'

'But you have a feeling.'

'Like you said, I'm curious.'

Ray glanced away from the road. His eyes met mine. 'I'm curious too. I want you to find out who did it.'

'You've got a long reach. Why don't you find out for yourself?'

He took one of his hands off the wheel and grasped my elbow. I felt the strength of his grip. 'You're within my reach, Rilke. I'm reaching out to you.'

'What do I get in return?'

'A free pass.'

'For Les too.'

'Thought I told you to cut him loose.'

'You also told me I should marry Rose Bowery.'

'And I was right about that as well.' We drove on in silence.

Ray said, 'Someone has to pay for this fuck-up. Les is the obvious candidate.'

'Not if you want my help.'

He glanced at me again. 'What is it? You queer for each other?'

'We've been friends a long time. He has my back. I have his.'

'I'm guessing you have his back more than he has yours.'

The heater was on, the Merc stuffy. I slid a finger inside the collar of my shirt, felt clammy skin. 'Les is the price.'

Ray hit a button on the dashboard and his hands-free came alive. It rang for a while and then a woman's voice answered with a ward number. Ray said, 'How are the kids doing?'

'No change.'

'Okay, let me know when there is.' Ray cut the call. 'Les is a fuck-up. Out of jail less than a week and he pulls this stunt. There'll be an investigation. Scanlan will probably pick him up anyway. Why not save him and me time and bother?'

'I didn't realise you and Thurso Scanlan were on the same side.'

It was the kind of statement that could refresh my features, the way Les's had just been freshened.

'You're sailing close to the wind, Rilke.'

'At least you know where you stand with me.'

'That's a laugh. You're trickier than Tam Shepherds Trick Shop.'

'I can't guarantee I'll find Manderson's killer.'

'You've got a good track record.'

Ray knew I had been involved in the successful investigation of two murders, neither of which I had volunteered for.

'I've been lucky.'

'Not sure I believe in luck.'

Ray turned into his housing estate. He eased the Merc over the series of speed bumps designed to stop boy racers getting their kicks. The list of things people did not believe in was growing longer. I filed luck beside coincidence and wondered what they had in common. An absence of control, a pantheon of gods rolling dice.

Multicoloured lights flashed in a top-storey window where someone was having a party. Ray glanced up at it, lips pursed. His brand of gangster relied on strictly set moral parameters that only he was allowed to cross.

He drew the car into the kerb a block before his house. 'I'll do a deal with you. If those kids pull through and you find Manderson's killer, I'll consider letting Les off the hook.'

There are no guarantees in this world, and gangsters' promises are fragile as mayflies, but I said, 'You're asking me to stick my neck out. I need more than consideration. Do me a deal.'

'A deal? We're not in your auction house now.'

'I know that.'

Ray stared into the grey and rain, the parked cars and scruffy hedges that edged the street. He was a dealer as well as a gangster, a pawnbroker who could not be seen to be an obvious cheat. His handshake was worth something.

He turned and held his right hand out to me. 'Okay, it's a deal.'

We shook, and I asked, 'Who will pay instead?'

'What's it to you?'

'You said someone had to be dubbed in to keep business on an even keel. Who's next on the list after Les?'

'Not you, not Rose, not any of the Bowery crew.'

It was as much as he was going to tell me. 'And if I fail?'

'All bets are off. Les is an easy score. This other candidate, not so much.'

'So far all I've found out is that Mandy was a nasty piece of work with wandering hands who no one has a good word for – not his colleagues, not his sister, not his neighbour.'

I left out Mandy's white-haired Ian Paisley lookalike visitor, the list of names still rolled tight in my wallet and the sexy woman who had bought the hatpin that had killed him.

Ray looked at me. 'You never asked why I'm so interested.'

'You play things close to the chest. I reckoned you wouldn't tell me.'

'Mandy paid me a licence fee every month for trading jewellery on my turf. He was under my protection.'

'Maybe the killer wasn't aware of that.'

Ray gave a thoughtful nod. 'That occurred to me.' He reached into the darkness of the car and took a folder from the back seat. 'This is purely FYI. We went to bad-boy school together. I want to know if what happened to him had something to do with back then.' He passed me the folder. 'Something in this stuff might help set you on the right road.'

I placed the folder on my knee. 'Anything else you can give me?'

'What? You want gumshoe rates? Fifty dollars a day plus expenses?' Some spends would have been nice, but Ray's voice was slick with sarcasm. He tapped the folder with his fingernail. 'It's all in there. There's a plastic bag in the glove compartment. Make sure none of this stuff gets wet.'

It was confirmation that no one would be driving me back to the West End. I retrieved the bag from a forensically clean glove compartment and slid the folder inside. 'Can I have my phone back, please?'

Ray grinned and reached into his pocket. 'You're going to need it to get yourself an Uber. Might have to walk a distance first though. They're not keen on coming out this way.'

We both knew that Ray simply needed to click his fingers to get me a lift. I took the phone and SIM from him. 'Shall I take Les's too?'

'Stay away from Les. You've got a job to do, and it won't do Les any harm to sweat. Let him think on where he screwed up.'

A blast of rain spattered the car windows, sharp as hail.

I pressed the folder to me. It was slim. Whatever information it held did not take up much space. 'Don't suppose Abomi would give me a lift back? It'd be a shame if I got mugged on the way home and something happened to your info.'

A car drove past, taking it slow over the speedbumps. Ray's teeth shone white in the brief bar of light thrown by its headlamps. 'Don't worry. No one's going to mug you, Rilke. You belong to me.'

Twenty-Four

I WAITED UNTIL I was home before texting Rose to tell her I was safe. The flat was cold, and there was nothing much to eat. I poured myself a tot of malt, topped it with milk and drank it by the light of the fridge door. I slipped Ray Diamond's folder under my mattress, turned my phone to silent, got into bed and slept.

It was still dark when I woke, unsure of what day it was. I had walked a long way through the rain from Ray's place before I had managed to snare a black cab to take me to Bowery to collect my car and drive home. My calves were tight. I wanted to pull the covers over my head and sink back into dreamless sleep, but I was aware of Ray's folder — dossier/list of accusations/mad-map serial killer theories/whatever it was — lying beneath me. I reached for my phone and turned it on. The time glowed 5 p.m. A cascade of notifications of missed calls from Rose chimed in the silent bedroom. Between us, Les and I had brought police and gangsters to her door. I wondered if we were still on the same side and if I would have a job at the end of whatever this episode was.

I searched local news sites for updates about the overdosed students. Yesterday's reports had shifted down the headlines. Perhaps they had been discharged from hospital and were recuperating in the bosom of parental homes. Drug deaths were a front-page splash. Recoveries unnewsworthy.

I scrolled through saved photos in my phone's gallery, past images of saleroom lots I had researched and silly memes Frank and Abomi had shared until I found the positive test result I had photographed the last time I contracted Covid. I attached it to a text, wrote *Quarantining alone in bed. Nothing to worry about except the usual shitshow. Les was masked so should be ok* and sent it to Rose. She would be able to read between the lines. I was not coming into work for a couple of days and Les was okay, for now.

I left Ray's folder until I had ordered two bacon rolls to be delivered from the Criterion Café. I made myself a coffee while I waited and set the folder on the table in the sitting room. The room was sunk in semi-darkness save for a pool of light thrown on the table by an Anglepoise lamp.

The Just Eat courier looked me up and down, taking in my naked feet and brocade dressing gown. Some other time I might have asked if he was hungry too, but I shut the door and ate standing in the shadows by the window, watching the street below. The trees were bare, their branches black and reaching. There was no man in a homburg and raincoat reading a newspaper beneath a streetlamp. No telltale glow of a cigarette from some hidden watcher. But someone might be stationed in the dark of an unmarked car, keeping an eye on my progress. I wondered if I was becoming paranoid.

I did not have the stomach for my second bacon roll. I bundled it in its wrapper and stowed it in the fridge for later. The whisky bottle was still sitting on the kitchen counter. I tightened its cap, poured myself a glass of water and took it through to the sitting room, feeling the dark dread of a man about to unlock the hotel-room door of a suspected suicide. I sat at the table, flipped open the folder and slid out its contents.

It was a thin sheaf of printouts from the internet and photocopies of newspaper articles. Another man might have emailed me a selection of links and PDFs. Was Ray's insistence on hard copy the product of a life focused on flesh-and-blood transactions or something else? Ray was getting on, but he negotiated online auctions with ease, and I recalled faint rumours of a cyber scam he was reputed to have made a quick fortune on. Paper could be shredded and burned, but electronic text left traces that were harder to erase.

A quick shuffle told me the papers in the folder related to Gallowhall School for Boys.

Gallowhall had been one of the institutions Les and I had been threatened with when we were boys. It loomed in my imagination, somewhere out of town, a dark Bates Motel structure. We had managed to dodge incarceration until Les's recent bad luck, but Ray Diamond had not been so fortunate. Gallowhall had helped make him the man he was.

The first page in the folder was a simple account of Gallowhall gleaned from a local history site. It had been established in the late 1880s as a Truant Industrial School, a place where persistent school dodgers and neglected boys were 're-educated', drilled into fodder for overseas colonies and the armed forces. Later it became a reformatory and later still a List D school which had only closed its doors in 2004. I had thought that List Ds housed young offenders, but the potted history told me they were catch-all facilities for vulnerable kids. A boy whose widowed mother had been admitted to hospital might find himself living side by side with precocious young murderers.

The sitting room felt cold. I turned up the heating, took the tartan blanket from the couch, draped it over my shoulders and read on. Ray had a tidy mind. The following pages contained a description of pre-World War Two conditions in the home. Cockroaches in the porridge, a master stabbed by a boy, 'not without cause' according to another master (Ray had highlighted this section), boys cheering a fire in the attic. A tragedy had occurred some years later when three boys tried to abscond using bedsheets to lower themselves from an upper floor to the ground. Two of them had made it, but a third plummeted to the courtyard, where he had lain broken and later died of his injuries. Ray had underlined this section and written POOR LITTLE SOD in neat block capitals in the margin.

The pages jumped to the 1950s and a report by the school nurse of some of the ailments the new arrivals were suffering from: malnutrition, tuberculosis of the bones, joints and lungs, pneumonia, whooping cough, rheumatic fever, a few cases of VD.

I turned the page, uncovering a selection of architectural plans. Gallowhall had started life as a panopticon built of local stone. Over the years it had grown, with low-rise outbuildings and a recreation pitch guarded by high fences. I wondered if Ray had done the internet searches himself or set a researcher onto them. Ray was a man used to delegating, but this had the feel of a personal project.

The documents homed in on the interior of the main building. The cold outlines of architectural plans gave way to colour photographs from a site devoted to explorations of abandoned spaces. Years of dust and rubble coating floors of decaying classrooms and dormitories, discarded school reports, children's pictures painted on brown paper still hanging on walls the same institutional yellow as the cell Thurso Scanlan had locked me in.

Graffiti decorated the rooms. Most of it was incoherent tags and scrawls whose codes I could not decipher, but an oversized cartoon face gaped across the wall of the assembly hall, where rows of plastic chairs sat as if waiting for the boys to return. Its mouth was formed of the open doorway. Red letters dripped across the wall, WELCOME TO HELL FUCKERS! It looked like a set from one of the horror movies Rose laughed at, clichéd but capable of sending a shiver though me.

Les and I rarely talked about our schooldays, Anderson never, but the crumbling classrooms roused glimmers of memories. School was the place where I had learned to be vigilant. It was a raised leather tawse slamming against an outstretched palm, fear of standing out, a scramble to escape at bell time, metal chair legs screeching against tiled floors.

I pulled the blanket tight around my shoulders and turned the page. Next came a report of an independent inquiry into allegations of abuse in the home. It was written in detached language — *values, restraint, regrettable mistakes, unfortunate exceptions to good rule* — and stank of backs being covered.

The final pages were newspaper reports into the prosecution, ten years ago, of two former employees of the home, men who had used their privileges to abuse boys under their care. Pupils' names were withheld, but reporters had described in graphic detail the acts the men had carried out. They described a hypersexualised atmosphere and allegations that boys had learned to target each other, to reproduce the bullying and sexual exploitation amongst themselves, carrying on a spiral of abuse that involved younger children.

I wondered where Ray Diamond and Mandy Manderson fitted into the story. It was hard to imagine either of them as boys. They were men beyond youth. Ray was nicknamed Razzle for several reasons: one, he was a pawnbroker, second, in irony, because of his unflashy wardrobe, and finally because of his surname. Diamonds are the hardest of gemstones, scalpel-sharp, and Ray was the hardest man in a hard city, quick with a cutting blade. It suited him well.

Mandy Manderson lacked Ray's heft, but he too had a sharp edge and a disregard for sexual boundaries. He had lured Hannah into an unwelcome kiss. And then there was the intimate manner of his death. Someone had murdered him for a reason – something personal.

I scanned the summary of the investigation into the Gallowhall abuse allegations. Its author was Andrew Cronin. I took my wallet from the inside pocket of my suit, hanging neatly on the back of my bedroom door, and slid out the list of names I had discovered in Manderson's safe. Andrew Cronin was last on the list, below Urquhart Murchison.

I lifted my laptop from its hiding place under the couch, fired it up and, one by one, typed the names on the list into the search engine. James Campbell, Stuart Jamieson, Robert McRobert and Kenneth Mackenzie turned up too many results to be useful. I added the words 'child abuse' to each of them and a depressing litany of men stared out from local news reports across the country. Adding 'Glasgow' did not narrow the results enough to be useful.

The search for Urquhart Murchison was different. The Right Honourable Lord Justice Murchison stared out from beneath a white horsehair wig, a thin, pale-faced man with a pronounced thrapple. His robes were white and scarlet. I read on and saw that he was a senator of the College of Justice, a member of Scotland's Supreme Court, the highest court in the land. Adding 'child abuse' to the search brought up a litany of cases he had presided over. I wondered if his prosecuting role accounted for his inclusion on Manderson's list or if there was another, more sinister reason.

I had never phoned Ray Diamond regarding anything unrelated to the sale of jewellery, but I picked up my phone and called his number.

'Rilke . . .' My name sounded like a threat. 'You got something for me?'

'Maybe.'

'Get on with it then. I don't need a fan dance.'

'I've come across a couple of names, Andrew Cronin and Urquhart Murchison.'

'Quick off the mark, right enough.'

'Do they mean anything to you?'

'Cronin's dead, roasting on a barbecue with Manderson if there's any justice in Hell. Murchison's untouchable.'

'You think either of them had anything to do with Mandy's demise?'

'Not unless Cronin came back from the grave, which is a disturbing but unlikely thought.'

'I found their names on a list among his effects; there could be a link.'

'There's a link, but Murchison doesn't have the balls for murder. He likes little boys in white panties.'

'He's still active?'

There was a warning note in Ray's voice. 'There's only so active you can be at his age, and like I already told you, he's untouchable.'

The face on my computer screen looked elderly, somewhere in its seventies, but still vigorous, a man inclined to vitamins and food supplements, capable of bagging a Munro or sailing a yacht. I shut my eyes, like a reluctant bungee jumper waiting for the shove that would send me plummeting.

'You think maybe I should go to the police?'

'I think you should listen to what I'm telling you. He's a protected species.'

I remembered what Ray had said about Jamie Jetpacks being a young man who, with a bit of training and cultivation, might make himself useful. Urquhart Murchison, a judge with a reputation clean as Fairy Liquid, had proclivities that made him open to blackmail. He was a corrupted force at the very heart of the legal system.

Ray was still talking. 'The brass have been turning a blind eye for years. Why do you think they got Murchison to chair the investigation into police corruption? He's a toothless fucker.'

'His son's in charge of the investigation into Manderson's murder.'

'So I heard. Sandy Murchison's cut from different cloth. Here's hoping he doesn't cotton on to what his old man's been up to. He's probably the only guy who'd put our friend the judge behind bars.' Ray told me to photograph the list, message it to him, delete it from my phone and to 'stop barking up the wrong tree. Maybe Mandy was putting a sting on Murchison, maybe he was thinking about it, maybe he just liked the feeling of power he got from having the judge's name written on a bit of paper locked in his safe. Either way it's nothing to do with you. Clock's ticking. Get on with the job I set you unless you fancy visiting your pal Les in Barlinnie again.'

I did as Ray told me and then went to the window and stared out at the trees again. Ray Diamond had exposed a sliver of his life to me. It is dangerous to know too much about men like him. Knowledge is power, and Ray would not hesitate to crush anyone with power over him.

I went back to my computer and typed 'Gallowhall List D School abuse' into the search engine. The same articles Ray had copied appeared alongside a confusion of historical information, government claim forms, reports of abuse inquiries, newspaper articles, first-hand accounts, survivor support group chatrooms. The internet is the antiquarian's friend, invaluable for locating objects, verifying sales prices, valuations and authenticity. It has recreational uses that go beyond ordering a quick snack, but I felt out of my depth.

These chatrooms were different from the down-to-business sites I usually favoured. They pulsed with details I wished I could unread, but there were few specific mentions of Gallowhall beyond what Ray had already given me. I turned to newspaper archives and found a tranche of articles reporting on the most recent inquiry and subsequent trial. A familiar name kept recurring.

Prentice Baxter had been a journalist on one of the Scottish broadsheets until cutbacks combined with a love of whisky had resulted in redundancy. Prentice was keen on the Scottish Colourists, a quartet of easy-on-the-eye Post-Impressionists who fetch high prices. For a while he had tried to subsidise his passion by dealing in fine art, but it is a job that requires knowledge, sharp wits and deep pockets. Alcohol had dulled his faculties, and experienced dealers, keen to unload dead stock, had taken care of his redundancy package. He had given me his mobile number back when he was optimistic and looking for stock.

I checked my watch. It was nine o'clock. I dialled the number. He picked up straight away, his voice clear as refrigerator ice.

'My walls are full but tell me what you've got.'

I could hear chatter in the background of wherever he was — some pub, I supposed — and realised I would like a pint to wash away the bad taste Ray's folder had left in my mouth.

I walked to the window and looked out on the night. 'I'm not phoning about a painting. You wrote some articles about Gallowhall School—'

He cut in quick. 'Were you a Gallowhall boy?'

'Not personally.'

'But you know someone who was.'

'Yes.'

'You have information about Gallowhall?'

'No, I'm looking for some.'

Prentice sounded wary. 'What do you want?'

I wanted names. I wanted to know the identity of the white-haired man who had visited Mandy Manderson every Wednesday. I wanted to know if Mandy's death was related to the outrages that had taken place at Gallowhall. I wanted to know who had murdered him, so Rose and I would be off the hook. I wanted to satisfy Ray Diamond and save Les from a long stretch in Barlinnie. I wanted the overdosed students to recover. I wanted peace in our time and goodwill to all men.

A car drove along the street. Its headlights sliced across the room, and I stepped back into the shadows, aware of my nakedness beneath my open dressing gown.

'Just to talk.'

'Okay, no time like the present. I've just left a meeting. You can buy me some dinner in Same Same, St George's Road.'

'I'll be there in twenty minutes.'

I dressed in a fresh white shirt and slate-grey suit. My black Crombie had almost dried out. I pulled it on and added a burgundy Tootal scarf spotted with white polka dots in the hope of looking less like the Grim Reaper.

Rain spattered the windows as the heavens opened into one of the sudden monsoon-like deluges that never used to be a feature of our rainy city. I slid Ray's papers back into their folder, slipped it beneath the sofa cushion and slung the tartan blanket on top. It was a poor hiding place, but no refuge is secure for ever.

Twenty-Five

SAME SAME'S PLATE-GLASS windows were steamy with condensation, but I could make out Prentice Baxter sitting at a window table holding a large menu close to his face. The tables beyond him were packed with Chinese families and students chatting and sharing food.

I opened the door onto heat and fragrance. A small queue of people sat on chairs by the entrance, waiting on takeaway orders or free tables. A waitress carrying a large tray bearing a steamed seabass garnished with curls of spring onion and thin slivers of ginger said, 'Forty-minute wait for a table.'

Prentice saw me and raised a hand. 'Rilke.'

The waitress was quick on the uptake, already ushering me towards him.

The journalist was a big man, six foot two, broad-shouldered and barrel-chested, equipped to carry a large beer belly. He stood up to greet me and I saw that he had lost a good portion of his bulk.

I took the seat opposite him. 'You're a shadow of your former self.'

'What would you say if I told you it was cancer?'

'I'd say that's no joke.'

'And you'd be right.'

'Ah, Jeez, man. I'm sorry.'

His grin widened, happy to have got one over on me. 'I kicked the drink, joined AA.'

A schoolboy waiter slid a menu and a bamboo basket of prawn crackers in front of me. The waitress reappeared and set a fresh pot of jasmine tea and a second cup on the table. 'Drink?'

I was the kind of parched that only alcohol will quench but I nodded at the teapot. 'This is fine, thanks.'

Prentice helped himself to a prawn cracker. 'Get him a pint of lager before he starts greeting.' The waitress departed for the bar. 'Wouldn't be much cop if I couldn't be around folk who drink, not in this country and not in my job.'

I took a prawn cracker and placed it whole in my mouth, savouring its crunch and melt. 'I thought you'd retired.'

'Who can afford to retire these days? I went back to the paper part-time, working harder than I ever did. I've got the energy for it now I'm dry.'

The waitress returned with my pint and asked if we were ready to order. Prentice requested his usual. I realised I was starving and asked for duck noodle soup. The journalist's eyes were on my pint, sweating and golden on the table, like an advertisement for the good stuff. I lifted it to my lips and drank, feeling guilt and relief at its earthy citrus scent.

Prentice helped himself to another prawn cracker. 'I was toiling, Rilke, heading towards the exit door. Now I think I might make ninety, a hundred even. Why not?'

I took another sip of my pint, wanting to finish it and kill the longing in his eyes. 'It's taken years off you.'

He slapped his reduced belly. 'Aye, I'm reborn.'

The waitress set chopsticks and a bowl in front of each of us and added a china spoon for me. A child at the next table said something that set his family laughing. His mother, or perhaps an aunt, put an arm around the boy and pulled him close, singing a few words of a song that made the table laugh again.

Prentice turned his thirsty eyes on me. 'What's your interest in Gallowhall?'

Same Same was noisy with chatter, but I lowered my voice. 'Did you hear about Mandy Manderson, the jewellery dealer who was murdered outside Bowery Auctions?'

'It crossed my radar. Must have been hard on Rose.'

'Not just Rose. I found his body. It shook me up.'

'Thought you were looking rough.'

I tipped my pint to my mouth again. Prentice had been struck by the curse of the newly sober, a judgemental edge that disapproved of people who could handle their drink.

'It's been preying on my mind. The polis are their usual useless selves.'

A different kind of hunger crossed Prentice's face, an appetite for a story. 'And you thought you'd go sniffing around.'

'It wasn't a random killing. It was close up, personal. Elaborate.' I remembered Manderson's mutilated eye and a nerve in my face twitched. 'I thought maybe if I could find out why it happened . . .'

The waitress brought our food. Prentice's usual turned out to be Hong Kong-style sweet and sour chicken and fried rice. He ordered another pot of jasmine tea. I waved away the offer of a second beer and sank my spoon into my large bowl of steaming soup. We ate in silence for a while. The waitress returned and topped up our teacups.

Eventually Prentice paused his chopsticks. 'So what have you come up with?'

I picked the bone from a piece of duck and set it beside the others. 'Not much.'

'Not much but something?'

'Manderson went to Gallowhall School.'

'So did a lot of kids.'

'It's been suggested that his death might have had something to do with his connection to the school.'

Prentice looked up, suddenly alert. 'Suggested by who?'

'I have to protect my sources.'

He rolled his eyes. 'That's my line. Come on, Rilke, you're hardly Bob Woodward.'

I resisted pointing out that neither was he. 'Maybe not, but I know how to look after my health.'

Prentice snorted, 'That's debatable.' He rolled a piece of chicken in his fried rice and ferried it to his mouth. 'So this source is someone you wouldn't want to get on the wrong side of?'

I gave a mute nod.

He raised his eyebrows. 'Ah, like that, is it?'

I waited for him to list potential candidates, but he said, 'What do you want from me?'

The schoolboy waiter delivered a tray of bubble teas to a table of stylish youths who might have stepped out of the frame of a boy band video. One of them had hair dyed the same iridescent, crow's-wing colours Les had sported when I last saw him. The memory of Les, blood seeping from his newly scarred face focused me.

'I thought you might know of support groups or survivors I might talk to. Someone who might have been there at the same time as Manderson and would be able to shed light on why he might be targeted.'

Prentice shook his head. 'You don't just rock up and start interrogating folk about traumatic experiences. Investigations like this take time. You have to gain people's trust.'

'I see that, but if Manderson's death had something to do with his time at Gallowhall—'

Prentice interrupted, 'I've yet to be convinced of that.'

'If his death had something to do with his time at Gallowhall, other people might be at risk.'

'That's a bit of a leap.'

'Mandy was murdered.'

'Boys who ended up in schools like Gallowhall have a higher mortality rate than the general population. Don't get me wrong: some of them thrived, but alcoholism, risky behaviour, poor health choices, self-harm, suicide, even murder, it's all par for the course. His death isn't a reason for me to risk relationships I've spent a long time cultivating.'

Beyond the restaurant window traffic drifted from the M8 slip road into the city. I knew the frustration of drivers who a moment ago had been speeding along the motorway and were now reduced to the slow crawl of city streets. I thought of what old Jack next door had told me.

'I don't know if this is relevant, but apparently he was visited regularly by a white-haired man who looks like Ian Paisley Senior. I wondered if he might have anything to do with the school.' Prentice leaned forward, and I saw that I had hit on something. 'You know who he is?'

The journalist poured himself more tea but did not bother to lift his cup to his lips. 'What makes you say that?'

'It's written all over you.'

He was only halfway through his meal, but Prentice put his jacket on and got to his feet. 'Wait here.'

A waitress approached the table. 'Is your friend finished?'

I told her I did not think so and asked for another pint. Maybe Prentice was right, and I did have an alcohol problem. But now was not the time to dry out.

Raindrops beaded the restaurant window. Prentice was talking to someone on his phone, his expression sharp in the shafts of light thrown by passing cars. I drank my pint, ate my soup and waited. I wondered what it would be like to be a family man, eating a meal with my wife and children, sharing the same dishes before going home to bed.

Perhaps the fathers and grandfathers grouped with their families around the restaurant tables envied me, a lone agent, with no responsibilities to anyone but myself. If so, they knew fuck all. My life was all responsibility and an empty bed at night.

Just when I was in danger of slipping into maudlin reverie the restaurant door opened with a cold blast of air. Prentice returned to the table, his face flushed from the sudden heat after the rain.

'That's it sorted. We're meeting him at Gallowhall tomorrow morning.'

'Meeting who?'

Prentice had stared to dig into his chicken and rice again. He looked up at me and gave a small smile. 'Let's just call him Iain for now.'

Twenty-Six

PRENTICE INSISTED ON driving. 'I only just got my licence back. I need the practice.' He glanced at me, hunched in the passenger seat. 'Don't look so nervous. I'm a decent driver when I'm sober.'

We hit the M8 at 8.30 a.m. and joined faltering lines of commuters, works vans and lorries. It was another dreich day, and rainwater flew from the tyres of pantechnicons and juggernauts, spraying the windscreen of the car. The rubber on the wipers needed replacing. They kept up an irritating squeal that formed a chant in my head – *go home, go home, go home, go home* . . . Prentice hit play on his CD and Bruce Springsteen lamented being bruised and battered on the streets of Philadelphia. We left the city stretch of the motorway behind, the traffic cleared, and Prentice pressed his foot to the accelerator. He was right: he was a good driver, quick on the clutch, easy on the brakes. He hummed along to the Boss, joining in when he sang about not knowing his own face and the friends he had lost. The journalist had a decent voice, low and gravelly, shades of Johnny Cash in his later years. I tightened the scarf around my neck, dipped my hat and closed my eyes.

When I opened them, Van Morrison was glorying getting stoned. We were driving uphill on a B-road that twisted and turned beside sodden fields occupied by miserable-looking black-and-white cows and a few grey sheep.

Prentice was no longer singing. I glanced at him. 'Wouldn't have thought you'd be keen on songs about getting high.'

'You don't need drink or drugs to get high. Beauty can do it too.' He took his right hand from the wheel and waved towards the great outdoors. 'You can get stoned on nature.'

I am uneasy when out of sight of concrete pavements, twenty-four-hour shops and city pubs, but I humoured him. 'If you say so.'

The road slid into a forest, trees rising on either side of us. I can identify ebony, mahogany, walnut, oak, pine, New Zealand Rimu and a multitude of other woods, once they have been cut, planed, polished and crafted into something. Trees in their natural state are a mystery, but I knew enough to know these were not the usual tax-dodge conifers that have colonised the Scottish countryside. They were older and more varied. Ancient woods of the type inhabited by grandma-scoffing wolves and gingerbread houses.

'You woke just in time.' Prentice steered the car around another twisting, uphill bend in the road. The forest ended on a final line of trees clean and straight as a ruler and revealed Gallowhall on a plateau above us, looming like a horror house upon a film set.

Prentice turned the CD player off and slowed the car to a crawl so we could take in the view.

'Gets me every time,' he said quietly.

The building had been someone's idea of Scottish baronial. High, storm-grey walls, each corner topped by a ruined turret. Four storeys of dead-eyed windows glowered into the forest. At its centre a blackened clock tower whose clock was long gone: time stopped. The vacancy where its face had once stared made me think again of Manderson's empty eye socket.

I imagined being a young boy from a city seeing Gallowhall for the first time. 'Fucking terrifying.'

Prentice glanced at me. 'You don't know the half of it.'

'Why does he want to meet here?'

'He's obsessed with the place. Said forget taking schoolkids to Bannockburn to learn Scottish history, bring them here.'

'That would be a Doors Open Day to remember.'

We had reached a small village that might have been established to serve the school back when it required a small army of staff. It was a mean-looking place with an air of neglect. We passed an off-licence and then a church fronted by a polished granite war memorial in the shape of an Egyptian needle. The obelisk looked out of place against the Presbyterian symmetry of the church. Prentice parked the car outside a Co-op and turned to me.

'Iain's a good source, but he's also a man on a mission. I've not managed to verify half of what he's told me, which means I've not finished writing the story. Strictly speaking, I shouldn't have brought you along.'

I had wondered at the journalist's willingness to share his source. 'Why did you?'

'A fresh face can break the routine, prompt new memories, but there's something else. Iain looks like your typical man's man. But he's vulnerable. What happened when he was a kid fucked him up. It'd be good to see him get some closure.'

'I'm not qualified to help anyone get closure. I'm just trying to find out what I can about Manderson's murder.'

'But if the two are connected . . .?' Prentice let the question hang in the air.

'I never figured you for a good Samaritan.'

He started the car and steered it into the main street. 'All journalists are good Samaritans, trying to bring truth to the nation. Maybe it explains our propensity to addiction. We're fighting a constant losing battle.'

Gallowhall was three miles up a ruined service road from the village. Prentice parked in a large, empty car park whose concrete surface was cracked and colonised by weeds. It reminded me of photographs I had seen of Chernobyl.

The slams of our car doors echoed across the empty expanse. A couple of black crows hopping sinister across the grass flapped their wings and took to the air. Prentice led the way towards the school. It was an Edward Hopper painting, except that Hopper's lonely buildings stopped short of complete decay. Gallowhall had been left to rot.

A glint of metal caught my eye. I bent and picked up a pin badge that had lost its pin. It was crusted with mud and decorated with a picture of the Wombles, *Wombling Free*. It was trash, but I could not bring myself to toss it back on the ground. I rubbed some of the mud from the badge's surface and shoved it in my coat pocket.

'Maybe he's got cold feet.'

It was as if my doubt conjured him. A figure stepped from the gloom of the building and walked towards us. Prentice raised a hand in greeting. The man raised his own hand, and for a moment they looked like shadows of each other, a broken spectre. He came into focus, a stocky man in his fifties, dressed in a sensible winter jacket, corduroys and work boots. The illusion receded. He was not wearing a hat, despite the cold, and his white hair shone against the black of the building.

Prentice introduced us. I pulled off my leather gloves and we shook hands.

Iain's grip was firm, his palm dry. 'Prentice tells me you're interested in Rodney Manderson?'

I put my gloves back on. 'I found his body. It was a sorry sight.'

Iain nodded. 'There's a lot to be sorry for in Rodney Manderson's life.'

'Did you know him well?'

'Not really.' He started to walk towards the building, to the grilled metal fences that had been erected around the site, across tufted grass still wet with dew and dampness. 'Watch out for rabbit holes. There's some size of a warren under here.'

Prentice and I fell in beside him. The ground bounced beneath our footsteps. I pictured the network of rabbit tunnels, branching and intersecting beneath the precarious surface. I paused to look at a long-abandoned digger overrun by grass and weeds, admiring the way the vegetation wove through and around the machinery, like flesh and veins on a skeleton.

Iain paused too. 'There were plans to convert the place into luxury apartments ten years ago. The firm went bust almost before they started and then vandals set the school on fire. The fabric of the building has deteriorated a lot since then.'

Prentice pulled a strand of sticky willy from the digger and stared at it as if wondering why he had picked it. 'I would have thought the site was too far from the city to be much use as commuter belt.'

Iain shrugged. 'The city's closer than it used to be. Back in the day, Glasgow might as well have been on the moon. That was one of the attractions for the authorities of siting the school here. It was nigh impossible for boys who ran away to make it home.'

We resumed our walk. I asked, 'Did a lot of boys try to escape?'

'A fair few.' Iain gestured to the forest below the plateau. 'There were rumours that a gang of lads had set up a camp in the woods. The usual Big Rock Candy Mountain fantasies.'

Prentice threw the strand of sticky willy away. 'Cigarette trees and lemonade springs.'

Iain did not smile. 'Aye, all that stuff. Nonsense of course. There weren't many good ways out of this place.'

We reached the metal fencing, and I saw that an opening had been cut in one of them. Iain was a big man, but he bent his body and slid easily through the small gap. Prentice and I followed. Close to, the building had an earthy smell of damp and mortar undercut by a tang of piss and fox skunk. Graffiti bloomed across the exterior. The space between the metal fence and the building narrowed. We slipped into single file, Iain leading the way, me last, Prentice between us. The clock was ticking on Les's liberty. For all I knew it was ticking on my own freedom, too.

I drew a finger along the fence. The metal rattled loud. Iain turned towards the sound, and I asked, 'Did you know Manderson when he was here?'

'I wouldn't say I knew him exactly, more knew of him. Rodney Manderson was well kent in his day.' Iain went left through an archway and led the way into a courtyard. He paused and pointed upwards, to the windows high above. 'Three boys tried to escape from one of the dormitories up there. Well before my time. Two of them made it, but story goes that the knots on their sheets slipped and the third boy hit the cobbles.'

'I read about it online. Tragic.'

Iain nodded. 'His ghost is meant to haunt the courtyard. Some boys claimed to have heard him screaming. Still gives me the shivers.'

I felt a tingle on the back of my neck. I looked back the way we had come, but there was no one there, just another iron-beaked crow pecking at the ground.

Iain moved his finger, as if drawing the building in the air. 'You used to be able to get up there, but it's too dodgy since the fire. Some of the floors have given way.' A pigeon flew from one of the unglazed windows. Our eyes followed it as it glided over the open courtyard and out towards the countryside beyond. 'Sooner or later this place will collapse. Eventually it'll disappear as if it was never here at all.'

'Would that be such a bad thing?'

His eyes met mine, grey and mild. 'Better this place never existed, but it did. People need to remember what happened here.'

Prentice said, 'Iain's determined the truth should come out. We don't want any more children suffering the way the Gallowhall boys did.'

The journalist was sincere, but his words sounded trite. I kicked at a bundle of dead leaves that had somehow found their way into the treeless space. 'Wasn't there an inquiry?'

Iain made a sound between a laugh and a raspberry. 'Aye, that's what they called it.'

I wondered what he wanted for Gallowhall, to make a shrine of it? Restore the building into a monument to cruelty? An oversized grave marker?

The house where serial murderers Rose and Fred West committed their horrors had been demolished and then ground into dust to prevent twisted souvenir hunters. Maybe Gallowhall deserved similar treatment. But I had never seen a memorial to victims of child abuse. The big man had a point. Perhaps the derelict school should continue to stand in remembrance.

We crossed the courtyard. Iain took a chisel from the inside pocket of his coat and slid it into the jamb of a closed door. His voice strained as he levered the chisel against the lock. 'They keep shutting the place back up, but they can't keep us out.'

I wondered who 'they' were and how often they patrolled the abandoned school. It was as if Iain read my thoughts. He favoured me with a weak smile. 'Don't worry. They're hardly ever here, and when they are they turn a blind eye. No one wants any trouble. Not like the old days.'

The lock gave with a crack. Iain had a few more goes with the chisel and managed to force the door open. He stepped over the threshold. After a beat of hesitation, Prentice and I followed.

We were in the entrance hallway I had seen photos of online. It was dark inside, the smell of decay stronger. Somewhere above us birds rose in a flutter; a solitary grey feather drifted to the ground. Our boots crunched glass and plaster. Iain opened the torch app on his phone. Light bounced off walls illuminating a wide staircase with an oak banister and holes where steps should be that gloomed like traps. My eyes adjusted to the bright beam of the torch. Coils of paint retreated from the walls in fragile curls that resembled tropical flowers.

I glanced upwards and had an impression of upper galleries, a broken ceiling lantern, a faint glimmer of dusty light.

Something sounded above, in the dormitories where Iain had said the floors were too fragile to hold a man's weight.

'Ghosts.' The big man opened a door, and we followed him into the same assembly hall I had seen on the urban explorers' website. The chairs were still there, but instead of being arranged in neat rows they were scattered across the room as if subjected to a riot or a tantrum. The face with the door for a mouth glared, its eyes creased in gleeful malevolence. The greeting WELCOME TO HELL FUCKERS! dripping red, a visual scream.

Iain righted one of the chairs and seated himself facing the doorway. Prentice and I took a chair each and sat facing him. I imagined the arrangement echoed the AA meetings Prentice credited with saving his life. Somewhere above us a door slammed. Prentice and I started at the sound.

Prentice gave a nervous grin. 'Just the wind.'

The big man remained impassive. He looked from me to the journalist and back. 'What do you want to know?'

I leaned forward in my chair. 'Someone killed Rodney Manderson. It wasn't a hit and run or a fist fight that took a bad turn. Someone pierced his eye with something sharp and drove it into his brain.' I paused for his reaction, but Iain was as still as a basking snake on beta blockers. I continued: 'What I mean is, it wasn't a chance killing, wrong place, wrong time. Someone deliberately did him harm.'

Iain nodded. 'I heard about the murder. It was in the papers. What I don't know is why you're involved.'

It was a fair question. I told him the same half-truth I had told Prentice Baxter. 'I was the one who found his body. I can't stop seeing it. I thought maybe if I could find out who did it . . .'

Iain had been staring at the crazy face painted across the wall. He turned his eyes on me. 'That's the job of the police. They haven't been to see me. They would have been in touch if they thought there was a connection with this place.'

I wondered what the police knew about Iain's relationship with Gallowhall and why they would contact him. 'You still have faith in the police?'

Iain shrugged. 'Some of them try.'

My sometime friend Anderson was a trier, Inspector Murchison too, but Thurso Scanlan was a nasty prick. There were plenty of his kind in the force, and then there was what Ray Diamond had referred to as 'the brass', content to let corrupted judge Urquhart Murchison thrive in return for a toothless investigation into police corruption.

I said, 'The police are lazy. They think an asylum seeker did it.'

'And you don't?'

'There was hatred behind Manderson's killing. It was personal, intimate.'

Iain nodded his head, a man who knew about hate. He turned his eyes back to the grinning graffiti face. 'We used to call him Kapo.'

For a second, I thought he meant the face on the wall, but Prentice leaned forward, his voice encouraging. 'Manderson?'

Iain nodded. 'One of our history teachers was obsessed with the Nazis. All he seemed to teach us about was World War Two, with an emphasis on the death camps. Do you know what a kapo was?'

I had a fair idea, but I shook my head. 'No.'

'A concentration camp prisoner who collaborated with

the guards. The camps couldn't have operated efficiently without them.'

'And that's what Manderson did?'

'They called him a prefect, but he was a kapo. You read about the kind of things that happened here?'

'Some of it.'

'You're right to say some. Most of it hasn't seen the light of day. Boys were tortured, humiliated, broken. Manderson was a victim before he became a kapo, but he took to cruelty like a whore to hard liquor.'

I did not have the stomach to ask for specifics, but Prentice was well-practised in the art of interrogation. 'Did that include sexual abuse?'

'Sexual abuse is another form of cruelty and humiliation. Maybe it is to do with desire, but it's not desire as most people know it. It turns reality upside down, an act of love into an act of hate. Manderson was good at lessons. He took what he learned and applied it to younger, weaker boys.'

I said, 'You called Manderson a victim. Does that mean you forgive him?'

Iain turned his mild eyes on me again. 'It's not up to me to forgive anyone, especially not the dead. Could you forgive?'

'Probably not. It depends.'

'On what?'

'What they did. How much they suffered. How much they hurt me.'

Iain smiled. 'I can't say if someone from here murdered Manderson, but I can say that he liked to hurt people. Odds are that didn't go away.'

'I heard you visited him regularly. Were you friends?'

Iain gave a half-laugh. 'Word gets about. Friends? No. I want ex-pupils to take a class action against the school. It's not as easy to get folk on board. It was a long time ago. Those who survived, if survived is the right word, have made some kind of a life. Who can blame them if they want to lock what happened in a box and never look at it again?'

'Manderson agreed to be part of the class action?'

Iain gave a smile that was no smile at all. 'Some days he did. Some days he didn't. He liked to string me along.'

'A different kind of torture.'

'Bullies like Rodney Manderson are good at spotting people's weaknesses. The fact that I care about righting the past makes me vulnerable. Caring about anything makes you weak. In his own way, Rodney Manderson was invincible. He protected himself by making sure that he didn't care about anything.'

I remembered how Manderson had been at auctions. Even hardened dealers occasionally fall in love with an object and blow more than they should on acquiring it, but Manderson was all knowledge and no heart. He had never risked his profit margin.

'He cared about money.'

'Everyone cares about money. But Rodney Manderson kept his needs simple. As far as I could see, the only pleasure he got was from trying to wind me up.'

'Did he succeed?'

'Of course, but I didn't kill him. I use my anger constructively. Taking the government to court isn't just about revenge, it's about stopping the cycle of abuse that creates men like Manderson. Men worse than Manderson.'

Laughter sounded somewhere in the house, shrill and high-pitched. Prentice and I stood up and turned towards the door. There was a babble of indistinct chatter and then more laughter.

Iain remained in his seat. 'Just kids.'

On cue two teenagers dressed in sweatpants and hoodies dashed into the room. They saw us and their laughter died.

Iain stood up. 'Fuck off, boys, or I'll set Mr Cronin onto you.'

The shorter of the teens straightened up. Their voice was high and girlish. 'I'm not a boy.'

Iain grinned. 'Cronin doesn't care. He'll take you anyway.'

The kids hooted and ran away, their laughter echoing in the hallway and then dying. The light was fading beyond the assembly room's windows, the atmosphere of the old school darkening. Iain had been harder with the teenagers than necessary, threatening.

I glanced at my watch. Time was ticking: Les's chances of freedom shrinking, the asylum seeker still in jail. Ray Diamond had told me to leave well alone, but I said, 'The same Cronin who wrote the report on this place?'

Prentice said, 'One and the same. Cronin was one of the head honchos at the Social Work department back in the day.'

Iain leaned his elbows on his knees and looked at the floor. 'He used to bring groups of men here of a night. Stinking of smoke and booze.'

'Who did? Cronin?'

'He was the most prolific of them all.'

It sounded too far-fetched to be true, another horror-movie trope where the respectable lead turns out to be the monster. I looked at Prentice, who nodded his head. 'It's true.'

'Why wasn't he prosecuted?'

Iain kept his eyes on the grinning face with a door for a mouth. 'Friends in high places, and anyway it's hard to jail a dead man.'

'How did he die?'

'Drowned in a car crash, went off the road and into Loch Lomond.'

'Suspicious circumstances?'

Prentice leaned forward. 'Not according to the police report. It was February, a sharp, unlit bend, prone to ice. The tread on his tyres was low. Cronin had alcohol in his system. Skid marks suggest he took the corner at speed.'

'The fact that you read the police report suggests you suspected foul play.'

Prentice shrugged. 'It's my job to be a suspicious bugger, but I spoke to the officer in charge, read the accident report. It stacks up. Cronin was a drunk driver who died on an accident blackspot. Could have been suicide, but there's nothing to indicate the involvement of any third party.'

'So, back in the day, Manderson was part of Cronin's crew?'

Iain turned his eyes on me. They were the pale grey of washed sea glass. 'He was a boy. They corrupted him.'

Prentice asked, 'Was Manderson one of the people who fetched boys from their beds?'

Iain nodded. 'Aye, he was one of them. I'm not sure I want you printing his name in your newspaper though. I promised him there'd be no reprisals. I'm not after corrupted boys. They were victims too. It's the grown-ups who knew what they were doing that I want punished.'

I did not dare mention Judge Urquhart Murchison in front of Prentice Baxter; he would be on the story like an XL Bully on a postie.

I said, 'One of them? There were others?'

Iain nodded. 'A few. Boys who reckoned it was better to give others up to save themselves, and there was a woman,

Mrs Hurst. She was meant to be the matron. We called her Nurse Hurts behind her back. She sounded posh, like something off the telly, but her accent slipped when she was angry, became local.'

I did not recognise the name from the articles I had read. 'Did she give evidence at the inquiry?'

He shook his head. 'I've searched for her, but no trace. Staff records were patchy. Hurst isn't a rare name. I don't know her date of birth, where she's living now or even if she's alive. She was Nurse, Matron or Mrs, but I don't know if she was married or even a qualified nurse.'

Prentice chipped in, 'Women change their names when they get married. It can make them harder to find unless you have something solid like a National Insurance number, court records, date of birth or the like.'

Iain's eyes met mine. 'She was just a woman. I doubt I'd even recognise her. We thought she was old, but we were wee boys. She might have been any age from her twenties to her fifties. There are some photographs of those times, but she isn't in any of them. Maybe she guessed that one day there'd be a reckoning and covered her tracks.'

'Did Manderson know who she was? Where she'd ended up?'

'He said he didn't, but then he would smile, as if he did.'

'Can I see any of the photos?'

Iain took his phone out of his pocket. He stabbed at it and held it out to reveal a traditional group shot of boys and teachers ranged in front of the school. I thought that perhaps I had seen it already in the papers in Ray's folder.

Iain pointed at a small boy with tousled black hair, kneeling at the centre of the front row. 'That's me.' He moved his finger to the last boy on the right of the top row. 'And that's Rodney Manderson.'

I leaned closer. The photograph was black and white, blurred by the phone's pixels, but I recognised Manderson. He was smiling the same smile he had worn during auction sales. A sly grin that hinted he knew more than anyone else in the room and would use his knowledge to win whatever he wanted.

'He didn't change much.'

'His path was set early.'

'Do you think he carried on abusing kids?'

'If I thought that, I'd have set the polis on him. Manderson was a bully and a sadist, but when he talked about sex he talked about grown women.'

The building was creaking as if it was impatient to be rid of us. The damp was creeping into me too, my knee joints aching in sympathy with the old school's decaying frame.

Iain got to his feet. 'There aren't many people involved in the class action. I know all of them, and no one knows who Nurse Hurts is, or even if she's still alive. People are dying off. Every time one of them goes, our chances for justice grow slimmer.'

'It must be hard to keep going.'

'What happened here has defined my life. I wish it hadn't, but it has. I'll keep fighting till I'm in my grave. Maybe beyond the grave.' A crash sounded deep in the building, as if confirming the possibility of an afterlife. Iain got to his feet. 'That's all I can tell you. Bad things happened here. Manderson was part of them.'

I stared at the grinning face painted on the wall. The old school had forged Mandy's life too. Had it also informed his death?

Twenty-Seven

I WAS BRACED for another encounter with the teenagers who had crashed into the assembly hall, but we met no one as we retraced the lower corridors of the building and stepped out into the fading day. Iain walked with us to Prentice's car. There were no other vehicles in the car park, and I wondered again how the big man had got there.

I fingered the child's badge in my pocket. 'If Nurse Hurst was in her twenties, she would be somewhere in her fifties by now.'

Iain's face was as blank as a brick. 'If she was in her fifties, she would be in her eighties, or dead perhaps.'

'You can't remember?'

The grey sky dulled his white hair; his pale skin had a livor mortis glow. 'No.'

'A lot of people from that time are dead. Maybe she is too but, bad as he was, I don't imagine Manderson had anything to do with it. He was the kind of guy who boasted of his misdeeds. Murder would have been too much to keep to himself.'

'Murder's nothing to boast of.'

Prentice and Iain exchanged a look. Prentice said, 'You never struck me as naïve, Rilke. Murder's a big fucking deal.'

I asked a question that I had been hesitating over all afternoon. 'Did you know a boy called Diamond? Ray Diamond?'

'Handy with his fists.'

I could not imagine Ray on the side of authority, but I asked, 'Not a kapo?'

Iain gave a small smile that I could not read. 'No, Ray was never a kapo.'

It was dangerous, asking a stranger Razzle Diamond's personal business. 'Where did he fit in?'

'If you want to know something about Ray Diamond, ask him.'

'Is he part of the class action?'

Iain repeated, 'Ask him.'

We made good progress back into Glasgow. The Streets were on the CD player, Mike Skinner advising a lovestruck mate who had been dumped to dry his eyes and not turn stalker. I scoured the local news on my phone, but there was no fresh information about the stricken students. I hoped it was a good sign.

Prentice dropped me at Bridge Street, and I caught a train west. Old-timers call the Glasgow subway the Clockwork Orange. I'm old enough to remember the wooden carriages which were replaced in the 1970s. The new rolling stock is brightly lit and sci-fi sleek, but the carriages still shoogle and I still have to lower my head as I step inside.

The schools were breaking up for the day. A group of

Glasgow Academy boys in blue blazers and long trousers crowded the carriage, a mixture of slouching assurance and spotty cringe. A tall prefect with a loosely knotted tie gave me a bold stare. There was a hint of an invitation in his tilted head and lowered eyelids, but he looked around sixteen and I have never been tempted by what some folks call Greek love.

Gallowhall's mouldering fragrance still clung to me. The internet search I had done into abuse in List D schools had brought up enquiries into private-school abuse too and similar stories of boys hauled from beds in the dark. The abusers were as sly as privilege.

I had my own past, my own demons, and as the subway carriage snaked and lurched my head filled with ghosts I would rather not raise.

I tramped up the escalator at Kelvinbridge, lit a cigarette and smoked it leaning against the parapet of the bridge. I stared into the black water of the River Kelvin churning below and tried to decide my next move. I was tempted to sneak into Les's building via the back close, but Ray had warned me to stay away. I was on the big man's radar.

My phone rang and a bright gemstone emoji I could not remember setting flashed on the screen. 'Think of the Devil and smell smoke' was another of old Jim Bowery's sayings.

Ray Diamond's voice had a Covid quality, hoarse in my ear. 'It's been twenty-four hours. You got anything for me yet?'

I took a last gasp of smoke and tossed my dout over the edge of the bridge, the sparks glowing briefly like a dying galaxy.

'Nothing much. I spoke to Iain, the guy who's leading the class action against Gallowhall. He didn't give me his second name.'

'I know who he is. What did he tell you?'

'Probably nothing you don't already know. It was a bastard regime. Manderson played his part; they called him Kapo.'

Ray gave a phlegmy cough. 'He was a quisling. I told you he paid me a licence fee every month?'

'You mentioned it.'

'Made him hand it to me in hard cash. Nothing like seeing a bully get the shakes. Guess there was someone else he should have been scared of.'

'Who?'

'Whoever killed him.'

'Iain told me about Cronin. He died before anyone could bring him to justice.'

'Hope they buried him deep.'

'Iain also mentioned a woman, some kind of matron. Nurse Hurst.'

'Ah yes, Nursey Hurty. Made Dracula's daughter look like Snow White.'

'What happened to her?'

'Went to ground. Reinvented herself.'

'What as?'

'A human being.'

There were monsters among us clothed in flesh. Ray's voice was as final as a slamming door, but I asked, 'Could she have had anything to do with Manderson's death?'

'If I thought that, I wouldn't be talking to you.'

'You know where she is?'

'I know what you had for dinner last night.'

It was Ray's way of telling me to drop the subject. I dropped it.

'That's all I have. How are the students?'

'Out of danger, in their parental homes and under Thurso

Scanlan's beady eye. Your mate Les better hope they don't start cooperating.'

Les was not the one who had sold the students dodgy goods, but I knew better than to argue the odds. I took my tobacco tin and rolling papers from my pocket, propped the phone beneath my chin and started to roll another smoke. 'Les isn't the cooperative sort.'

'Better not be.' I heard Ray inhale and breathe out and knew he had lit a cigarette of his own. He coughed a deep and fruity smoker's cough. 'What's your plan?'

It was the question I had been musing as I stared into the Kelvin. 'There's more than one person involved in the class action against Gallowhall, but I suspect talking to them might just turn up repetitions of the same story.'

'Boring you, is it?'

'It's not that, just—'

'Just what?'

'I don't think it'll tell me who killed Manderson. The reason why he was murdered might lie in the past, but I think the answer to who is much closer.'

A sigh travelled across the miles from wherever Ray was into my ear. It was soft, but it muted the rumble of traffic, screech of buses, the plash of the river below and bustle of commuters exiting the underground station.

'Okay. Bring me a name. If it checks out, your pal Les is off the hook. But the clock's ticking. You've got until Sunday.'

The cigarette I was rolling slipped from my fingers and tumbled downwards, into the waters below. 'That's only three days. I need more time . . .'

But the line was dead.

Twenty-Eight

I SAT ALONE in the bitter cold at one of the Belle's outside tables, nursing a malt. The pavement was rain-stained and littered, the warm glow of electric light beyond the pub window enticing, but I needed another cigarette. I was lost. Tangled in too much and not enough information. I took out my notebook and pen and jotted a list of what I had learned so far, with fingers that felt more stone than flesh.

The hatpin might be a sharp compass pointing a link between the murderer and Bowery Auctions, or it might have been grabbed on impulse by a stranger. Manderson's bank card had been found in the asylum seeker's possession. How had it got there, and did it mean he was guilty after all? And then there was Gallowhall. Was Manderson's childhood the key that would unlock everything, or simply an unfortunate past?

I pulled up my coat collar, smoked my cigarette and sipped my drink. I thought about the sexy spy blonde who had bought the hatpins. Commissioning Ronnie Kerrie with his boozy breath and wizened-jockey looks was a bold act. It felt incriminating.

Thanks to Abomi, I knew the make, colour and personalised numberplate of the blonde's car. I considered phoning Ray back and asking if he could set his unofficial army of rogues onto the search or use his influence with men in dark places. But Ray was apt to go straight to source. If he found the woman, he would question her himself. My conscience had enough weight without burdening it with the torture of a fragrant blonde.

Anderson was my only friendly(ish) police contact, but he was irritatingly straight. There was no way he would source the car owner for me. I fished out my phone and dialled Rose. The number rang out. I returned it to my inside pocket, and it juddered back to life.

Rose's voice was brittle in my ear. 'I thought you'd joined Les in Ukraine or Yemen or whatever war zone he legged it to.'

I heard the hurt-disguised-as-anger in her voice and felt bad for not calling sooner. 'I've been busy. I texted you.'

'Anyone can text if they've got your mobile. Last time I saw you, you were being frogmarched into the night by Ray and his goons. There was blood all over the kitchen.'

I raised my malt to my mouth. The burn of it stung my lips and thawed my throat. 'Les got mouthy. Ray opened his face. It looked worse than it was.'

It had looked fucking horrible.

A burble of background chatter reached down the telephone line and into my ear. I pictured Rose standing in the middle of the busy saleroom and felt a pang of homesickness. A door slammed. The chatter ceased, and I knew she had entered the privacy of her office.

'My imagination's been running riot. I thought he'd diced you into little pieces and buried you under the M8 repair stretch.'

A passing Heinz 57 with a grey muzzle and long tail stopped to take a sniff of me. I patted its head, fur rough and beaded with rain. It grinned and trotted off. A man with a dog lead wrapped around his fist followed in its wake. He gave me a look that might have been an invitation or a threat.

Rose said, 'Did you hear me? I worried you'd ended up like Jamie Mitchell.'

Jamie Mitchell had been a gangster on the rise, with aspirations to expand his territory. He had been beaten to butcher meat after I inadvertently led Ray to his cannabis farm. I had been out of my depth, meddling with things that should not have concerned me. Ray's intervention had saved me from a thrashing or worse. It occurred to me that Ray might think I owed him my life and that finding Mandy's killer could clear the debt.

'It could still happen. Ray wants to know who murdered Manderson. He's given me until Sunday to find out.'

There was the trickling sound of something, red wine probably, being poured into a glass. Rose took a gulp of whatever it was. 'What's it got to do with him and why you?'

A couple of smokers exited the pub and lit up at the next table. I glanced in their direction. They were discussing a skiving workmate whose long Covid they doubted, more interested in each other than me.

I took a sip of my drink and kept my voice low. 'Apparently Mandy and Ray went back a long way. Ray seems to think I have a talent for detection, and he's got a lever on me. He'll dub Les in for the students' ODs if I don't come up with anything.'

'Good.' Rose and Les had a fractured relationship, but the violence in her voice shocked me. She took another gulp of her drink. 'Les has had this coming for a long time. Walk away before he drags you down with him.'

I slugged back the last dreg of malt. Now there was nothing left to keep me warm.

'Too late. Les knows there's something fishy about the hatpin, remember? Les is no grass, but Ray has a way of getting things out of people.'

Rose took another quick swig of her drink. Her voice rose a notch. 'There's nothing we can tell him. We don't know anything.'

'It might take a bit of time and a lot of pain to convince Ray Diamond of that.'

The street was busy with people. I cursed myself for using Ray's full name in public, even though I had whispered it beneath my breath out of well-worn habit.

Rose said, 'Ray Diamond knew my dad. Christ, he practically dandled me on his knee.'

'It doesn't matter that Ray knew you when you were a sweet kid or that your da used to fence for him. Ray's a stone-cold psychopath who's learned decent manners. He'll break you and not lose any sleep.' There was silence on the line. I said, 'I'm sorry, Rose. If I could turn back time, I'd leave Mandy lying where I found him, pin through the eye and all.'

I wondered if she had hung up, then her voice was back in my ear. 'It's not just down to you . . .' I thought she was going to mention Les again, but she said, 'You did what you did because you were worried I'd be implicated, and you were right. I waved that stupid hatpin around on national TV, raving about what a great murder weapon it would make.

I threatened Mandy in front of witnesses the day before. I didn't kill him, but since when did being innocent save anybody?'

The smokers finished their cigarettes. Warm air gusted from the pub door like cloudy breath as they slipped back into the pub. I envied them.

'Anderson would save you.'

'He'd try, but Anderson isn't flavour of the month at the cop shop. He says he's out of step with the current regime. According to him, it's like the Vatican. You've got to back the right faction if you want to get on.'

'No chance of him making Pope then?'

Rose gave a small laugh. 'Not even polis Pope.'

'But he's still got full privileges?'

'Suppose so. Whatever they are.'

'Good. I need you to ask Anderson to identify the owner of a car for me.'

This time her laugh was incredulous. 'Are we talking about the same person? No chance. He's funny about that kind of thing.'

'It's important, Rose.'

'To you and me maybe, not to Anders. He's always banging on about corruption in the force and slippery slopes.'

'Just ask. You'll find a way.'

'He'll start hassling me about why I want to know. Last thing I want is Anders cottoning on to this mess.'

I could feel her slipping away from me. 'The woman this car belongs to went out of her way to buy the hatpins without anyone knowing her identity. Maybe she was cleaning up for the killer. Maybe she *is* the killer. Her car's the only link I have.'

'So why didn't you get on her trail before?'

'Things happened . . .'

'Christ, that's your fucking mantra. Things are always happening.'

There was no point in listing my hours in a police cell or the visit to Gallowhall. 'Anderson's our only chance.'

'You know Anderson. He's not a pushover.'

'Use your womanly wiles.'

'Since when did you become a pimp?'

The mention of pimping reminded me of Cat and Dickie Bird. 'You've always been your own woman, Rose.'

Her breath was ghostly soft in my ear, and I had the brief illusion that I felt it warm against my face. 'I'll do my best.'

I gave her the information I had on the car, and she repeated it back to me.

'Red sports MG, licence plate H.E.L.3.N.'

'I need it soon.'

'I told you. I'll do my best.' She hung up without saying goodbye.

It was growing colder, a faint smirr turning the flesh of my face wet. A man could dissolve into rot if he stayed outdoors in Glasgow for too long. I looked at my notes and added Nurse Hurst beneath the heading 'Gallowhall'.

If the blonde driver of the MG turned out to be her, then everything would fall into place. Perhaps Mandy had located the nurse, decided to go in for blackmail, and she had responded with the same ruthlessness she had shown towards the small boys in her care. If that was so, then I could hand her to Ray Diamond with a clean(ish) conscience.

I drew my coat around me and got to my feet, not bothering to return my empty glass to the bar for fear I would not be able to resist another drink. The car, the blonde, the hatpin. I had been worrying Manderson's murder for days and found nothing to save Les from prison and keep me and Rose clear of Ray Diamond's grasp.

Twenty-Nine

MY PHONE WOKE me early the next morning. Abomi's face flashed on the screen, the selfie he had insisted on adding to my contacts, his smile guileless. I put him on speaker and reached for my dressing gown.

'Hi, boss.' Abomi was the only one who called me boss without a hint of sarcasm.

'Hi, son, how's it going?'

I walked to the window and drew the curtains. A dreich night had ushered forth a dreich morning. A couple of wood-pigeons were hunched in the tree outside my bedroom window. The road below was empty except for a tumbling polythene bag caught by the wind. It wheeched upwards, caught on an air current, tossed around like flotsam in a storm.

'Are you coming in today, Mr Rilke?'

'Afraid not, son.'

'Rose is in a bad mood all the time. She gets on Frank's case and then he gets on mine.'

'That's the way of the world, kid. Everyone kicks the monkey beneath them on the ladder.'

'But I'm the bottom of the ladder. I don't have anyone to kick.'

'It's only a matter of time, Abomi. You'll not be a junior porter forever. Sooner or later, there'll be a hairy wee ape you can try your boots on.'

A year ago, the boy might have taken me seriously, but he had learned to tell when I was joking.

'I'm not the kicking kind, Mr Rilke.'

'No, son, me neither. What can I do for you?'

I expected him to ask when I would be back at work, but a smile entered his voice and he said proudly, 'It's more like what can I do for you, boss.'

I walked through to the kitchen, filled the kettle and switched it on. 'What can you do for me?'

He took a deep breath, gathering enough steam for the words to tumble out all at once. 'You know Rose went to the car auctions last week?'

Rose had a long line of love affairs with classic cars that were a bargain until you lifted the bonnet. She was a favourite of Stevie Bell, whose garage specialised in vintage motors.

'What did she get this time?'

'A Hillman Husky, 1969 model, green paintwork.'

'Good condition?'

'The starting motor's been playing up, so she got me to take it to Stevie's.'

'How many times did it break down on the way there?'

A note of impatience entered the boy's voice. 'It cut out twice, but that's not why I'm phoning.'

I dropped a teabag into a mug, took a half-pint of milk

from the fridge and sniffed it. It smelt faintly sour. I poured hot water over the teabag and added a splash of milk.

'Why are you phoning?'

'That car you were talking about, H.E.L.3.N.? It was on the ramp.'

I froze, milk bottle in hand. White, scummy gobs congealed across the surface of my tea. 'You sure?'

'The lady brought it in. Snapped clutch. Stevie had to pick her up from the side of the road.'

'Is it still there?'

'Yep. I'm waiting outside. Frank said he'd collect me but he's not here yet.'

'Okay, stay where you are, and if the woman turns up, I want you to follow her.'

'I can't do that, Mr Rilke.'

'Yes, you can, Abomi.'

'She'll be in a car. I won't be able to keep up, and anyway it's not nice to follow women. It's creepy.'

'I've got something I want to give her.'

Abomi giggled at the unintended double entendre. 'Sorry, Mr Rilke.'

'Just do your best. I'll be there in twenty.'

Frank had arrived by the time I reached the garage. He and Abomi were sat in Bowery's removal van, which was parked outside the garage, the name of the auction house painted cherry-red on its sides. I parked beside them and lowered my car window like a drug dealer in a narco drama.

Frank followed suit. 'Abomi said you need us to follow some woman. I told him he must have the wrong end of the stick.'

Abomi leaned over Frank. There was a packet of milk chocolate digestives on the dashboard and a chocolate mark on his chin. 'That's what you said, wasn't it, Mr Rilke?'

I felt an uncomfortable combination of embarrassment and irritation. Embarrassment at what I had asked the young porter to do and irritation that Frank had announced Bowery Auctions' presence in bright red letters.

'Don't worry about it. I'll take it from here.'

Abomi said, 'She's coming to collect her car before four o'clock.'

'How do you know that?'

'Stevie said he couldn't look at Rose's Husky until he finished with the MG. I asked when that'd be, and he said it'd be sometime after four, cause that's when the lady was coming to pick it up.'

'You're a superstar, Abomi.'

The boy grinned and helped himself to another chocolate biscuit. 'Thanks, Mr Rilke.'

Frank looked from him to me. 'I'm not going to ask what this is all about. I'm better off not knowing.'

Abomi piped up loyally, 'Mr Rilke wouldn't do anything dodgy.'

Frank raised his eyebrows. 'And bears never wear pointy hats.' He rolled up the cab window, started the engine and steered the van into the street. I slid my car into his vacated parking place. It seemed like no one bothered with goodbyes anymore.

Waiting is hard. I leaned back in my seat and tried to look like a man with legitimate business. The front of the garage was open, and I could see Stevie Bell in the gloom of the building working on the red MG. I pulled my cap low on my head, but he was intent on his task. It was an hour before he lowered the ramp and drove the MG into the street. Thirty minutes later a slim woman crossed the road dressed in high-heeled black boots Rose would covet and an understated grey coat I suspected she would find dull. The woman went into Stevie's garage. I slumped lower in my seat, opened the camera on my phone and snapped a couple of photos, feeling like a sleaze, feeling like a detective. Five minutes later she steered the MG onto the street. I started my engine and followed.

For once I was lucky. It was rush hour, the roads jammed with stop–start traffic. Despite her flash car, the mystery woman was a cautious driver. I kept at least two cars between us and somehow managed not to lose her at the lights. The midday news came on the radio: reports of wars in places that had once seemed far away, another local council going bust, a man who had thrown acid in his ex-girlfriend's face, a president who had lost his mind. I pressed play on the CD and Kris Kristofferson started growling 'Sunday Mornin' Comin' Down', complaining of a sore head, beer for breakfast and feeling so alone he might as well be dead. It was too upbeat for my mood. I turned the CD off and concentrated on the road ahead. We were heading south towards Shawlands.

I am not a stranger to the south side of the river, but it feels like foreign territory colonised by the trendy middle classes, pushing buggies that cost more than my car. It is no coincidence that the word 'nuclear' is applied to families and bombs with the power to blast the world to mushroom clouds.

The red MG turned off a busy main road into a residential street. I dropped my speed and kept it in sight. Traffic was sparser. Soon it would be hard to conceal that I was following her. The car turned another corner. The roads were widening, the neighbourhood becoming leafier, tenements replaced by detached mansions that made you wonder where the money came from. The MG slowed and turned into the driveway of 117. I drove on.

I parked a few yards along the block and typed the address into Google. The Streetview photograph had been taken on a bright spring day. Daffodils bloomed sunny in blue pots on either side of the doorstep. A brass knocker and letterbox gleamed against the sober front door. A holly hedge with crisp edges bordered a gravelled parking area big enough for four cars, more if you did not mind playing Jenga. The house looked corporate in its respectability.

I typed the postcode into Companies House. A cosmetics concern named Pretty Baby was registered to the address. Its sole director was Mrs Helena Todd. I did another search and brought up Pretty Baby's website. The faces advertising her unguents were young and fresh enough not to need any cosmetic help. There was a photo of Mrs Todd on the contacts page, a honey blonde with pale rose lips and a healthy bloom. Her white shirt was open at the throat, revealing a gold necklace bearing a diamond charm. She looked like someone's favourite aunt, the kind a young man might have impure thoughts about.

Apart from a couple of experiments with mascara and guy liner I have never dabbled with make-up, but looking at the glass pots, slim tubes and vials displayed on the website, it struck me that the cosmetics industry had a medicinal aspect. I took a screenshot of the photo and texted it to Prentice, asking him to check with Iain if Mrs Todd might be Nurse Hurst.

A silver Jaguar drove along the street and turned in to the driveway of 117. It was too distant for me to see the driver. Abomi was right: tailing women was creepy. I started the engine and headed towards the West End.

Rose was standing at the back door of Bowery Auctions wearing her long, shaggy white coat and smoking a thin Panetella. It was a bad sign. She watched me cross the concrete. Dark eyes narrowed, red lips tight.

I climbed the wooden steps that led to the door, a dead man walking. 'I found her.'

Rose exhaled and turned to look at me. A fug of cigarillo smoke floated in the air between us and faded.

I coughed. 'I guess I should have let you know.'

'That would have been nice.'

'Did you ask Anderson?'

'Yes.'

'And . . .?'

The collar of her coat was turned up against the cold, giving her the look of a Russian princess waiting for a train to throw herself under. 'He's like a dog with a bone. I told him she was a client, but he isn't buying it.'

It was almost closing time; only my car and the work vans remained in the car park.

'He didn't join the dots?'

'Not yet, but he knows there's something going on, and what's the biggest story round here? Mandy's murder. Anderson's a policeman. He's at a loose end and his nose is twitching. Plus he's always been overprotective.'

'What do you mean, he's at a loose end?'

Rose took another pull at her Panetella and shook her head. 'Don't let on I told you. Anderson had a bad result on his medical. They've put him on desk duties. He's at a constant simmer, his lid rattling.'

'What's wrong with him?'

'He fucking hates paperwork. Anderson's a man of action, you know that.'

I resisted the temptation to say more action and fewer Killie pies might have improved his medical. 'I meant what's wrong with him physically?'

'Nothing much. High blood pressure, high cholesterol, high BMI. He's a middle-aged west coast of Scotland man. It's normal, part of our cultural, class heritage, but Anderson won't accept that. He's gone on a health kick. He's taking it to extremes.'

'Kicked the fags?'

'Worse than that – he's off the drink.'

'Christ.'

Rose puffed at her Panetella. 'Exactly. Anderson's not a tea and biscuits in front of the telly type. He's starting to stick his neb into things. It could have been avoided if you'd told me you'd already found her.'

The door opened and Hannah and Lucy emerged. I had not seen Hannah since she'd accidentally dropped the tray of hatpins and confided in me about Manderson.

I dredged up a grin. 'How are my two favourite reprobates?'

Hannah looked as pale as her Angie Bowie mullet. 'Good, thanks, Mr Rilke.'

Lucy's smile outshone mine. 'On our best behaviour.'

'Glad to hear it.'

I watched them cross the car park. Lucy was talking ten to the dozen, but Hannah seemed subdued. I looked at Rose. 'Something up with Hannah?'

Rose gently stubbed her half-smoked Panetella against the wall, checked it was not still smouldering and pocketed it for later. 'She turns up on time and does her job. I've enough to worry about without mothering little madams who already have mothers.' The two girls walked through the gate into the world beyond Bowery Auctions. Something on the other side of the car park caught Rose's attention. 'For fuck's sake, that's all we bloody need.'

I followed her gaze and saw Les, dressed in a black boilersuit and black leather jacket, walking towards us.

Thirty

'I COULDN'T STAND it any longer, Rilke. Stuck in the flat like a rat in a trap, waiting on Razzle Diamond's dogs to bite.'
'So you thought you'd put me and Rose in the frame too?'
'You're already in the frame.'
Les and I were sitting in my car, a short distance from 117, fragrant blonde HQ, waiting for something – anything – to happen. I checked my phone again. Prentice had not been in touch.
Les's scar was still red and angry, but he had applied some self-dissolving stitches from his emergency first aid supplies and it was healing. Ray Diamond was skilled with a blade. He could have taken Les's face apart if he had wanted to. Instead, he had left him with a zigzag that could be mistaken for a duelling scar.
I turned the key in the ignition, lowered the electric windows and took out a roll-up I had made earlier. 'Does it hurt?'

Les lit a cigarette. 'What?' I touched my left cheekbone. He made a face. 'Just my vanity.'

'It'll be a memorable feature once it's healed.'

'I'm already fucking memorable. I didn't need to be mutilated to stick in people's minds.'

'There'll be a million TikToks on how to conceal it.' I found my phone and summoned up Helena Todd's website. 'Talking about make-up, what do you make of this?'

Les took the phone from me. 'Strange fucking name for a beauty site.'

'She's implying she can make women look young and beautiful.'

'Aye, but Pretty Baby? It's a bit close to the bone.'

'How?'

Les adopted the queeny tone he uses when lecturing on the University of Gay. 'I forgot, you're more of a Bruce LaBruce kind of guy. *Scotch Egg* is your fucking life story.'

'Just tell me what you're getting at.'

'That you're a big poofter.' He raised his eyebrows, overdoing his incredulity. 'Seriously? You never heard of *Pretty Baby*? 1970s vanilla porn? Fourteen-year-old Brooke Shields flouncing around in a frilly nightie while her mother auctions her virginity to the highest bidder?'

'Fourteen?'

Les took my phone and checked his brain extension, Wikipedia. 'Whoops – I tell a lie. She was twelve.'

'Jesus Christ.'

'Mild compared to what you can get these days, but it made a lot of people hot under the collar. Gave me the boak. Old dudes competing for poor wee Brookie.'

'You've seen it?'

'You remember how my da was. Had the idea that if he

showed me the right porno I'd straighten out. I've seen more quim than most straight guys.'

Les's fingers tapped at my phone. He found what he was looking for and held the screen up, showing me a poster of a very young Brooke Shields, plastered with make-up, wearing a white dress and straw hat, a doll wearing the same costume perched on her lap.

I took a last drag of my cigarette and tossed it out of the window. 'Sure it wasn't a horror movie?'

Les was staring at the poster. He opened the Pretty Baby cosmetics website again and then returned to the poster. He turned the screen towards me and flashed between them. 'Notice anything?'

'I might do if you slowed down.'

He passed the phone to me, and I compared the two pages. 'The title fonts are the same. Same colour, same lettering . . .'

Les finished my sentence. '. . . same name. This isn't a coincidence, man. She's totally channelling the child porno thing.' We stared at each other. Les whispered, 'This is circles inside circles. We'll be lucky to get out of this one with our heads attached to our necks.'

A loud rap on the driver's side window made us both jump. Inspector James Anderson's face loomed level with mine. He opened the back door of my car and slid into the seat. 'This is an interesting coincidence. Dig out your passports, did you?'

Les's voice was high-pitched with fear disguised as indignation. 'Why would I need a passport?'

I knew his passport was tucked in his manbag along with a healthy supply of dope and his stash of emergency cash.

I touched Les's arm. 'Jim's just yanking your chain. He

means we're on the wrong side of the river.' I turned to looked at Anderson. His face was ruddy, and he was well over his fighting weight. 'Never pegged you for a funny man, Anderson. With material like that you should think about headlining the polis Christmas party.'

'Christmas is a long way off. What happened to his face?'

'Played with the wrong cat.'

Anderson nodded, grim-faced. 'I might have heard something of the kind. What are you doing outside Mrs Todd's? I wouldn't have thought it was your kind of place.'

Les asked, 'What kind of place is it?'

Anderson grinned. 'You don't know?'

I met his eyes in the rear-view mirror. 'I'm getting an inkling.'

'An inkling. You've some vocabulary, Rilke.'

'I kill at Scrabble.'

'Scrabble's harmless fun. I wouldn't have thought it was your kind of thing.'

Les turned around to look at Anderson. 'We're fans of harmless fun.'

'That's not what I heard.'

A man leading an apricot labradoodle on a leash was strolling along the pavement. He clocked the three of us sitting in my Skoda and gave us a curious look. We fell silent. The man walked past Helena Todd's place, glancing up at it before turning a corner.

Les said, 'Poncy-looking dog.'

Anderson laughed. 'I would have thought it'd be right up your street.'

Les muttered, 'Useless curly fucker.'

I said, 'What did you hear?'

Anderson looked from me to Les and back. 'That you've

turned detective and Zorro here's pissed off the wrong people.'

I wondered how the word had got out. 'So what is Helena Todd's place?'

'Tell me why you're here first.'

I paused, getting my story straight. 'Mandy Manderson went to Gallowhall School . . .'

Les muttered, 'Nae luck.'

I ignored him. '. . . and someone mentioned that Mrs Todd might have worked there.'

Les said, 'It was a prison, not a school. You and me were always getting threatened with it.'

Anderson ignored him. 'What's that got to do with Manderson's murder?'

I chose my words carefully. 'I wondered if maybe his murder had something to do with his past.'

Anderson leaned forward. I caught a blast of his cologne, the Rive Gauche Rose had bought him for Christmas. 'What, or should I ask who, made you think that?' I hesitated and he said, 'It wouldn't be a well-known pawnbroker and alumnus of Gallowhall?'

Les said, 'Alumnus? Bet you're a dab hand at Scrabble yourself, inspector. You and Rilke should start a league.'

Anderson shot him a harsh look. 'Don't try to distract me.'

I touched the rolling papers in my pocket but resisted taking them out and making myself another smoke. 'I can't tell you.'

Anderson sank into the back seat. 'That's an answer in itself.' We sat in silence for a while, then he said, 'Best way to find out if Mrs Todd worked at Gallowhall is to ask her.'

'Just like that?'

'Just like that.' He opened the car door, stepped onto the street and opened my door. 'You're coming with me.' He pointed at Les. 'You stay here.'

I expected Les to object, but he was lying low and gave a relieved smile. 'Watch out for those pretty babies – beauty can be beastly.'

Thirty-One

THE PAVEMENT WAS slippy with mulch. A blackbird bold on a gatepost piped out its territory.

I fell into step with Anderson and straightened my coat. 'Are you sure it's a good idea to alert her?'

Anderson pulled up the collar of his jacket. 'Sometimes alerting people is the best chance you've got. A bit of friendly interest can flush a guilty rabbit or two out of the long grass.'

'You think she's guilty of something.'

'I don't think anything – yet.'

We reached the gateway and walked up the steep path that led to the house. Helena Todd's place was as neatly anonymous as Streetview had suggested, the garden gravelled like a pub car park. There were four cars angled on it. High-end, the kind rich old men buy when they feel time is running out.

I smoothed the lapels of my coat. 'Do you want me to pretend to be polis?'

Anderson looked up at the video camera angled above the door, ensuring anyone monitoring its feed would get a good look at his face. 'Impersonating a police officer carries a minimum six-month custodial sentence. Just follow my lead and no fancy footwork.'

Three steps led up to an impressive front door equipped with a brass doorknocker in the shape of a lion's head and a Ring doorbell. Anderson slammed the lion's head smartly up and down, a policeman's knock.

I angled my face away from the video camera. 'Did they teach you that at Tulliallan?'

'First day, alongside how to detect when someone's pissing up your leg.'

The door opened, and there was Mrs Helena Todd, in the flesh. A good-looking, well-groomed woman not afraid of a flashy accessory. The kind Anderson was attracted to.

Her smile shone with professional warmth. 'Inspector Jim Anderson, it's been a while.'

I expected her to ask what we wanted but she opened the door wide. We climbed the steps and entered a long hallway, black-and-white tiled floor, cerise walls hung with Russell Flint prints of unselfconscious ballerinas, peasant girls and female bathers in various stages of undress.

Anderson glanced at the Russell Flints as we passed through the hallway, and I remembered Rose telling me he had a Jack Vettriano print of a woman in black stockings on his bedroom wall. She had laughed and said, 'He claims she looks like me. I said he could have a nude painting of the real thing, but he told me that would be vulgar.'

I got an impression of movement in other rooms of the house. Music played faintly somewhere above us, a light plinkety-plunky piano melody whose tune I could not catch.

Helena Todd led the way to a ground-floor sitting room-cum-office and closed the door behind us. My phone buzzed in my pocket. I took it out and glanced surreptitiously at the screen. A message from Prentice. *Iain's not sure. Could be but maybe not. Hurst's hair was black 30 yrs ago.*

Anderson gave me an enquiring look and I put my phone away. Helena Todd gestured towards the couch. Anderson and I sat side by side like men on a crowded bus. She settled on the only easy chair, stretching her long legs out in a way that managed to evoke both HRH the late Queen and a page three glamour model.

'What can I do for you, gentlemen?'

Anderson leaned forward and clasped his hands. 'Mr Rilke is a consultant who occasionally helps us out. He has a few questions he'd like to ask you.'

Helena Todd turned her eyes on me, her pupils the same shade of violet Elizabeth Taylor was famed for. 'What do you consult on?'

I fished my handkerchief from my pocket and gave an explosive cough. 'Can I have a glass of water, please?'

'Of course.' Helena Todd got to her feet, a mildly pissed-off Stepford wife, and left the room.

I hissed, 'What's going on?'

Anderson kept his voice low. 'This is your show. I got you through the front door. Ask what you want to ask.'

'I can't just ask if she abused young boys at Gallowhall.'

'That's a step up from asking if she worked there. If you think she was involved in child abuse, you should have called us in pronto.'

'It's just a theory.'

'A pretty explosive theory. Did you consider mentioning it to Murchison?'

'He's not half the polis you are.'

'I'm enough of a polis to know there's something dodgy going down when you start flattering me.'

'I'm just dancing in the dark. What is this place anyway? It feels like a weird B&B.'

'That's one way of putting it.'

The cars out front, the risqué paintings, activity upstairs, mature, good-looking blonde welcoming us inside without asking the purpose of our visit.

'Ah, shit, it's a knocking shop.'

Anderson grinned. 'Helena Todd's popular with the judiciary. She runs a clean premises and doesn't disturb the neighbours.'

I had always thought of Anderson as the straightest of straights. 'Rose would hand you your marching orders for good if she knew you frequented this place.'

Anderson snorted, 'Behave yourself. I don't frequent this place, or anywhere like it, but there are things it's better to turn a blind eye to. Your lot weren't legal until 1980, but we didn't target gay bars in Glasgow.'

I was sick of history being rewritten, as if equal marriage had wiped the slate clean of beatings, sackings, humiliations, accusations and arrests.

I snapped, 'God help us if we were found winching in public though.'

'What you call winching's an act of gross indecency.'

'Fuck off, we couldn't hold hands or kiss in public. Christ, stand too close and you'd get your features rearranged.'

We were still crammed together on the couch, our thighs touching, voices risen to urgent hisses.

Anderson flushed maroon. 'I saved you from getting arrested in Kelvingrove Park. Remember that?'

'I wouldn't have needed saving if your mob hadn't bloody arrested me.'

My lot. His mob. We were dangerously close to name-calling.

Anderson muttered, 'They wouldn't have arrested you if you hadn't . . .'

The door opened, and Mrs Todd entered carrying a carafe of water and three glasses. She gave us a curious look. 'Everything okay?'

'Yes, thanks. Frog in my throat.'

She set the glassware on a low table. 'Sorry to abandon you. The kitchen's at the back of the house. Please, help yourself.'

Anderson smiled. 'You should get one of those Water at Work things.'

Helena Todd took her seat. 'I prefer a fresh flow.'

Anderson grinned. 'So I've heard.'

I dug him discreetly in the ribs to stop him flirting. Helena Todd noticed and gave a smile that sharpened her high cheekbones. If she was involved in Mandy's murder, or its aftermath, she would surely suspect the reason for our visit, but she raised her drink to her lips with a steady hand.

Anderson took a sip of his water. 'This isn't an official interview. Your name came up in the course of an investigation into Gallowhall School.'

Helena Todd injected a light note of surprise into her voice. '*My* name?'

'A name that seems to be associated with yours. Do you have any connection to Gallowhall?'

Her eyes gave nothing away. 'I've read about it in the newspapers of course – ghastly affair – but I've never been there. What name did you associate with mine?'

Anderson glanced at me. I cleared my throat. 'Hurst, Nurse Hurst.'

Helena Todd took another sip of water. 'I don't know anyone of that name. We are permitted to carry out aesthetics here . . .' She must have seen the incomprehension on our faces because she added, 'Non-surgical cosmetic procedures. Other than that, I've no medical training.'

Anderson nodded. 'Someone's obviously got their wires crossed. Happens more often than we'd like to admit.' He got to his feet. 'Sorry for wasting your time.'

In cop shows detectives often ask a leading question as they leave the premises, but Anderson chatted affably to Helena Todd about the weather, rolling out clichés about soft rain and the Dear Green Place.

I paused in front of the Russell Flint prints in the hallway. 'These are nice.'

Her eyes met mine, and I was struck again by her lack of laughter lines, the smoothness of her lips. Gays are accused of fetishising youth, but the young-old cast of her face was unsettling, like a doll brought to life.

She reached out and straightened one of the prints. 'Reproductions — I'd have thought an antiques expert like you would spot that.' The realisation that Helena Todd knew my identity was an electric jolt to the spine. She opened a glass display cabinet by the door and handed me a miniature pot of cream. 'Take one of these samples for your boss. And do recommend Pretty Baby to her if she ever wants aesthetic work undertaken. We come highly recommended.'

Anderson's smile lost its lustre. 'I'll be seeing you, Helena.'

She opened the door. 'Any time, inspector.'

Anderson strode off down the driveway, but I hesitated on the doorstep, remembering what he had said about flushing guilty rabbits from long grass. It was the first time we had met, but I said, 'I've seen you at the salerooms. You collect jewellery and costume wear? Edwardian period?'

Helena Todd held my gaze. 'What woman doesn't like jewellery?'

'Edwardian stuff is probably a good investment. It's unfashionable at the moment. Too ornate for modern tastes, hard to wear without giving people a fancy eyeful.'

Helena's lips parted in a small *oh*. Her Bearsden tones gave way to Calton and Gallowgate. 'What are you after?'

Suddenly it was easy to say it out loud. 'I want to know who murdered Mandy Manderson.'

Her eyes were as cold as a waiting blade. 'I don't know anything about that.'

'Rilke.' Anderson was waiting at the bottom of the drive. He gestured at his watch.

Helena Todd had regained her composure. 'I'm protected. Bring polis to my door again and I'll make sure your friend Rose is beyond cosmetic help.'

'That's quite a threat.'

'It's a promise.' The door shut smartly in my face.

Anderson waited until we were back on the tree-lined street, beyond the reach of security videos. 'Pass it over.'

'What?'

'That tub of whatever it is.'

I took the small white pot branded with Pretty Baby's logo from my pocket and read the label. 'Anti-ageing serum.'

Anderson took it from me and tossed it into one of the domestic refuse bins that lined the pavement, waiting for collection. 'Cheeky bitch. I always thought something about her set-up stank. I don't know how, or what, but she's up to her manicured elbows in something.'

'I don't think a manicure goes much beyond the fingertips.'

Anderson gave me a hard stare. 'Fuck only knows what what's in that cream. Belladonna, probably. What took you so long, anyway?'

'I asked her who killed Manderson.'

He turned to look at me. 'Jesus, a wee bit of subtlety wouldn't go amiss.'

'You said alerting people can flush them out.'

'Aye, but you leave room for uncertainty. Let them think there's still a chance of covering their tracks. What did the old witch say?'

'She threatened Rose.'

Anderson's face turned red. I thought he was going to hit me. 'Fuck's sake, Rilke.'

'I know. I'm sorry.'

We had reached my car. Les was asleep, slumped against the passenger door. Anderson opened it and caught him as he tumbled towards the tarmac.

Les snatched at the door handle. 'Jesus Christ, just kick me into the gutter, why don't you?'

Anderson snapped, 'Get in the back. I need to have a word with fuckwit.'

Les rubbed his face as he limped into the street. He touched his scar and winced. 'How did it go?'

'Shitly.'

I spotted a familiar figure dressed in a long black parka and chunky boots, jogging along the other side of the road in the direction of Helena Todd's place. A black baseball cap hid her eyes, but I saw enough of the jogger's face to know it was Cat. I ducked into the car, but, although darkness would not be long in coming, it was still daylight, and I could not be sure she hadn't seen me.

Les said, 'You see who I saw?'

'Maybe.'

'Wonder where she's going in such a rush.'

I had a good idea but did not answer him.

Anderson turned round and looked at Les. 'You're moving into Rose's place to keep an eye on her.'

Les laughed. 'I don't think so.'

I said, 'Les is a marked man.'

There was no need to tell Anderson who was after Les. He already knew.

Anderson pointed his index finger at Les. 'Anything happens to Rose, and I will personally eviscerate you.' He turned to me. 'And you'll be next.'

Les snapped. 'C'mon, man, I've got enough problems.'

Anderson looked like he might even up the scar on Les's face. 'Your problems are nothing compared to what they'll be if I take against you.'

I started the engine, steered the car into the street and drove away from Helena Todd, towards Rose's place.

Thirty-Two

ANDERSON MADE ME stop at Celino's on Dumbarton Road. Ten minutes later he emerged with two bags of deli food, a bunch of chrysanthemums and four bottles of red wine. He stashed them in the boot and got into the front seat.

Les slumped low in the back of the car. 'Rose can't stand me.'

Anderson glared at him. 'You look after her like she's the Queen of bloody Sheba. You stay straight and you stay indoors.'

I parked outside Rose's building and waited while Anderson persuaded her to accept Les as a temporary lodger. At one point I thought I heard shouting. I turned the radio on and stayed put.

My mobile rang, number unknown. I picked up and a stranger asked if I was me. I hesitated, then said that I was, in a voice that sounded unsure.

'Your property is available to collect from Partick Police Station.'

The Lidl bags containing Manderson's stock.

I told the stranger I would be there within the hour. Anderson got into the car, his face redder and more crumpled than usual.

I started the engine. 'I've got to go to Partick cop shop. Want me to drop you there?'

'That's the last place I need to go.'

'Where then?'

Anderson turned the car radio off and took out his phone. 'Just drive.' I heard a distant buzz and then a faint voice saying Anderson's name. Anderson leaned back in his seat and smiled a chummy smile that told me he was speaking to another policeman. 'How's the Manderson investigation going?' Whatever the person on the other end of the line said made him frown. The voice said something else, and Anderson forced a laugh. 'Good to hear. I'll tell Rose you've got the right guy. One less bloody menace to contend with.' He killed the call.

I glanced at him. 'They're still convinced the asylum seeker did it?'

'He had your man's credit card on his person. Also, he confessed.'

'It's too easy.'

'This is real life, not a Sunday afternoon drama. You want your mate's death to be meaningful . . .'

'Mandy Manderson was an arsehole.'

'So what are you getting all knicker-knotted for?'

'I found him.'

'Then be glad we did our job.'

'Don't take this personally, Anderson, but Police Scotland don't always get the right man.'

'Murchison's a good officer. His dad's Judge Urquhart

Murchison. He literally wrote the book on police corruption. Young Murchison's following in his footsteps. He's clean as Doris Day's panties.'

The thought of Ray Diamond's hands around my throat stopped me from telling Anderson what I had learned about Judge Urquhart Murchison.

'No one's that clean.'

'If you know something, now's the time to tell me.'

I hesitated, but Anderson was straight as William Tell's arrow. If I told him about the hatpin, he would have me up on a charge of attempting to pervert the course of justice or worse. Rose would be dragged into the mess. We would end up in prison. Bowery would collapse, and a bunch of people would lose their jobs.

I changed the subject. 'Why would Helena Todd threaten Rose if she had nothing to do with Manderson's death?'

Anderson snorted. 'First it was child abuse, now it's murder. Where's your evidence?'

'I'm just saying she's pretty touchy for an innocent woman.'

'I never said Helena Todd was innocent. She's running a brothel. You turn up with me in tow and start asking stupid questions about child abuse.'

I improvised a half-lie. 'I saw her with Manderson. One of the boys he was at Gallowhall with thought she resembled the matron there, Nurse Hurst.'

'It's a big leap from that to murder.'

'Maybe Manderson was blackmailing her with something from back then. You said yourself her set-up stinks.'

'There are many reasons why something might have a bad smell about it. You've no proof of any of this. Drop it, and drop me at that taxi rank.'

It was none of my business, but I asked, 'Where are you going?'

'I left my car in Helena Todd's street.'

'Are you going to have a word about Rose?'

Anderson got out of the car and slammed the door. His coat fanned out behind him as he strode towards the rank without a backward glance.

A heavy-set man in a football top, jogging trousers and sliders was leaning against the counter in Partick Police Station, complaining about persistent dog fouling in his back green. The desk sergeant looked like he wanted to bang his head against the cracked Perspex screen between them.

'Like I already said, sir, an officer talked to your neighbour. He insists that he disposes of his dog's mess. It's a case of your word against his. Nothing we can do about it.'

The man set a carrier bag on the counter and took out a white cardboard box, the type usually used for doughnuts and cream cakes. 'That's where you're wrong.'

The desk sergeant rubbed his forehead with his hand. 'That better not be what I think it is.'

'DNA test it. I guarantee you it's proof.'

The desk sergeant tapped his fingers against the counter. 'There's such a thing as a chain of evidence. How do I know you picked that up from your back court? Anyway, we don't have a budget for DNA testing dogshit.'

'How much can it cost?' The man opened the box, and a powerful smell enveloped the reception area.

The desk sergeant took a step backwards. 'Remove that now, or I'll put you on a charge.'

'Ah, get to fuck.' The man tipped the cake box upside down and landed a large turd on the counter.

'That's it! You're fucking nicked.' The desk sergeant sprang towards the door connecting the backroom to the reception area, but the man was already away, legging it into Dumbarton Road at a faster speed than I would have credited him capable of.

Thurso Scanlan walked into reception just as the desk sergeant returned, red-faced and out of breath. He looked from the sergeant to the turd to me.

I held up my hands. 'I'm an innocent party. I'm in to collect the goods you took off me on my previous visit.'

Thurso Scanlan barked at the officer. 'For fuck's sake, clean that up.' He pointed at one of the interview rooms and ordered me to 'wait in there'.

He returned with the two carrier bags and the receipts I had signed. It was the same dull room, smelling of bleach and despair, where he had interviewed me before. I worked my way through the contents, ticking items off the list as I took them from the bag. It took just under forty minutes. Thurso Scanlan watched me like I was television.

I held up the list and showed him an entry for a diamond ring with no tick against it. 'We're an engagement ring short.'

Thurso Scanlan's eyes were pale blue, like a Weimaraner's. He did not blink. 'How's your friend Leslie getting on?'

'Les has learned his lesson. He's keeping his nose clean.'

Thurso Scanlan nodded. 'I wondered if he maybe knew something about a couple of recent ODs, two lads, students.'

'You'd have to ask him, but I doubt it. Les doesn't hang about with students.' I pointed at the unticked ring on the list. 'This is missing.'

Thurso Scanlan sighed. 'Take a moment and look properly. If you want to make a complaint, we'll have to take the property back and launch an investigation.'

'How long will that take?'

Thurso Scanlan picked up a couple of necklaces lying on the table between us and regarded them. 'How long is a rope of pearls?' He smiled as if he had said something witty. 'Low-priority investigations of that kind take time. Could be six months, could be a year, longer.'

Les was adamant Thurso Scanlan was bent. A man with more moral courage might have stood his ground, but I was in a vulnerable position. I folded the receipts into my pocket and started to pack the jewellery away.

Thurso Scanlan's grin was muted, but there was a gleam in his eyes. 'Wise choice. Don't want to lose a sale because of sloppy bookkeeping.'

I got to my feet and shoved the Lidl bags into my rucksack. We did not shake hands. The desk sergeant was not at his post. The counter was bare, the reception room Jantex-fragrant.

Thurso Scanlan had a bounce in his step as he walked me to the door. 'Sad to see Inspector Anderson go, but we all reach the end of the line eventually.'

It was my cue to say that I did not know that Anderson was going anywhere, but I embraced the fashion for no goodbyes and let the door swing to without a word. Dumbarton Road was knife-cold. An undersized traffic warden in an oversized uniform was sliding a ticket under the windscreen wipers of my car.

She gave me a sympathetic smile. 'Sorry, pal. Doesn't matter if it's three hours or three minutes – late is late, as far as the council's concerned.'

I took the ticket and folded it into my pocket. 'Late is late and dead is dead.'

She pointed across the road towards the police station.

'I'm just doing my job, son. Threaten me, and I'll set the polis on you.'

I wanted to say that it was just an observation, a simple truth in an untrue world, but I was learning to hold my tongue. I got into my car and drove towards Bowery Auctions.

Thirty-Three

IT WAS AFTER hours, the car park empty except for Bowery vans shining white beneath the arc lights. I unlocked the gates, drove my car inside, relocked them and walked across the vacant tarmac, my loaded rucksack heavy on my back. I wondered if I would ever cross the car park without seeing Mandy Manderson slumped against the wall.

A couple of lamps shone dimly in the dark of the main saleroom, casting shadows against the walls. Portraits and landscapes were hung floor to ceiling, a patchwork of faces, rustic pastures and wind-tossed seas. The best we could hope was that a pub or hotel, keen on the kailyard, would buy them cut-price.

Music was playing somewhere deeper in the dark. A woman singing about a messy night on the piss that she could not remember. The beat shifted from mournful to the rhythm of high heels pounding concrete as she rapped out her anger. I followed the sound to a jumble of furniture. A light shone from the depths of a wingback chair. Hannah was curled up, small and pale, her features illuminated by the glow of her phone, facial piercings shining. She whispered, 'I don't know what to do.'

A woman's voice, filtered tinny through the phone mic: 'I told you, you don't have to do anything.'

My shadow touched Hannah's face. She gave a small scream and dropped her phone. I caught a quick glimpse of the woman onscreen: white skin, violet eyes and honey-blonde hair. Hannah leapt from her seat, grabbed the phone and hissed, 'Gotta go.' The screen went to black.

Half a dozen bentwood chairs from a recently bankrupted café were tangled amongst the furniture. I pulled one free and sat opposite Hannah. 'I didn't mean to startle you.'

She sank back into the armchair and smiled, but her feet shifted, as if she wanted to burrow into its cushions. 'I know I shouldn't be here after hours. I didn't feel like going home yet.'

'You've probably blown our insurance, but I won't let on to Rose, this time. Are you okay?'

'Fine. Thanks for asking, Mr Rilke.'

Normally I would have left it at that, but I had seen who Hannah was talking to on the video call. 'Mandy Manderson's death still bothering you?'

Hannah shook her head. 'Not really . . . I mean, yes . . . of course . . . but . . .' A tear rolled down her face and she brushed it away. 'I just want things to go back to normal.'

'You know you'll get no judgement from me. Is Helena Todd bothering you?'

Hannah's eyes widened. 'I don't know anyone called Helena Todd . . .'

'I saw her face on your phone when you dropped it. I was

with Mrs Todd this afternoon. She's not a woman you forget.'

Hannah shut her eyes. She had dyed her eyebrows and lashes pale pink. Another tear eased its way down her cheek. 'It isn't what you think.'

'What do I think?'

She shook her head. 'I don't know.'

'I think you're keeping dangerous company.' It was the kind of prissy phrase people had used on Les and me a million times when we were young, but it was true. 'Helena Todd is poison.'

'You don't know anything about her.'

'I know she runs a brothel called Pretty Baby. I suspect it specialises in young girls. What else should I know?'

I expected Hannah to deny everything, but her face flushed rosy. She wiped away her tears with the back of her hand. 'Helena Todd's a survivor who's created a safe space for women to be themselves.'

'Sounds like she's selling you a line.'

'Sex work is work. She's not selling me anything.'

'Bet she takes her cut though.'

'Class costs.'

I detected Helena Todd's voice in Hannah's choice of words.

I am prone to brief encounters with strangers. I know Grindr, secret sexual codes, an edge of danger and knowing glances that lead to more. Hannah was an adult, entitled to her own sexuality, but I still remembered some of the cruelties that had cut me when I was young, the close shaves and not-quite escapes. Perhaps it was the bleached hair and sugar-pink eyebrows, her dedication to dressing up, that made me think there something pure about Hannah. She was wild and naïve. I did not want her tainted by Helena Todd.

'We're living in a digital world. You don't need to get up close and personal to make money.'

Hannah uncurled her legs and sat up straight, like someone readying themselves for a fight. 'Who said I was getting up close and personal? I appreciate your concern, Mr Rilke, but my choices are none of your business.'

'Helena's been linked to Mandy Manderson's death.'

Hannah's eyes widened. 'That's a lie.'

Lying was easy. 'The police visited her this afternoon. They seem pretty certain there's a connection.'

A door slammed in the main saleroom. Our heads turned towards it. I said, 'You expecting anyone?'

Hannah shook her head. 'No.'

Had I locked the auction-house door behind me? I was tired and could not be certain. I scanned the overstuffed corner where we were hidden, looking for a weapon. An Anglepoise lamp rested on a nearby occasional table, like a depressed dinosaur. I put a finger to my lips, telling Hannah to keep silent, picked it up and crept in the direction of the main saleroom. The route between the stacks of furniture was narrow, so I turned sideways. The lamp's electric flex snaked around my ankles, and I stumbled into the pile of bentwood chairs which clattered into an unruly heap, legs tangled like a parody of an orgy. Footsteps ran towards us, metal segs loud against the wooden floor.

Our head porter, Frank, appeared, a brass poker raised in his right hand. 'Jesus, Rilke, you gave me a fright.' He looked at Hannah and then back to me. 'Am I interrupting something?'

I set the lamp back on the floor. 'We're putting Mandy Manderson's stock up for sale. Hannah was about to help me catalogue it. What about you?'

'Keyholder duty. A neighbour phoned the cops to say there was suspicious activity.'

'And they called you? Nice to know the force is taking things seriously.'

Frank shrugged. 'I guess Mandy's murder made the neighbours jumpy, the polis not so much.'

'Hannah and me are hardly suspicious.'

Frank put the poker down. 'Hannah's not. You on the other hand—'

A noise interrupted him before he could make a quip about me looking dodgy. The three of us turned our heads towards it. Frank picked up the poker. I reached for the Anglepoise and held my breath as we edged forward. A shape moved in the darkness. I half-hoped it was Mandy's killer ready to put the whole mess to bed one way or another.

I whispered, 'Did you lock the door?'

Frank hissed, 'I didn't know who was here. I might have needed to make a run for it.'

'Brilliant, cheers for that.'

A woman's voice called, 'Hannah? Is that you?'

I reached for my phone, slid the torch app open and pointed it in the direction of the voice. Light and shadows bounced across the saleroom. Chairs, cabinets, paintings, rugs, boxes, a table crowded with ceramics, a shop dummy that made us gasp, and then a slim figure raising a hand to shield their eyes from the sudden brightness.

Cat was still dressed in the long, dark coat she had been wearing when I saw her running in the direction of Helena Todd's. She saw Frank and me bearing our strange weapons and let out a small scream.

Hannah pushed past us. 'What are you doing here?'

Cat let her arm fall by her side. 'You weren't answering your phone. Your grandma's worried. She called me.'

I remembered that Hannah was close to her grandmother and wondered why she had not asked the old lady for money instead of selling kisses and more. Hannah had always seemed middle-class, able to weather Bowery's low pay in return for cultural cachet, but it seemed I had read her wrong.

Cat recognised me and took a step backwards. 'Did you follow me?'

'I was here before you arrived. I work here.'

Frank put the poker down. He took his keys from his pocket, ready to lock the door. 'Does everybody know each other except me?'

Our head porter is handsome. Young women are usually shy or flirty around him before they realise he is gay. Cat looked at him with indifference.

Hannah said, 'Cat and I went to art school together.'

It made sense now. Cat had introduced Hannah to Helena Todd.

I nodded at Frank. 'Sorry you got dragged in after hours.' I lifted the rucksack containing Mandy's stock, ready to stash it in the safe. 'Why don't you head off?'

Frank gave me a strange look. 'You sure?'

'Positive. Hannah will give me a hand.'

Frank shrugged. 'I'm here now. It makes no odds.'

'I'll manage.'

He nodded at Cat. 'What about her?'

'She can see Hannah home once we're done.'

Frank tossed his keys in the air and caught them, then clenched his fist in a not-quite power salute. 'Okay, boss, see you tomorrow.'

Frank only called me boss when he thought I was being a prat. He touched his fingers to his forehead and headed for the exit.

Cat stroked Hannah's shoulder. 'Your grandma's getting her knickknacks in a twist, worrying where you are.'

Hannah glanced in the direction of the exit but stood her ground. 'You go to Gran's if you want. I'll see you there.'

'It's you she wants to see.'

The saleroom door slammed behind Frank. The locks barrelled home.

I turned to Hannah. 'Do you want to tell me what's going on?'

Cat snapped, 'What's anything got to do with you?' She turned to Hannah. 'This fuckwit's a friend of my brother Hari. He's already been on my case about stuff he knows fuck all about.'

Hannah muttered, 'Cheers, Cat. This fuckwit's my boss.'

The name was threatening to stick. 'Stop calling me fuckwit. Les is the one who knows your brother. I've never met him.'

I was still holding the torch. It illuminated Cat's face, the jut of her cheekbones, the tight line of her jaw. 'Didn't stop you sticking your nose into my business though, did it?'

It was Hannah's turn to touch her friend's arm. 'Rilke's one of the good guys.' She glanced at me. 'Unfortunately, he has an overdeveloped sense of responsibility. He thinks Helena Todd's exploiting us.'

'Who cares what he thinks?'

I switched off the torch app and shoved my phone in my pocket. The saleroom sank back into shadow.

'Usually I'd agree with you. Doesn't matter what I think, but Helena Todd's a special case.'

Hannah made a face. 'Remember I told you about Mr Manderson's murder? He thinks Helena's involved.'

Cat laughed. 'That's a pile of crap.'

Hannah nodded. 'Obviously, but we promised Helena we wouldn't cause her any trouble. Mr Rilke's tenacious when he gets the bit between his teeth.'

Cat scoffed. 'Which bit?'

Hannah's chin had regained its determined upward jut. She looked at me. 'Can we use the office computer?'

I lifted the bags of jewellery. 'I'll log you in.'

Cat had caught a strand of her hair between her fingertips and was twisting it. 'You don't have to prove anything to him.' But she followed us into Rose's office.

I stashed Mandy's jewellery in the safe, making sure to block sight of the code with my body. Rose's desktop computer was ancient, and there was an awkward moment while the three of us stood silent in the small room while it hummed and chuntered into life. Rose's screensaver emerged, a photo of her with old Joe Bowery, not long before the hit and run that had killed him. Joe was holding a pint of Guinness and Rose had her hands around his neck, pretending to strangle him. They had each stuck out their tongues and crossed their eyes. I remembered taking it, at a drunken end-of-sale party, what seemed a long time ago.

Hannah sat in Rose's chair and started typing.

Cat took the visitor's seat. She glanced at me. 'Sure you're ready for this?'

I leaned against the filing cabinet. 'I won't know until I've seen whatever it is.'

Hannah tapped at the keys and a website appeared. A pink and blue floral background that recalled Hokusai and that rip-off merchant Damien Hirst. Two words throbbed neon pink, GLASGOW KISS. Kiss vanished and was replaced in rapid succession by

        CARESS

                      TOUCH

            LICK

      EAT   FUCK

GLASGOW vanished, and the word FUCK flickered alone onscreen, off and on like a faulty lightbulb. I did not know much about websites, but I knew enough to realise that this one had cost a lot of money.

I said, 'This cost someone a lot of money.'

Cat tried not to smile, but pride shone on her face.

I raised my eyebrows at Hannah, reminding her that I knew she was skint.

She looked away. 'Mates' rates.'

A keyhole labelled ENTER appeared onscreen. Hannah clicked on it and a menu emerged. HOMEPAGE, CINEMA, STILLS, TEASERS, PERFORMERS, CONTACT . . . She moved the cursor to Homepage. A sepia photograph of her and Cat in peach vintage lingerie. A mission statement in hot neon pink.

Glasgow Kiss is an ongoing exploration, redefining new artistic vistas in erotic experience. Alchemical, taboo, dangerous, consensual, magical, darkness, DIY, DI-DO, Do You Dare?

Me-Me Meow and AhA Ha-Ha are artists and filmmakers slip-sliding beyond gallery walls and cinema screens for their own pleasure and yours.

Sign up for more content.

Hannah's facial piercings shone like a constellation in the glow of the computer screen. Her skin was basement-dweller pale. I had noticed her style becoming more edgy, but I had not savvied that she was shifting from vaguely hip to full-on vamp.

She turned to look at me. 'More?'

I nodded, and she went to the Cinema page. A dozen octagonal tiles, tinted in a carnival of bonbon colours, shone like Amsterdam windows. I leaned closer. Each tile contained a photograph of Hannah and Cat: semi-dressed, naked, wrapped around each other, covered in flowers, draped in tulle, compressed in PVC, frothy with lace. A bearded, heavily tattooed man appeared with them in a couple of the windows. His face was obscured, but I thought I recognised Dickie Bird.

Hannah said, 'Choose one.'

I hoped that Rose's malware was up to date and pointed at the least explicit-looking film, the two women lying together on a bed of bright petals.

Cat laughed. 'Vanilla.'

Hannah gave Cat's hair a playful tug. 'No kink shaming, no judgement, remember?'

She opened the virtual room, pressed play, and a film started, accompanied by a gentle fractured melody, bright with temple bells. The girls' bodies were androgynous, thin and hairless. They ran their hands over each other's small breasts, smiling, occasionally laughing, nymphlike in a midsummer arcadia. There was no edge, no sense of transgression. I wondered if anyone found it sexy.

'I'm the wrong audience for this kind of thing.'

Cat leaned over and took the computer mouse from Hannah. 'Show him Lickspitty.'

The camera zoned into a close-up of the two women's profiles. They were facing each other, eyes bright. The camera zoomed slowly out, revealing their naked breasts, then zoomed in on their faces again. Cat's hair was pulled back from her face in a high ponytail. She opened her lips and liquid seeped down her chin. The women started to kiss, their tongues pushing into each other's mouths, viscousness on their lips, their chins, inside and outside each other's mouths. They were smiling. Making eye contact with each other, with the camera, with the viewer, with me.

I leaned over and pressed pause.

Cat grinned, pleased to have prompted a reaction. 'Too much?'

The image of the two girls' faces, shiny and sticky, their tongues touching, was frozen on the screen. I had seen much worse, done much worse. There was nothing to be scared of except that Cat and Hannah were not making the film independently in some bedsit or rented hotel room. Helena Todd's Pretty Baby business was in the mix.

I reached out and rotated the desk chair until Hannah was facing me. 'How come you're broke?'

She ran a hand over the shaved nape of her head. 'Things take time. We need to build subscribers.'

'How many members do you have?'

'Six.'

I burst out laughing. 'How long has the site been live?'

Cat snapped, 'Not long.'

Hannah said, 'Two months.'

I shook my head. 'You tried something new. It didn't work out. No biggie. Maybe you should take the site down and move on.'

Cat leaned against the desk. 'How long have you worked here?'

'Thirty years.'

'Never felt like leaving?'

I considered walking out on Bowery at least once day, but there was nowhere I wanted to be more. 'Guess I'm lucky I found my niche when I was young.'

'Or maybe you don't have any ambition. Hannah and I want to change things.'

'By getting your kit off?'

'By showing there are ethical ways to get your rocks off. Porn doesn't need to be exploitative, trafficked women and revolting old men.'

Hannah nodded. 'This is more than porn, more than money-making. It's a shared art practice.'

Cat chimed, 'Empowered activism.'

'Fair enough. Good luck to you both, but why do you need Helena Todd? She's not a revolutionary artist. She's old-school, catering to the establishment, geriatric old judges and lawyers.'

Cat rolled her eyes. 'You can't see past your conditioning. Helena's part of a continuum. Engaging with her practice is a way to effect change.'

'She doesn't have a practice. She runs a knocking shop.'

'You're a whore-phobic prude.'

'I've nothing against whores or renters; it's pimps and madams I don't like.' The frozen still of Hannah and Cat was getting on my nerves. I hit a keyboard key, intending to close the site. It was a clumsy move; the screen reverted to the menu of teasers for full-length videos on offer. I stretched out a hand to complete the shutdown and paused. A familiar building was in the background of one of the stills. I pressed the cursor and maximised it onscreen. 'Tell me about this.'

Cat made a noise that was half sigh, half raspberry.

Hannah looked at the screen. 'Some people are turned on by the idea of outdoor sex. We filmed it early morning at the end of last summer before the clocks went back.'

'I don't need educated on the thrill of the outdoors. What made you choose that place?'

'We were going for a sexy vampire vibe. It's a dramatic backdrop, full-on gothic.'

'But how did you find it?'

Hannah looked confused. 'You mean what was it like?'

'No, how did you hear about it?'

Hannah shook her head, as if she could not quite remember. 'Maybe Helena mentioned it?'

Cat stretched a hand towards the computer mouse. 'It's none of his business.'

Hannah pulled the mouse beyond her friend's reach. 'I remember now. Dickie suggested it.'

Cat snapped, 'Shut up.'

Hannah's expression was mischievous. She knew Cat wanted to close the conversation down and was teasing her. 'I remember because he said he would drive us out there if you covered a shift in the pub for him.' She moved the mouse and positioned the curser, circling it like a military drone about to drop a bomb. 'It was Dickie who suggested we go there, Dickie Bird. Cat works with him at the Lismore.'

The onscreen image shivered in the dim light of Rose's office. Hannah and Cat, naked in the early morning sunshine, too young and skinny to be sexy, laughing at the camera, curled together on a tartan picnic rug, in the ruined shade of Gallowhall.

Thirty-Four

IT WAS ALMOST last orders by the time I reached the Lismore. The place was busy with late-night dog walkers who had nipped in for just-the-one and committed drinkers, three, four or more pints down and determined to get another one in before last orders. Dickie Bird was alone behind the bar: same shaved head, leather and tattoos. He gave me a quick nod and kept on serving. I worked my way towards the bar and waited.

'What'll it be?'

The last time we had met he had told me to leave, but there was no malice in Dickie's expression. I ordered a pint, told him to take one for himself and waited some more.

The bell clanged like a North Sea shipwreck and Dickie called, 'Time now, ladies and gentlemen, please.'

He propped open the barroom door, letting the heat and chatter of the evening escape into Partick's winter bite. The rumble of conversation shimmered and continued. No one moved. Dickie rang the bell again. 'Time! Home now, please!' Drinkers downed their dregs and gathered themselves in a raggle-taggle jumble of hats, scarves, gloves, coats and bags. They braced for the outdoors, some tottering, others chipper for the next phase of the night. A dogwalker saluted the barman. 'See you tomorrow.' Dickie gave him the same noncommittal nod he had given me. A gaggle of half-cut students attempted to bribe him into a lock-in, but Dickie turned his mild gaze on them and they retreated.

Some people lack the right muscles for smiling. I wondered if Dickie Bird was one of them. I waited for him to tell me to sling my hook, but he locked the door and started to clear the tables. If we had been friends, I would have pitched in. But I stayed by the bar and waited until he had finished.

Dickie loaded the dishwasher and began wiping the bar down. 'Thought you were told to keep your nose out of other people's business.'

'I saw the website. Glasgow Kiss.'

Dickie started sluicing out the wine measures. His expression darkened, but I thought it was irritation rather than embarrassment. 'Didn't think you were into girls.'

'I'm not. I'm investigating the murder of a colleague of mine, Rodney Manderson.'

Dickie's eyes met mine. They were wary, but mention of murder tends to make men wary. 'Never heard of him. You police?'

'I'm an auctioneer. Manderson was a small-time jewellery dealer.'

'Someone murder him for his jewels?'

'Doesn't look like it.'

'You're wasting your time. I never met any jewellery

dealers. I'm pretty sure Cat never did either. Glasgow Kiss has nothing to do with your dead friend.'

'He was a Gallowhall boy. Helena Todd's name came up in connection to him.'

Dickie nodded. 'Helena Todd's a busy woman, fingers in a lot of pies. What made you pick on Glasgow Kiss?'

'Hannah works at the auction house. She had a run-in with Manderson not long before he died. She showed me Glasgow Kiss, and I saw a still of the video you made up at Gallowhall. That and the connection with Helena Todd feels like more than a coincidence.'

Dickie nodded. 'Everything's connected somehow, right?'

'Maybe, if you want to get philosophical about it, but when one step leads straight to another you've got to start asking questions.'

'You're an auctioneer, not a polis. All you need to ask is who's the highest bidder.'

'If Helena Todd is involved in Manderson's murder, Cat and Hannah could be in trouble.'

Dickie Bird considered this for a moment. 'I try to look out for Cat, but she doesn't make it easy . . . Glasgow Kiss.' He shook his head. 'Daft name, right?'

'Not the best.'

'Makes me think of someone putting the heid in.'

It could have been a threat, but Dickie's tone was soft.

My pint was well below the midway mark. I did not ask for another. 'You appear on the website.'

Dickie was neither cocky nor self-conscious. 'Cat was determined. I thought better me than some other prick.'

His lips curled at the unintentional double entendre. He had the right muscles for smiling after all.

'How do you know Helena Todd?'

Dickie Bird rolled up a sleeve to display the tattoos roaming across his muscled arms.

'This is my art. Cat and Hannah think they're making something special. Seems like girl porn to me but I never went to art school, so I'm not qualified to say. I know a fly old bag when I see one though. I wouldn't trust Helena Todd as far as I could throw her.'

'Why not?'

'You met her?'

I nodded, 'Yes.'

'Then you know why not.'

The dishwasher beeped. Dickie Bird opened its door. Steam clouded outwards like dry ice in a schlocky horror.

I nursed the last of my pint. 'Cat said you suggested Gallowhall as a location.'

Dickie started to unload the dishwasher, using a cloth to wipe away excess moisture. 'I come from round that way. When we were kids, we used to dare each other to go inside. It was closed by then, but still in one piece. You could explore the whole building. Creepy as fuck. All kinds of stuff left behind. Things that probably shouldn't have been, official records and the like. We'd look at them, but they didn't mean much to us. I guess it all went up in the fire. Cat and Hannah said they wanted a vampire vibe; I thought, why not? We went early doors to avoid dog walkers, took the camera, I did the filming.' He smiled his mild smile. 'It was a nice day out, as far as these things go. Personally, I'd have preferred it if we'd just gone for a walk, but things are as they are. Sooner or later, Cat will get bored and move on to some other mad scheme.'

'Is she prone to mad schemes?'

'Cat worked here all through her art degree. First off it

was club nights: she deejayed and put crazy projections all over the walls like an acid trip. That was art too, but it never really caught on. Next it was some kind of food project: roadkill and hedgerows, baked squirrel and boiled nettles. I body-swerved that one.' He stuck out his tongue in disgust, revealing a pointed metal stud. 'Now it's art porn. She should settle for painting pictures. She's a good artist. You should see the painting she did of me. My maw has it pride of place in the sitting room next to the telly. It was your girl Hannah that started it. None of this would have happened if Hannah hadn't introduced her to Helena.'

'Hannah introduced them?'

'Yep, Hannah and Helena are tight.'

Hannah liked to push boundaries, but it had not occurred to me that she might have been the catalyst. Cat had seemed the dominant force in the partnership.

'How did Hannah meet Helena?'

Dickie Bird took my empty glass from me and ran it under the tap. 'How would I know?'

It was cold outside, the street quieter now, but fast-food shops were still open and there were a few cabs and the occasional car on the road. Dickie had put on his leather jacket and a knitted black cap. I wondered if anyone had ever told him he looked like a leather queen. I waited while he locked the security shutter before I asked the question that had been in my mind ever since he told me he had grown up in the vicinity of Gallowhall.

'Did any of your family work at the home?'

For the first time he looked wary. 'You know it was full of nonces, right?'

'I heard something along those lines.'

'My da and grandda were miners, worked down the road at Gallowrig. Before my time. When Thatcher pulled the plug my da got taken on by the chemical plant. He retired just before it closed.'

I sensed a 'but' and injected a note of encouragement into my voice. 'A lot of good people must have worked there who didn't have a clue what was going on. Abusers are clever. They find their own tribe and hide in plain sight from the rest.'

Dickie nodded. 'My granny and my aunty Mo worked in the kitchens. My granny beat herself up for years after it all came out. Couldn't forgive herself for not spotting what was going down.'

'Is your granny still around?'

'Died of Covid in 2020.'

'I'm sorry.'

'I'm guessing you're not asking about my gran for no reason.'

'There's a suggestion Helena worked at Gallowhall at one time. The home used to take group photos of the staff and children. I've not been able to find one. I wondered if your aunty might have any.'

'I doubt it. She and my gran fucking hated that place. They weren't exactly looking for souvenirs.'

'Will you ask her for me?'

'Was Helena involved in what went on there?'

'Maybe.'

Dickie Bird nodded, processing the possibility. He pocketed the pub keys. 'I keep out of her way, but she owns some decent video and editing equipment. Let's us use rooms at her place too.'

'Sounds like she's been helpful.'

'She's all smarm with the girls, but she thinks I'm a scumbag.'

'Maybe she recognises your accent from her Gallowhall days and worries you'll connect her with the home.'

I could see he liked the idea that Helena feared his insight. He suppressed a smile. 'Maybe she does.'

I passed him my card. 'Will you ask your aunty to check if she has any photos of Helena? She might have gone by the name Nurse Hurst back then.'

He shook his head. 'She's long done with that place – doesn't need to be reminded of it.'

But he pocketed my card before he disappeared into the night.

Thirty-Five

IT WAS EARLY Sunday morning. Time was almost up for Les, and I had nowhere new to go.

Anderson's phone rang out. Rose's mobile was turned off. Hannah's was dead. Les's went straight to message. I did not bother to call Ray Diamond. He would be in touch when the time came.

I ordered two bacon rolls from the Criterion Café. They were delivered by the same Just Eat courier as before. He gave me the same knowing look. I tipped him the usual amount and shut the door gently in his face, just as I had last time.

Ray's dossier was hidden under my sofa. I took it out and leafed through it, but there was nothing there I had not already read. I ate standing by the window. The sky was gunmetal grey with the threat of rain, maybe even snow.

The telephone rang and a voice I recognised as Manderson's neighbour Jack asked, 'That you, Death?'

'I'm not sure I like this new handle.'

'Handle?'

'Nickname.'

'Then try dressing like you're one of the living. You popping round for a roll on sausage?'

'Sadly not. I've just had a couple of bacon rolls.'

I put the call on speaker, went through to the bedroom and selected a wool suit the same shade of grey as the sky, a white shirt and black tie – get-up fit for a funeral.

The old man was talking about his two laddies, the visit they were due to make that afternoon, the chocolate doughnuts he had bought at the Co-op in their honour. He drifted back in time to a Post Office strike he had been involved in. The demonstrators had used oil drums as braziers, burned rubbish in them to keep warm. 'Strikes always happened in the winter. We'd hold their Christmas cards to ransom. Fucking freezing on the picket line. Didnae matter how many socks you wore, the cold came up through the soles of your boots. And what was it for? The union aye sold us down the river. Took from the Russians with one hand and the Tories with the other.'

I fastened the top button of my shirt, slid my tie beneath the collar and around my neck. 'You did all right from it, Jack. You've got a nice house – it must be worth a bob or two.'

'Right place, right time, son. Aye, we were lucky . . .' He wandered off down memory lane. I let him ramble on in the background, took the phone through to the sitting room, set it on the table and flicked through Ray's folder again. There were angles beyond my reach. Manderson had been under Ray's protection. Was his death an attempt to undermine the pawnbroker's authority? If it was, there would have been more moves, an escalation of violence.

The old man mentioned Rodney Manderson and my ears pricked up. 'He was a bad boy when he went away and a worse boy when he came back. No wonder his sister left the house young. She was a nice wee girl, ten years between them. Mr and Mrs Manderson tried for years to have another kiddie after her. My wife aye said they spoiled him, but I think he was spoiled in the womb. He was an evil wee bastard, like something out of one of those horror movies, like Darren in *The Omen*.'

'I think you mean Damien.'

'Isn't that what I said? He was the Devil's spawn, though to be fair I can't imagine Mrs Manderson dancing with the De'il. She was more of a mince and tatties, soup on the stove, scones in the oven type.'

'I didn't realise there was such a big age gap between Rodney and his sister.'

'Och aye, I remember it well because we took her the night Rodney was born. Ten years old she was. A pretty wee thing, nae bother to anybody. By the time Rodney was ten she was out the house. Married the first man that would have her. I don't think it lasted. She went to France after that. I hadn't cast eyes on her for years until she came back for the funeral. Wouldn't have recognised her if she hadn't told me who she was. She's still bonny – what they call "well-preserved".'

The phrase made me think of Helena Todd. I said, 'What kind of phone do you have, Jack?'

'A wee one, pocket-sized.'

'A smartphone?'

'Smart enough for me, son.'

'Can it take photos?'

'Selfies and the like? Course it can. Why? You want to send me a cock shot?'

'I want to send you a photo to see if you recognise someone.'

I downloaded Helena Todd's photo from Pretty Baby's website and texted it to him. There was silence on the line. I wondered if he had lost the connection, but his voice returned, still bright with energy.

'For a moment I thought it was Steph Manderson – Manderson as was; I don't know her married name.'

'She still goes by Manderson.'

'Is that right? Well, it's not her. I don't know who that is. Another well-preserved woman. Lotions and potions, no doubt, plus folk eat better than they did – those that don't go to fat, the couch potato brigade.'

I promised that I would visit soon and brought the call to a close before he could embark on a monologue about obesity, at odds with his love of square sausage and doughnuts.

I looked at the photograph I had sent the old man. I saw what he meant. Helena Todd and Steph Manderson's styles chimed. They were both well-groomed blondes in fragrant middle age. I found the paperwork Steph Manderson had completed and phoned the number she had given. It rang out. No one wanted to speak to me.

My phone burst into life. Les's name flashed on the screen. 'Ray just called. I've to make myself available at six tonight.'

Ray was putting the screws on, warning Les of his intentions, like a jailor handing a condemned man a rope.

I glanced at my watch. It was 8 a.m. 'That gives us ten hours.'

'Enough time to get to London. Enough time to catch a plane to somewhere.'

'You still at Rose's?'

'Aye.'

'Look out the window. Anyone hanging around you don't like the look of?'

There was a pause on the line. I imagined Les crossing the room to the tall windows of Rose's front room and peeking from behind the shutters down into the square below. He whispered, 'What does Ray drive?'

'Whatever he wants. Usually high-end. Last time I saw him it was a black Merc.'

'There's a black Merc parked opposite.'

'Could be rent day, a cash landlord doing his rounds?'

'It was there last night. I had a smoke on the doorstep. It was parked opposite, exact same spot as now.'

'Not worried about traffic wardens.'

'Not worried about anything. I can't see if there's anyone inside, but there was yesterday.'

'How could you tell?'

'Rose and me had a couple of bevvies. I was feeling bold, went over and had a look. Wished I hadn't. There was a bloke at the wheel. Ray's usual type. Big enough not to need any finesse. There's a lot of street trading goes on round here. I was hoping it was someone selling blow, nothing to do with me.'

'Sounds like Ray's got eyes on you. He gave you a deadline hoping you'd bolt. You make a move in the direction of a train, plane or automobile, and he'll have you in that Merc before you can tell him where you'd like your new scar.'

'I don't have to leave by the front door.'

'He's watching you, Les. He'll pick you up and grind your bones to make his bread. I'm the only chance you have. Ray promised to let you off if I find out who killed Manderson.'

Les's voice held the dead calm of despair. 'And how's that going?'

'I've got someone in the frame. I just need a bit more evidence to be sure.'

'Christ, Rilke. What am I meant to do?'

'What Anderson told you to. Stay sober, keep an eye on Rose, and keep your wits about you. I'm close to wrapping it all up.'

'Ten hours close?'

'I think so.'

'You *think so*. You're deluded if you think I'm going to stay sober, and the last thing Rose needs is a minder. She's not even here.'

In the twenty-plus years that I had known Rose, she had never emerged from bed before midday on a Sunday. 'Where is she?'

'Someone called. She went to meet them.'

'Who?'

'I don't know. I heard her talking to someone on the phone, she said their name . . . Alanna? I think maybe it was Alanna. I was half-asleep.'

'Could it have been Helena?'

'Maybe . . . I don't know.'

'Hannah?'

'I've got a stinking hangover. I'd just woken up and she was in the hallway. Alanna, Helena, Hannah . . . they sound the same when your heid's under a feather pillow.'

'You didn't think to go with her?'

'I'm under house arrest, remember? Anyway she shot off like a bullet. Up, dressed and gone in thirty minutes.'

Thirty minutes is slow for a bullet, but lightning speed for Rose. She usually takes several cigarettes and three cups of coffee to get out the door.

'No note on the mantelpiece?'

'We're not married. She stuck her head round my bedroom door, told me to keep out of her wardrobe and then she was gone. Cheeky bitch. As if I'd want to try on her tatty frocks.'

'You're wearing one right now, aren't you?'

'It's good manners to lend a guest a nice dressing gown.' Les's tone sharpened. 'Don't get distracted and start looking for Rose. I'm the one Ray's gifting thirty years in Barlinnie. Even with time off for good behaviour I'll be an old, old man when I get out. No one ages well in a joint like that. Carby scran, zero sunshine, fuck-all skincare . . .' I heard the fear in his voice and remembered the sunset of bruises that had marked his body when he left prison. He whispered, 'I won't survive a long stretch, Rilke. I'm trusting you with my life here.'

'I know you are, pal. I promise I won't let you down.' I had never told anyone I loved them before. I said it now, to drive home the vow I was not sure I could keep. 'I love you like a brother, Les. I swear, you're not going to jail.'

He knew me too well to be reassured. 'Ah, Christ, now I'm really fucking worried.'

Thirty-Six

HANNAH OR HELENA? Helena or Hannah? I called Hannah's workmate Lucy and told her Hannah had left her purse at Bowery. I wanted to drop it off but was not sure where she lived. Lucy sounded half asleep, but she recited an address near the Maryhill stretch of the canal.

'Is Hannah happy working at Bowery?'

'You're asking the wrong person, Mr Rilke. I hardly see Hannah outside of work.'

'I thought you two were best buds.'

'Not these days. She moves with a cool crowd now.'

I told Lucy I thought she was pretty cool, and she laughed. 'I'm cool enough not to want to be cool.'

I heard a male voice in the background and envied her, wrapped up in bed on a Sunday morning with a lover who would reassure her she was both hot and cool.

I pulled my Crombie on top of my suit and added a yellow Tootal scarf to stop me looking too ghoulish.

Hannah's building was modern, art deco-style with a white-painted exterior, well-placed balconies and a good view of Stockingfield Bridge that spanned the Forth and Clyde Canal. Too expensive for Bowery wages or the Glasgow Kiss website's non-existent profits. I pressed Hannah's buzzer, wondering where the rent was coming from. Dead air on the entryphone.

I had taken a large buff envelope from the car as a precaution. I pressed random buttons until someone answered, put a smile in my voice and said, 'I've got a package for one of your neighbours,' and was buzzed in. Hannah's flat was on the third floor. I took the stairs and rang her doorbell. There was no response. I rattled the letterbox.

A door across the hallway opened and a slim man in his mid-forties stepped out accompanied by a Jack Russell trussed up in a heather-tweed dog coat.

'She's out. May as well put that through the letterbox.'

Our eyes met. I favoured him with a smile. 'Needs signed for.'

Hannah's neighbour was dressed for the weather in a Barbour jacket and tweed cap, like an aristo ready for a grouse shoot.

'I'll sign if you want.'

'Needs signed for by the recipient.'

'Ah, like that is it? Court papers?'

'I couldn't possibly say.'

He gave a sage nod. 'Course not.' The dog sat down,

anticipating a delay to its walk. 'Hannah's not a bad girl. She's just going through a bit of a wild phase.'

If the clock had not been ticking, I might have said that some of us were still wild, and seen where that took us, but there was no time for even a fleeting dalliance.

I slapped the envelope against my open palm. 'Don't suppose you have any idea where she went? It'll save her a lot of trouble if she gets this today.'

'Save you a lot of trouble, you mean.'

I bent down and scratched behind the dog's ears. 'Save us both a lot of trouble.'

The dog rolled onto its back and offered me its belly. The man raised his eyebrows in mock disgust. 'Oh, Dolly. She lets anyone tickle her tummy.' He looked me up and down. 'Want to come in and wait for her?'

I gave Dolly a last pat and straightened up. 'I'd love to, but I've not got much time for tummy-tickling today. I need to track Hannah down.'

'Maybe some other time?'

'Maybe.'

He touched the dog gently with the toe of one of his Hunter wellies. 'She went off with a woman in a snazzy motor, if that's any help.'

The description could apply equally to Rose or Helena.

'Blonde or brunette?'

'Brunette. Very brunette, if you know what I mean.'

I did. Rose was as brunette as they came: black hair, pale skin, dark eyes and red lips, with all the sex appeal of Sleeping Beauty's wicked stepmother. She was smart but she could be reckless too, especially when her blood was up.

I said, 'Maybe Hannah's aunt taking her out for Sunday lunch.'

Dolly got to her feet. The man gave the dog a fond look. 'I was on the balcony watering my plants. Hannah looked like she'd been taken hostage. Maybe her aunt's onto whatever those court papers are about.' He straightened Dolly's lead. 'I hope they sort it out. We were all young and stupid before we became old and foolish.' He took a card from his inside pocket and passed it to me. 'Ring when you're free for tummy-tickling.'

I pocketed it. 'Cheers.'

The *Ride of the Valkyries* ringtone I had assigned to Rose blared in my pocket. I made a face. 'The boss.'

He mouthed a knowing *oh* and took himself and Dolly down the stairs.

Rose did not bother with niceties. 'I'm with Hannah. She knows where the hatpin is.'

I waited until I heard the door to the building slam, then loped down the staircase, out into the freshness of new smirr.

'We went to a lot of trouble to get rid of that hatpin — why would we want it back? And how did Hannah even know about it?'

'Apparently she found the body before you did and legged it, like you should have.'

'Why would she let on now?'

'Because she's a grifting little bitch.'

I let the insult hang in the air. 'Is she with you?'

'Yes.'

I upped my pace and headed for my car. 'I've a pretty good idea where the hatpin is, and I don't think you should go there.' I got into the driver's seat and closed the door. 'Where are you?'

'I told you, on my way to collect it.'

My phone buzzed with a call from an unknown number. 'Do me a favour, Rose, and don't. I'll explain later.'

'Explain now.'

The unanswered call buzzed like a warning, but I needed to persuade Rose not to go to Helena Todd's.

'The person who's got it is bad news. You don't want to end up looking like Picasso's *Weeping Woman*.'

'What does that even mean?'

The unknown number cut out and started up again. 'Maybe they'll make a skin collage of your face.'

Rose's laugh was disbelieving. 'You better join us then. I'll get Hannah to text you the address.'

I should have known better than to repeat Helena's threat to rearrange her features. Rose was the kind who ran into burning buildings.

'I'm serious—'

'You're a fucking clown, Rilke. You've been drifting around, getting nowhere and keeping me in the dark. I should know by now that if I want something sorted, I've got to sort it myself.'

She hung up. I swore and redialled the unknown number. Dickie Bird did not bother with hellos either.

'I showed the photo you sent me to my aunty. She recognised her straight away. Said she looked like she'd hardly aged a day. That woman is definitely Nurse Hurst. Aunty Mo said she was a right bitch. She reckons she knew what was going on, maybe even took part.'

It chimed with what Iain had told me on our visit to Gallowhall, but I felt uneasy. 'I don't suppose she had an old photo, did she?'

'That's where you're wrong. She let me look through her albums and memory boxes. There wasn't much from

Gallowhall. Like I said, Mo and my gran didn't want any souvenirs of that place, but there was a picture from a Christmas party. It's a good one of my gran. I guess that's why she held on to it. Your woman's in the background, clear as anything. It's her all right. I'm sending it to you now.'

My phone pinged. I sat on the stairs and opened the message. It was an old Polaroid, the colours softer, more natural than those of a modern camera phone. Two women were sat side by side at a pub table covered with glasses and beer bottles. The camera had caught the dry froth on the empty glasses, the ashtray overflowing with cigarette stubs. The women were laughing. They were both round-faced, with short, practical haircuts under paper crowns. One was grey, the other ash blonde. I thought perhaps I could see a resemblance to Dickie Bird in their jawlines, their mild eyes.

I took in all of this in an instant, synapses snapping between my eyes and my brain. The women, the table, the drinks did not hold me, because standing in the background, caught full-face and unaware, was Helena Todd, her hair dark brown with a feathered fringe, her make-up thicker and less sophisticated than when we'd met, but unmistakably herself.

I let out a sigh of relief. 'Thanks, Dickie. This means a lot.'

'Too true it does. I told Cat she was an old witch, but I didn't know the half of it. She was around all those years.'

My heart was beating faster. 'I've got to go, but don't worry. This is all going to come out. She'll be brought to justice.'

I put the call to hands-free, turned the engine on and started to drive in the direction of Helena Todd's place. I knew now what I was going to do. I would phone Anderson and Ray Diamond. Anderson first so he could swoop on

Helena and get her to the safety of a police cell. Ray next so he would see I had done as I was told and given him a credible killer before the deadline on Les's freedom. A woman with a past linked to Manderson, who had made sure to get her hands on the murder weapon.

Dickie was still talking. 'I've set the dogs on her. She's got nowhere to hide now. I found the website of some vigilante paedophile hunters and emailed them her address. She won't know what's hit her.'

I pressed my foot to the accelerator. 'Dickie, these people don't muck about. They could kill her.'

It sounded like Dickie Bird had dredged up one of his rare smiles. 'She deserves everything she gets. I hope they rip her apart.'

Thirty-Seven

I SPED IN the direction of Pretty Baby, alternating between Anderson and Rose on the hands-free. It was a rerun of yesterday. No one wanted to talk to me. I wondered if Ray had connections amongst the vigilantes and what it would mean for Les if someone gave him Helena Todd's name before I did. It was four in the afternoon, two short hours before my time was up.

Rose's green Hillman Husky was parked outside Helena Todd's place. I drew in behind it and texted Ray: *I have the info about the stock you're interested in. Please confirm L's debt paid in full.* I hoped it would be enough to put him in a holding pattern.

There were no high-end cars stationed on Helena Todd's drive. Perhaps the lawyers and judges were slumped in armchairs sleeping off large Sunday roasts, striding across pristine golf courses or fiddling with little boys.

I pressed the doorbell and rapped at the letterbox,

imitating Anderson's police knock. There was no response. I texted Rose: *Outside HTs, calling the pigs if you don't let me in pronto.*

After a moment footsteps sounded on the tiled floor, locks turned, and the front door opened. It was less than a day since I had seen Hannah, but she looked older and harder, pale. Her hair now had a greenish hue; even her piercings looked dulled.

'Stay out of this, Mr Rilke. It's none of your business.'

'Is Rose here?'

Hannah gave a weary nod and stepped aside. She was dressed in a sleeveless vest and baggy black cargo pants strung with ribbons that swayed as she walked. There was no sense of activity in the upper rooms, no distant music or faint laughter.

Helena Todd was in the same small sitting room as before.

Hannah followed me in. 'I told him it was none of his business, but he wouldn't listen.'

Rose was on the couch, dressed in a black jumpsuit cinched at the waist by a gold belt with a filigree clasp. She looked up as I entered. 'No show without Punch.' Rose was playing tough, but I knew she was as relieved to see me as I was to see her.

Helena sat opposite Rose on the armchair, wearing a navy shirt dress that made her look matronly. Her legs were encased in sheer nylon, her court shoes low-heeled, the kind favoured by air stewards on long-haul flights.

The hatpin lay on a piece of tissue paper on the coffee table between them. The lighting was low, but the faceted amethyst glinted.

Helena nodded at me. 'I thought you might turn up.'

I felt out of place in this small room with three women,

as if I had interrupted some female rite I had no business interfering in. 'What's going on?'

Rose adopted the ultra-calm manner that meant she was close to blowing her fuse. 'Hannah phoned this morning to tell me she knew where the hatpin was and that I could have it for the princely sum of forty thousand pounds. I told her to shove it up her tight little arse and she said she would send it to the police with a letter outlining why it's bad news for me.'

I looked at Hannah. 'Better hope your website picks up. You don't work for us anymore.'

Rose touched her right earring. Victorian jet, mourning jewellery, perfect for a party or a showdown. 'I think that's my prerogative.' She addressed the girl. 'Hannah, consider yourself fired and blacklisted from every auction house, gallery and antique shop in Scotland and the north of England.'

Helena leaned back in her chair. 'I guess that counts as international, as far as you're concerned?'

I perched on the couch. 'We also operate in London, Paris and Milan . . .'

Rose did not add the usual punchline: '. . . but mainly in the Glasgow area.'

Hannah whispered, 'I didn't mean to . . .' Her face fell into the familiar expression she wore when she was caught out. Sometimes there were tears, always apologies, and promises.

Rose ignored her and focused on Helena. 'What's any of this to do with you? Seems like a lot of trouble for sweet fuck all.'

Helena's smile was superior. 'I'm Hannah's grandmother.'

Surprise spiked my voice. 'You're pimping your own granddaughter?'

Rose looked from me to Helena and back, then realisation dawned. The low lighting, the plush carpet, satin upholstery and erotic Japanese prints. 'Ah, I thought you just had ghastly taste.' She turned to Hannah. 'I guess you don't mind being sacked from Bowery now that Granny's put you on the game.'

Helena gave a professional laugh. 'The girls' films are art. I think they're rather beautiful, actually.'

Rose said, 'The girls? Don't tell me Lucy's—'

I shook my head. 'Lucy's nothing to do with this. Hannah has another partner in crime . . . *had* another partner in crime. Cat's checked out.' I could see the resemblance between Hannah and her grandmother now. The determined tilt of their heads, high cheekbones and slender hands. Their lack of boundaries. I turned towards Hannah. 'I thought your website was naïve but harmless. Why are you suddenly threatening Rose?'

Hannah looked at the floor. 'Rose is loaded. She splashes the cash on fancy frocks and vintage cars . . . I've got student debt and Gran can't pay my rent forever.'

Rose gripped the arm of the couch as if forcing herself not to throttle the girl. 'You're trying to blackmail me because you want to pay off your student debt?'

'I'm sick of being poor.'

'Boo-fucking-hoo.'

I touched Rose's arm, reminding her we were on enemy territory and said softly, 'Hannah, how did you know about the hatpin?'

The girl looked at her grandmother, who shrugged. 'You brought these people here. You might as well tell them.'

Hannah adopted the faintly aggrieved tone I was familiar with, the high-pitched whine of a radiator in need of bleeding. 'I found Mr Manderson first. I should have called the police, but it was horrible. I panicked and ran away. I was worried I'd get into trouble, so I didn't say anything. When no one mentioned the hatpin, I thought maybe the police were keeping it quiet to help trap the murderer. I decided to keep quiet too in case they thought it was me. I got a shock when I saw the pin on sale and realised that someone was trying to get rid of it. I wasn't sure what to do, but I knew it was important. I told Gran I wanted it for a film and asked her to buy it for me. I was shaking so hard while the auction was going on I dropped the pins.'

'That still doesn't explain why you turned on Rose.'

'I didn't turn on Rose. I like her.' She looked Rose in the eye. 'I like you. I like both of you, but you've been behaving oddly since Mr Manderson's body was found. I knew the murder had something to do with you. I don't care who killed him. He was a horrible man, and I'm glad he's gone, but I deserve something for keeping quiet.'

Rose shook her head. 'Someone should have strangled you at birth.'

Helena laughed. 'You're delightful.'

I said nothing, recalling how Manderson's body had been slumped face down, the hatpin jammed in his ruined eye concealed until I had turned him over.

Rose ignored Helena's jibe and looked at Hannah. 'Firstly, neither of us touched Mr Manderson. Secondly, you're deluded if you think I'm giving you a penny—'

Hannah snapped, 'You wouldn't miss it. I've seen the prices you get for old tat. Forty grand's nothing to you.'

Rose shook her head. 'Who are you? The Junior Apprentice? Ask your grandmother, Madame fucking du Barry, about profit and loss, overheads and outgoings, income tax, VAT and utilities. I bet it takes a lot of business savvy to run a whorehouse.' She turned to Helena. 'Tell your granddaughter to grow up.'

Helena shook her head. 'You know how it is. Once the genie's out the bottle it's hard to put it back in. Why shouldn't she be rewarded for her silence?'

I had sat in silence throughout the exchange. Now I played one of my aces. 'I know who you are.'

Helena's eyes were as mild as Dickie Bird's. 'You know nothing.'

'I know your real name is Hurst. I know you worked as a nurse at Gallowhall and that the boys there had some interesting stories to tell about you.' I glanced at Hannah, wondering if this was news to her. Her face was impassive. 'Did Mandy Manderson recognise you? Was he blackmailing you?'

Helena arched her eyebrows. Innocence, surprise and something else – calculation? 'I never met Mr Manderson.'

'He was a Gallowhall boy. He claimed to have known you very well.'

'From what I've heard, half the unfortunates of Glasgow were Gallowhall boys. Poor little lads who grew into wretched men.'

'Some of them never got the chance to grow up.'

Helena shrugged. 'Tragic, but nothing to do with me.'

I looked at my watch. Time was slipping away. Ray would throw Les to the wolves if I did not make a move.

Rose said, 'Any chance of a drink in this place?'

Helena nodded. 'I think we could all do with one. Hannah, fetch Ms Bowery a . . . ?'

She looked at Rose, who said, 'Gin and slimline.'

Helena nodded. 'I'll have the same. Make them doubles.'

Hannah's face flushed. I waited for her to tell her grandmother to get lost, but she got to her feet. 'Mr Rilke?'

I wanted the girl gone and my head straight. 'A glass of water.'

Hannah left the room. I got up and checked that she was not listening beyond the door. The corridor was empty. I returned to my seat opposite Helena. 'Apart from us, the murderer is the only one who knows about the hatpin.'

Helena looked me straight in the eye. 'Hannah told you: she found the body and ran away. When the pin went on sale, she spotted an opportunity and asked me to buy it. Enterprising of her.'

'Hannah's story is a crock of shit. Manderson was lying face down. Hannah wouldn't have seen the hatpin unless she rolled him over.'

Helena said gently, 'Hannah may have acted unwisely, but she's not a murderer. If I were you, I'd be very careful. Going to the police will expose you more than it will expose anyone else. One of you removed the hatpin.' She raised her eyebrows at Rose. 'You were seen wearing it by God knows how many witnesses on afternoon TV. Apparently, you even joked about what a great murder weapon it would make. You had an altercation with the victim the day before and, according to Hannah, your temper is legendary. Maybe you'd get off, maybe you wouldn't, but there's enough evidence to put you through a nasty trial, especially if Hannah were to say she saw you running away from the car park at the right time.'

I looked at my watch. It was close to 5 p.m. Ray Diamond would want a result very soon. 'You're forgetting something. The past has caught up with you, Helena. People are after you.'

Helena crossed and uncrossed her long legs. 'You have suspicions, but no evidence. I run a well-ordered house. It's brought me a lot of goodwill with people who matter. People in the law, like your friend, Thurso Scanlon.' She smiled at Rose. 'How's Inspector Anderson? It's always nice to see him.'

I felt Rose getting to her feet and grasped her hand in mine, keeping her on the couch. 'Anderson's fine. Not a big fan of yours as it turns out.'

Helena smirked. 'You'd be surprised.'

Rose started to say something. I squeezed her hand and spoke over her. 'There are some things that even people in the law are squeamish about. Child abuse, for example.'

Rose looked confused. 'Where's this going?'

Helena's voice was steel. 'Nowhere.'

I took my phone from my pocket. 'You're wrong. There's witness testimony and a photograph connecting you to Gallowhall.' I turned my phone on. There was a message from Ray Diamond – a GIF of a ticking alarm clock wired to a bomb. I found the photo Dickie Bird had sent me and held it out to Helena. 'The lady on the right is still around and willing to testify. There's an active Gallowhall survivors' network. Once word gets out, others will come forward.'

Helena squinted at the image on the phone. 'I've no idea who that is.'

'You're in the photo and the witness in question is certain who you are.'

'Her word against mine.'

'Like you said, once the genie's out of the bottle, it's impossible to get it back in. Dickie Bird's put your name and the address of this place all over the internet, and he's contacted some freelance paedophile hunters.'

Helena's face flushed. 'Why would anyone listen to that freakshow?'

Rose leaned back in her seat and flashed a smile. 'Sounds like time for you to sell up and skip town. Destroy the hatpin, and no one will be any the wiser. Mandy Manderson isn't much missed.'

I shook my head. 'Whose side are you on?'

'I'm on the side of letting sleeping dogs lie.'

'There are no sleeping dogs.'

My phone buzzed in my pocket. I glanced at it. A text from Ray Diamond. *Time's up in ten.*

Helena snapped, 'Rodney Manderson will look like a beauty queen compared to how you'll both look if anything happens to me or my granddaughter.'

I was suddenly alert. 'I never mentioned that Manderson's first name was Rodney.'

Helena flushed from her sternum to the roots of her neatly coiffed hair. 'I knew him. I know a lot of people. It doesn't mean I killed him.'

I saw murder in her eyes, and for a moment thought she was going to reach for the hatpin.

'No one accused you of killing him.' The picture was coming into focus. 'Did Manderson threaten to expose your past? Are you the reason he thought he could get away with taking liberties with Hannah?'

Helena's flush was shifting from scarlet to wine, her voice a scalpel. 'No one takes liberties with my granddaughter.'

Doubt shrank. My phone was still in my hand. I found Ray's number and pressed call.

Helena got to her feet. 'What are you doing?'

I seized the hatpin, shoved it into my jacket pocket and pulled Rose from the couch and out of the room, kicking the door shut behind us.

Rose snatched her hand away. 'What the actual fuck?'

'She killed him.' I opened the front door, pushed Rose

ahead of me, grabbed the keys from the door and locked it behind us. 'Helena fucking killed him.'

Helena's heels sounded on the tiles. She battered on the other side of the locked door shouting, 'What the fuck . . .?' Like an echo of Rose.

I strode down the driveway, stabbing at the buttons on my phone.

Rose shouted, 'Oh, come on! That's a pretty massive leap of logic. And will you slow down. I can't run in these boots.'

Ray Diamond picked up on the third ring. There was a clatter of cutlery and voices in the background, a faint hum of music. Ray sounded like he had taken a drink. His voice was slower, more relaxed than usual. 'I was beginning to think you'd left the country.'

I couldn't decide whether Ray drinking was good news for me or not. 'You'd know if I'd left the country.'

Ray gave an easygoing laugh. 'Yes, I would. Hang on, I'll take this somewhere quieter.'

Rose caught up with me. 'We're stuffed if she calls the polis.'

I muted my call. 'We're the ones calling the polis. Phone Anderson, tell him to get here pronto.'

Rose sensed the urgency in my voice and for once did not argue. She turned away and fished her phone from her bag.

Ray was back on the line. 'Have you got a name for me?'

I unmuted. 'Yep . . .' It was suddenly hard to get the words out.

Ray's easy bonhomie vanished. 'No point in getting squeamish at this stage. Not if you want your wee pal off the hook.'

'Helena Todd aka Nurse Hurst.' I recited the address of Pretty Baby.

Ray's voice was calm, as if I had passed on the details of a new restaurant he did not much fancy. 'Okay, fine.'

I stared at the house. It looked like a blameless suburban mansion. The front door was still shut, but I knew it would not take Helena long to find spare keys.

Rose waved her phone in the air and shook her head, letting me know that Anderson had not answered her call.

I asked Ray, 'What are you going to do?'

'Nothing you need to know.'

'Is Les clear now?'

He sighed. 'I'll never get what you see in that fuckwit.'

'That was the deal. I give you Manderson's killer and you take the heat off Les.'

'If she did it, then he's free.'

I still hadn't worked out how Helena had landed the asylum seeker with Manderson's bank card. Doubt wavered within me, but she was corrupt and cunning, and it was her or Les. 'She did it.'

'Okay. I may need a bit of corroboration on that. In the meantime, tell Leslie to keep his nose clean. This is a one-off. Next time I won't play nice.'

The line went dead. I stabbed out a quick text to Les: *It's sorted*.

A car drew into the other side of the road and parked. There were four men inside. Too distant to make out their features, but I got an impression of bulk and white skin.

The front door of the house flew open, and Helena staggered down the drive. She almost lost her balance before Rose caught her by the arm. Helena's hair blew across her face. She shoved Rose away. 'What the fuck are you doing?'

I kept my eyes on the car, the four men. They were staring

in our direction. 'Do you know Ray Diamond, aka Razzle Dazzle Diamond?'

'I'm protected. He can't touch me.'

'Thurso Scanlan's more Ray's boy than he is yours. Your protection is about to dry up. Best thing you can do is put yourself into police custody and confess.'

'Confess to what?'

Rose was calling Anderson again. I could hear the ringtone dialling out. 'Rilke, are you going to explain what's going on?'

Helena barked, 'Your boyfriend's deluded.'

Rose laughed. 'He's not my boyfriend.'

Another car joined the vehicle at the end of the drive. Four more men.

I took Rose by the arm. 'Time to get back inside.'

Helena and Rose followed my gaze, just as a third car drove up. The doors of the first car opened. The men started to emerge. Sports clothes and close-cut hair, weasel faces, soft fleshy features, big bellies, blue jeans, grey joggers, an Oasis T-shirt, bald heads, skinny arms, wire glasses, Reeboks, baseball hats, baseball bats . . .

Helena whispered, 'Jesus Christ, what have you done to me?'

We ran towards the house.

Thirty-Eight

THE FRONT DOOR was fitted with deadbolts that would hold off King Kong, Godzilla and a pack of flesh-eating zombies. I slammed it shut and turned the locks home.

'Is the back door secure?'

Helena was grey as day-old porridge. 'I keep it locked.'

Rose sprinted down the hallway towards the rear of the house, her high heels suddenly no impediment to flight. 'I'll make sure.'

I darted into the two reception rooms at the front of the ground floor. They were frowsy with velvet furnishings, heavy drapes and more love seats than could be considered respectable. Their windows were equipped with old-fashioned wooden shutters, designed to block prying eyes and Glasgow winds. I closed and bolted them.

The doorbell rang. Helena was frozen in the hallway, staring at the Ring camera feed on her phone. She held it up, and I saw two middle-aged white men onscreen. They looked like the kind of guys you saw smoking outside pubs, waiting for their kids at the school gate or pushing trolleys very slowly around supermarkets behind their wives. Unremarkable except for their hungry eyes and righteous anger.

I whispered, 'Christ, it's *Dawn of the Dead*.'

One of the men shouted, 'We know you're in there,' his voice a double echo onscreen and on the other side of the door.

I held a finger to my lips. Helena and I retreated to the centre of the house. Rose and Hannah were already in the small sitting room. A bottle of Roku gin and tins of slimline Fever-Tree sat on the coffee table, next to iced glasses garnished with lemon.

Rose was pouring herself a drink. She looked up as we entered. 'The back door's tight as Fort Knox. There are bars on the back windows at basement level. I got Anderson on the phone. He's on his way.'

Helena turned on me. 'Did you set these bastards on me?'

Things had moved on since I had asked Hannah for a glass of water. I poured a hefty measure of Roku into a glass of ice and drank it straight. 'These are Dickie Bird's new friends, but Ray's boys will be joining the party soon. Mandy was under his protection, and Ray's taking his demise seriously. The safest place for you is in police custody.'

Hannah poured her grandmother a gin, added a dash of tonic and handed it to her. 'Mr Manderson's death had nothing to do with Gran.'

Helena tipped her glass to her lips. Her throat pulsed as she swallowed and swallowed again. 'Keep out of this, Hannah.'

The girl flushed. 'He doesn't know what he's talking about.'

A pounding noise echoed down the hallway, louder than fists and boots. The vigilantes were hellbent on breaking the door down.

Helena glanced at the doorbell feed and took another thirsty swig of her drink. 'I've got cash upstairs. Maybe we can pay them off?'

My glass was empty. I poured another large shot and refreshed Helena's glass. 'These guys are fanatics. They'll take your money and then slit your throat. It's a race between them and Ray's goon squad. My money's on Ray. Slick as smoke. He'll slide through the keyhole if he needs to.'

Helena pushed her hair away from her face. 'I've nothing to do with Ray bloody Diamond.'

'As far as Ray's concerned Mandy was his property. Ray was a Gallowhall boy too. I've a feeling he's got other unfinished business with you. Take my advice and give yourself up to the police, if you don't fancy getting disappeared by Ray.'

I recalled the skinless mess that Jamie Mitchell had been reduced to after Ray Diamond captured him and felt bile in my throat.

Helena shook her head. 'I never touched bloody Manderson. You've no proof, no evidence. I bought the hatpin, sure, but that's not enough to convict me.'

'We're not talking the Supreme Court. I've enough proof to convince Ray.'

Hannah perched on the arm of Helena's chair. She raised her eyes sweetly at me, the hoop that circled her lower lip glinting. 'Gran didn't kill Mr Manderson – I did.'

Rose snorted. 'What is this? *I am Spartacus?*' She topped her glass up with more gin. 'You spend weeks looking for a killer and two pop up at once. Should we be worried about our safety?' A deafening bang came from the front door. She nodded towards it. 'Except for the obvious.'

Helena turned her anxious eyes on us. 'Hannah's loyal.

She's always been too quick to accept the blame for other people's actions.'

Rose laughed. 'Hannah's a little bitch. She'd throw us all to the lions for the price of a cheap pair of shoes.'

Hannah's chin tilted upwards. Her cropped hair and clean jawline resembled Joan of Arc on her way to the flames. 'I'm not sorry I did it.'

A shadow of dread touched my spine.

I touched Hannah's arm. 'We all want to save people we love, but sometimes we have to let them take what's coming to them. Your gran will be safer in jail than she is out here.'

Helena snapped, 'What planet are you living on?'

Hannah squeezed her grandmother's shoulder. 'Don't worry, Gran, you're not going anywhere.' She looked at me. 'The hatpin was lying on Rose's desk. I don't know why I picked it up. I probably would have put it back later.'

Rose was halfway down her third, maybe her fourth, gin. 'We should have fired you way back, saved ourselves a lot of trouble.'

I said, 'So all that stuff you told me about Mandy offering to give you the hatpin in return for a kiss was a lie?'

Hannah had cried when she told me that story. Now her eyes were dry. She was the only one in the room who was not drinking, and her expression was sober. 'Some of it is true. Mr Manderson was a sleaze. We all knew it.'

Rose's ice clattered in her glass. 'I warned you and Lucy to stay out of his way.'

'We did, but I was making some art films with a couple of friends. Somehow Mr Manderson found our website, Glasgow Kiss. He connected it with Pretty Baby and started pestering me for sex. I told him to go fuck himself, but the day of the sale he cornered me outside Bowery and said he'd out Gran as some kind of abuser if I didn't do what he told me to. He stuck his tongue down my throat. It was true what I said about him being strong for an old man. The hatpin was pinned inside the lining of my jacket.' She drew open her leather bomber and pointed to a flaw in the lining. 'I didn't even think about it. I grabbed the pin and jabbed it at him. I thought he'd move away, but he laughed and called me a silly slag. He thought he could say anything he wanted and get away with it.'

'But he couldn't?'

Hannah gave me a thoughtful shake of her head. 'I guess I saw red. Pretty soon after, he saw red too. I stabbed the pin in his eye and pushed until it reached the back of his skull.' She smiled like a girl recalling a good time. 'It touched bone.'

Rose groaned. 'Fuck's sake.'

Helena whispered, 'Hannah . . . it was self-defence . . .'

Her granddaughter gave another dreamy smile, and I knew that my desperation to save Les had led me to rash conclusions.

Hannah stroked her grandmother's back. 'I wanted to tell you, Gran. I thought maybe you'd understand. I didn't plan to kill Mr Manderson, but killing him felt good.'

Helena gave a low moan. Hannah slid onto the couch and snuggled beside her. There was something nauseating about the tenderness of the girl's embrace set alongside the savagery of Mandy's murder, like milk veined with blood.

'I took a bank card from his pocket and gave it to a guy begging outside Greggs on Argyle Street. I told him to use it once and then throw it away. I felt bad when I heard he'd been arrested. I guess he got greedy and used it more times than he should have.'

I believed everything Hannah told us except the part about feeling bad for the beggar. The wildness I had detected in her had tipped into something callous, almost psychotic, but I had known her since she was barely out of her teens. I could not hand her to Ray Diamond, not even to save Les.

A screech of police sirens cut through the clamour of the vigilantes, breaking the moment.

I knelt on the floor, my face level with Helena's. 'Ray Diamond has a biblical sense of justice. An eye for an eye. A tooth for a tooth. Your involvement in Gallowhall is out in the open. There's proof that you were there and witnesses willing to testify against you. There'll be a trial. You'll be found guilty and sent to jail.'

Helena understood what I was saying. She pushed her granddaughter away gently. Her skin was the texture of crepe, her violet eyes dull. I stood up and held out a hand to help her up, but she shoved me away and got to her feet by herself.

Hannah whispered, 'Gran . . .?'

Rose saw what was coming first and let out a sharp gasp.

Helena slapped her granddaughter hard across her face. 'You keep your mouth shut until this is finished and done with.'

Hannah's head snapped back with the force of the blow. A red hand mark glowed on her cheek. Tears sprang to her eyes. I expected her to start crying, but her lips pursed into a grim expression that suggested she had been slapped before and had learned to swallow the pain.

Helena's voice was steady. 'I killed him. I don't know if it was the film Hannah made at Gallowhall that alerted him to Pretty Baby, but somehow Rodney Manderson found our website and recognised me. He threatened to implicate me in the Gallowhall scandal if I didn't give him a lot of money.'

It was a rehearsal for what she would tell the police.

Rose said, 'That doesn't make sense. Why would you have the hatpin?'

Helena hesitated, searching for a story that fitted the evidence. 'I was sick of Hannah's petty thieving. I'd found the hatpin on her earlier that day and confiscated it. It was still in my bag when I confronted Manderson outside your auction house. You know the rest.'

Hannah whispered, 'That's not true . . .'

I stepped forward to stop Helena hitting the girl again, but she grasped Hannah by both wrists and stared into her eyes. 'It *is* true, and if you say anything else, they'll decide we both did it. I've had a good run. I always knew there was a chance I'd end up in prison. I've prepared myself.'

The banging at the door was replaced by shouting and scuffling. A dull thud that might have been the sound of someone's skull hitting wood.

The tears that had trembled in Hannah's eyes rolled down her face, coursing over the livid mark on her cheek. 'But you didn't do it.'

Helena gave her an encouraging smile. 'I did, darling. I did.'

The doorbell rang. Helena looked at her phone and then at Rose. 'Your friend Jim's here, with the cavalry.'

The doorbell rang again, long and impatient. Rose hurried from the room.

Helena turned to Hannah. 'Stop snivelling, for Christ's sake.'

Hannah wiped her eyes on her sleeve, her sobs subsiding. 'I love you, Gran.'

Rose returned with Anderson, accompanied by four uniformed police officers.

Helena stepped forward. 'I have a confession to make.'

Anderson was casually dressed in jeans and a leather jacket, his expression grave. 'I'm all ears, but first things first.' He turned to me. 'You're a fucking idiot, Rilke.'

He nodded at one of the uniforms who unclipped a set of handcuffs from his belt and stepped towards me.

'Mr Rilke, I am arresting you on suspicion of attempting to pervert the course of justice. You do not have to say anything . . .'

I felt a dizzying pull of gravity, like a man looking into his own freshly dug grave. I gripped the back of the couch, steadying myself.

The policeman was still reading me my rights. '. . . it may harm your defence if you do not mention, when questioned, something which you later rely on in court. Anything you do say may be given in evidence.'

Rose whispered, 'Jim, no . . .'

He gave her a harsh look. 'I'd keep very quiet if I were you.'

The wave of nausea passed. I straightened my spine, edged back the sleeves of my suit jacket to expose my wrists and held my hands out. 'Listen to him, Rose.'

The police officer told me to turn around and cuffed my wrists behind my back. The snap of the bracelets trembled my centre of gravity again.

I braced myself. 'Rose, there's a lawyer called Ali Grant, based in Finnieston. Let him know what's going on.'

Rose grasped Anderson's arm. 'Jim . . .'

He pushed her gently away. 'Be very careful, Ms Bowery. You're one wrong move away from a police cell.' He turned to Helena. 'Okay, Mrs Todd, what do you want to tell me?'

Helena took a deep breath. 'I want to confess to the murder of Rodney Manderson.'

Hannah started to cry.

Thirty-Nine

TWO POLICE VANS bore the vigilantes away, leaving their cars abandoned on the street outside.

'Stewart Street nick's going to be full tonight.' The police officer's hand gripped my shoulder, steadying me as we took the steps that led from Helena Todd's house onto the drive and towards the waiting squad car. He cradled my skull as I lowered myself into the back seat. 'Easy now.'

A black Mercedes with tinted windows slowed outside the house as Helena Todd, hands cuffed behind her, was helped into a separate squad car by a WPC. I watched from the police car as the Merc pulled away slowly and headed in the direction of the city centre.

Six Months Later

LES AND FRANK were leaning against the bonnet of a gold Ford Cortina. Frank met me halfway across the prison car park and took the transparent carrier bag bearing my belongings from me. 'Okay, boss?'

I was not sure, but I nodded. 'Okay.' I jerked my head at the car. 'Bit flashy?'

'Rose borrowed it specially from Stevie.'

Les was summer formal in a pale-biscuit 1970s suit with blaxploitation lapels, a chocolate-coloured shirt and cream tie. He grabbed me in a tight hug and clapped me on the back. 'Welcome to the land of the living.'

I was wearing the suit I had gone to court in, too dark and heavy for the weather. I returned his hug. 'Not sure I'm fully resurrected.'

'Don't worry, Frank and me will sort you out.'

He opened the passenger door, and I slid inside. The car smelt good, clean without the underlying scent of bleach I had grown accustomed to. I expected Frank to take the driver's seat, but he got into the back and Les got behind the wheel.

I raised my eyebrows, though Rose had already let Les's secret slip on one of her visits. 'What's going on?'

Les grinned. 'Provisional licence. Frank's been giving me lessons.'

'Does Stevie know you're driving his motor?'

Les turned the key in the ignition and drove towards the exit. 'He doesn't not know.'

Frank said, 'Remember your mirrors.'

Les turned to look at him without taking his foot off the accelerator. 'I checked my mirrors.' He turned his eyes on me. 'Your man's more obsessed with mirrors than Penn and Teller.'

Frank said, 'Eyes on the road.'

We headed west. It was a sun-drenched day. Trees were in full leaf and sandstone tenements shone gold and orange. The sunshine had drawn people onto the streets. Summer dresses and patterned shirts lounged outside bars and cafés and peacocked towards Kelvingrove Park. I had grown so accustomed to prison grey that the brightness stung my eyes.

Les was a happy driver, fond of the horn, adept with sign language. I had assumed we were going to my flat, but he turned on to Woodlands Road, drove past the Free Presbyterian Church of Scotland where a sign proclaimed, *Your Sins Will Find You Out*. Les swerved around a couple of potholes, almost dismounting a cyclist, turned on to Arlington Street and parked outside the private baths.

I kept my seatbelt buckled. 'Thanks, boys, I appreciate the gesture, but I'd rather go home.'

Les cut the engine. 'So you can lock yourself in and sulk in a darkened room? Fuck that, you've somewhere to be.'

'Where?'

'Relax, it's a surprise.'

I undid my seatbelt. 'If you've lined up a rent boy, I'll make my excuses and leave.'

Les was already out of the car, lifting a garment bag from the back of the boot. 'Don't worry. Everyone knows you're too tight to pay for it.'

'Just never been a fan of human trafficking.'

'Aye, you're an early riser, woke before woke.'

Frank took a shoebox from the boot. 'You're going to like the suit, Rilke. Rose picked it.'

'Tell me it's not red satin.'

Frank had shaved off his moustache. It made him look younger. 'It's your kind of thing. Sober, nice cut.'

Les was ringing the doorbell of the Arlington Baths. 'The kind of suit you can get buried in.'

Frank shot him a look. 'No one's getting buried.'

I climbed the stairs. 'Not today.'

Les grinned. 'Aye, aye, a pleasure postponed.'

The door to the Arlington opened and we stepped inside.

An hour later, skin pink from the steam room and Turkish bath, hair cut by Les's hairdresser, who had dropped by on a favour, dressed in my new suit and fresh brogues, I emerged into the street.

Frank held out his open palm to Les. 'Keys.'

Les shoved his hands in his pockets. 'How am I going to improve if I never get to practise?'

Frank closed and opened his palm in a gimme gesture.

'You've had your shot. Rilke's just out the jail. He can't afford to get pulled over.'

Les handed Frank the keys and got into the back seat. 'I object to that. I'm a good driver.'

I said, 'Where are we—'

They chorused, 'It's a surprise.'

I stowed my old duds in the boot and took a seat up front.

Frank passed me an envelope thick with bank notes. 'Rose said to give you this. Back wages with a bit on top.'

I put it in my inside pocket. 'Cheers.'

He drew another, thinner envelope from his jacket. 'The team had a whip-round to welcome you home.'

I hesitated, and he said, 'They'll be offended if you don't take it. It's not OTT, but I had to stop Abomi from donating his life savings.'

I smiled and took it from him. 'Thanks, Frank.'

He nodded and turned the key in the ignition. The Cortina's throaty engine coughed and thrummed.

Les leaned forward and squeezed my shoulder. 'Did you see Thurso Scanlan inside?'

'No, he's classed VP.'

'Christ, it's not often you feel sorry for rapists and paedophiles, but inflicting Scanlan on them is cruel and unusual punishment.'

Ray Diamond had used his networks to reveal Thurso Scanlan's side hustles and implicate him in the students' overdoses. Police Scotland's reputation was already reeling from a variety of corruption scandals, and Scanlan was unpopular. The thin blue line had distanced themselves by carrying out an uncharacteristically robust investigation. He was sentenced to twelve years at His Majesty's Pleasure and had his police pension rescinded.

It had been a good season for scandal. Helena Todd's life and career had lit up newspapers, websites and podcasts. Prentice Baxter had done a major exposé. The murder of Mandy Manderson was the glue that had held it together, but Helena's time at Gallowhall and her career as a high-end madam with a sideline in cosmetics excited more interest. A Netflix documentary was on the way, and there were rumours of a West End play. Helena would not profit. She had argued self-defence, but the jury had not been convinced and she was currently serving a life sentence for Manderson's murder. There were faint rumblings that Ray Diamond was waiting for the dust to settle before making his final move. I had sleepless nights wondering what Ray would do to me if he ever discovered Helena and I had got one over on him for the sake of saving Hannah.

Anderson had risked his police pension by shielding Rose. I was a brief footnote: *a man was prosecuted for attempting to defeat the ends of justice.*

Not everyone had got what they deserved. The Right Honourable Lord Urquhart Murchison was still snug beneath his wig in white and scarlet robes. I had glimpsed him occasionally on the small television in my cell, pronouncing on the law, pale and ascetic, except for his thrapple, which hung loose like a turkey's.

Hannah had sent Lucy a postcard from New Zealand. I suspected it was a decoy and that she was elsewhere, reinventing herself. I hoped things worked out for her, but doubted she would stay out of trouble for long.

We were driving east through familiar streets into the Gallowgate. I said, 'Tell me we're not going to the Sarry Heid.'

Les banged out a quick tattoo on the headrest of my seat. 'Wait and see.'

Frank glanced at him in the rear-view mirror. 'Keep schtum.'

Les said, 'I am keeping fucking schtum.' He took out his phone and dialled. Someone picked up and he said, 'With you in two.'

Sunlight caught the Barrowland Ballroom sign as we passed, sending it ablaze with colour, shooting stars electric. Frank turned the Cortina into the main drive of the Barras Market.

I said, 'It's Friday – the Barras isn't open today.' But even as I said it, I saw the bunting strung across the market trembling in the sunshine and the crowd of familiar faces. Frank killed the engine, Les opened the passenger door and I stepped into the day.

The old dealers were there, high-end and low, and so were the cowboy queers and young artists who were helping to keep the old market alive. Rose was dressed in a scarlet satin gown, cut on the bias, and high red wedges. Her hair was coiled in a loose up-do studded with diamanté and roses. She put her arms around me and whispered, 'Welcome home.'

A fiddle started up and a trumpet joined in. I returned Rose's hug. 'You didn't have to get dressed up on my account.' Now that I looked more closely, I realised that everyone was wearing their finery. Old suits that rarely saw the light of day, dresses stretched across bodies that had expanded since their last wear, cowboy boots and fringes, sparkles and kilts. The scent of mothballs, whisky and perfume wafted on the breeze. 'What's going on?'

Rose said, 'Everyone wants to celebrate your release.'

Anderson was at my side. 'Only took a decade and my resignation from the force. She said yes. We're getting married.'

Rose shook her head. 'Civil partnered. I'm nobody's wife, but I'm a decent partner.'

The fiddle was soaring. The trumpet hit a high note and somewhere a bagpipe droned. The crowd was already surging towards Saint Luke's. Hands clapped me on the back. Paper money was shoved into the pockets of my suit.

Anderson said, 'Who are these folk? We'll never fit them all in the venue.'

Rose ran a soothing hand across his back. 'They're friends, and that's what the pizza truck on the square outside is for.'

Abomi rushed from the crowd and smothered me in a bear hug. 'Missed you, boss.'

'Missed you too, son. How's your uncle Razzle?'

Abomi grinned. 'Top of the world. Almost forgot, he said to send his best.'

'Take mine back to him.'

Abomi fell into step beside me. 'Sure thing.'

Frank and Les were ahead of us, Les talking ten to the dozen, Frank occasionally nodding. Rose slid one hand into mine and the other into Anderson's, and we followed the crowd together through the marketplace towards the church and a new day.

Acknowledgements

RILKE AND I occupy the same city. We drive the same roads, walk the same pavements. Occasionally we visit the same bars, the same cafes and restaurants. Our style is different. It is true that we both wear a lot of black, but I do not possess a Crombie, and I like my outfits to have a splash of colour, usually red. Despite our similarities we never bump into each other, but I know he is out there, rolling another fag and swapping wisecracks with Rose and Les.

Like Rilke I also associate with a bunch of merry pranksters. Huge thanks go to my editor Francis Bickmore at Canongate Books whose nuanced understanding of character, plot, current events and more helps hone my words on the page. Copy Editor Alison Rae has a razor focus and comprehension of grammar, logic, etymology. She also has a smart eye for contradictions which has saved me from embarrassment more than once. Thanks too to my agents Sam Copeland of Rogers Coleridge and White and Katie Haines of The Agency who look after my literary well-being and interests – something I don't always have the sharpest concept of.

Friends are important and I too often neglect them for the page. Thanks for sticking with me, David and Cathy Fehilly, Paul Sheehan and John Jenkins, Clare Connelly and Laughlin Bell, Jude Barber, Iris Williamson, Neil, Citim and Nina McDonald, Yvonne and Gordon Blair, Carol Barclay, Stuart MacRae, Hazel and Stuart Strachan. Huge hugs to my sister Karen Sinclair, brother-in-law Chris Sinclair and niece Sophie Sinclair. Thanks too to my students and colleagues at University of Glasgow who help keep me relevant and the team at Woodlands Community who help to make our district a real community.

The City of Glasgow is home to Rilke and to me. The River Clyde runs through its centre. Jude Barber and I have been collaborating on a podcast, *Who Owns the Clyde?* https://podfollow.com/who-owns-the-clyde/view asking how it is that so much of our river, a site of ecological, cultural, economic and historic significance, no longer belongs to the people. We're asking who it belongs to now and suggesting some potential futures for our river. If you want to, you can sign our petition to the Scottish Parliament to grant the River Clyde, and other Scottish Rivers, Rights of Personhood via https://petitions.parliament.scot/petitions/PE2131

Finally, I am very lucky to have my partner Zoë Strachan as one of the centres of my life. She is my first and most insightful reader, a shrewd and compassionate critic. A fine writer herself, I am beyond fortunate to have her as a companion in literature, life and love.